She wonc

As though he _____ d,
"I just wanted _____
His voice trail _____ a thin
excuse.

"Thank you," she said, and felt the words were
inadequate.

"Get some sleep now, Janey." His voice deepened at
the use of her name, causing a riot of reaction in her.

She had to clear her throat before she could answer.
"I will…and, Dave?"

"Yes?"

"When I said 'thank you,' I meant for everything."

There was a long pause, and Janey imagined a blush
suffusing his face, his bared chest.

To her surprise, he chuckled. "Janey, honey, I haven't
done anything yet."

She half smiled, but his next words ripped the smile
away and started her heart pounding in a wild,
unmatched rhythm.

"And when I do, a 'thank-you' won't be what I'm
after."

MARILYN TRACY
No Place To Run

Silhouette Sensation

*First published in Great Britain in 1994
by Silhouette Books, Eton House, 18-24 Paradise Road,
Richmond, Surrey TW9 1SR*

© Tracy Le Cocq 1992

Silhouette, Silhouette Sensation and Colophon are
Trade Marks of Harlequin Enterprises B.V.

ISBN 0 373 59100 4

18-9402

Made and printed in Great Britain

Other novels by Marilyn Tracy

For my brother,
State Police Officer Glen Michael Huber,
killed in the line of duty, January 26, 1991:
the little boy who always wanted
to grow up and get the bad guys.
I miss you.

Chapter 1

Dave Reynolds hurried across the kitchen, a cold beer in one hand and a half a sandwich in the other. He glanced at the old, battery-operated clock hanging over the refrigerator, and even though he knew it was fifteen minutes fast, he didn't slow his pace. He ducked his head through the archway leading to the dining room, too tall to clear it otherwise. He didn't so much as glance at the littered table and five mismatched oak chairs before leaving the room, crossing the shabby living area and stepping outside onto his broad front porch.

Here he stopped, somewhat chagrined, too aware of his rush to get to the porch, too conscious that this daily dash had somehow, sometime between last week and today, become a habit. A need. He forced himself to remain still, to draw a deep breath of Portales, New Mexico's, yeast-scented air. The scent clung to the early spring breeze defining it, giving it clarity.

Porch needs painting, he thought, more to steady himself than in any real desire to upgrade the looks of the house.

Chips of paint, sun blistered by the previous summer's heat and made dusty by the dry February winds, clung together in the corners, mountains and valleys of dirt accumulated in a year's time in the dry desert town.

Maybe he needed to take a leaf from Janey Anderson's book; she'd had a fellow over at the Meeks place yesterday, sawing and hammering, fixing those old rickety steps. But she was smarter than the local sheriff, Dave thought, smiling, she had hired someone to do it and, best yet, hadn't even been home to listen to the racket.

Moving again, but much more slowly now that he'd glanced at her front door and found it still closed, Dave stretched a booted foot to crook one of the battered porch chairs closer. It too needed a coat of stain; it was weather dry and cracking. He hitched sideways out of habit, forgetting he'd already deposited his holster with its dark .357 magnum on his dining table.

The thought of his weapon drove home his odd behavior. He had stripped the gun from his hips before even going inside his unlocked house. He knew it was as safe on that battered table, in this town, as though he'd locked it in a vault. On the seat of the chair next to him lay his felt broadbrimmed cowboy hat. Both the gun inside and the hat lying on the chair were mute testimony to the fact that he'd been in and out of his house in less time than it would take to tell it.

Not that he was likely to tell anyone about it, he thought ruefully, sitting down, too casually facing the western sky—the direction of *her* house. He couldn't tell anyone about all this; he'd never hear the end of it. He'd either be teased unmercifully—and probably deservedly—by the single deputies in the department, or the married ones would all spill the tale to their wives and there would be a round of matchmaking dinner invitations and speculative glances at the supermarket the next time he swung by for groceries.

And Dave wasn't interested in dating the woman. Hell, she was as pregnant as a woman could get. No, he wasn't after anything. But for the past week or so he'd been skipping the usual rehash-of-the-day's cup of coffee with the boys and hightailing it home in time to watch her oddly graceful descent down her porch as she took her evening walk.

Dave found himself, like everyone else in town, wishing he knew more about her. He wanted to know more because he wished he could step off his dusty porch, hold out his arm for her and escort her for this nightly ritual across the street, down five blocks, across the street again and back.

He knew she walked for exercise, walked for her health and for the sake of her baby. But something about that walk always struck Dave with the notion that she was wrestling with some inner demon, as though the walk, in and of itself, were an act of bravery.

There were reasons why she would need courage. Lord knows she'd been through every stage of hell in the past year. What little Dave did know about the young woman was enough to give her every reason in the world to look over her shoulder and shy away from folks in town.

He'd seen her almost every day since she'd moved into the old Meeks place seven months ago, but had only exchanged the briefest of greetings with her. Tonight would be different, he swore to himself. Tonight he was going to make her smile. He'd seen that smile once, back at the ice-cream store a couple of months ago, and then again the other night, and something about it did funny things to his insides.

He'd have worked on making her smile months ago, but her very reticence made it impossible for him to just waltz on over there and hold out his elbow and tip his hat. She'd think he was crazy. And she'd probably be right.

Dave lifted his sandwich and took a bite. He chewed it slowly, not tasting Mrs. Jordan's deviled ham despite the fact her recipe always won first prize at the county fair. He was too busy wondering if Janey Anderson would forego her nightly walk tonight. Was she ill? Could she be in labor? She was already a couple of minutes later than usual.

The fact that he was following the time told him how ridiculous he was being, sitting on his front porch, beer and sandwich in hand like any spectator at a sideshow, worrying that his favorite performer might not walk onstage. But Janey Anderson wasn't a performer. She was simply and honestly the most beautiful woman he'd ever seen. And she was the widow of a state hero who had died a tragic death, and she'd chosen to settle in the town of Portales.

As usual, Dave's thoughts stumbled on her choice of New Mexico towns. Why Portales? Especially when she was pregnant, alone, and obviously skittish of everyone and everything. The people here all had solid reasons for living in Portales, reasons that went back to pioneer days or were tied up with the local university. Their daddies or their granddaddies had settled here, hacking at the sandy soil, scraping the money together to invest in grain, seedlings or ranch land.

The town was too small for Dave not to know practically everything the townspeople had managed to learn about her, and living across the street from her had provided many opportunities for him to glean even more. As a local himself, Dave was well aware that Janey Anderson had no kin hereabouts and hadn't ever been in Portales before that anyone could remember, so no one could figure out what made her pick the small crossroads town.

He told himself that in learning everything there was to know about her, he was doing her a favor. He could ease her transition into a new location, and he got the chance to keep an eye on her without her being aware of it. Telling yourself something, and believing it were two entirely different matters, he thought.

From the first day of her arrival, he'd known her name, and had known to the minute when she moved into the old Meeks place. Both suited her somehow, her name and the old house. Despite her solemnity, she possessed a gamin quality that fit the name of Janey. The dark curls, the slightly upturned nose, the elegant legs, the skittishness in her mannerisms, all these combined to underscore this pixie-like tag. And the house, old and stately, given over to ruin, was like her life, crumbling before everyone's eyes. But like her life, she had slowly enacted a restoration on that old place that was nothing shy of miraculous.

Norma Judson, Janey's next-door neighbor to the south, had been the first to discover the town's newest resident was the widow of the state police officer shot and killed in a brutal massacre eight months earlier. Norma said Janey didn't talk about the death of her husband, but that she'd recognized her right off from all the fuss on the news.

Norma had gone over to "the little girl's house" the first day she'd moved in, bearing a tinfoil-wrapped banana bread loaf, and had even invited the girl to attend her church on Sundays. "She was pleasant enough, I guess, but, well, distant. That's the word. Just plain distant. Made me feel kind of sorry for those old people out at that nursing home. I think I'd want somebody a might perkier changing my sheets and things."

Janey worked part-time at Los Abuelos, the hospice facility that had moved into Portales about four years ago. She didn't work as a nurse, but as a volunteer social worker. Dave couldn't imagine this lovely woman willingly going in and working with the terminally ill on a daily basis, and then, as he thought about it, he could. Who knew more about grief than she did?

The fact that she was widowed and he was single, and that she lived in such close proximity to Dave would have immediately given greater rise to possible matchmaking, except that the folk in Portales were too conscious of her husband's death. And Dave was too conscious of the living legacy her husband had left her.

In a way he was sorry the matchmaking ladies hadn't had their way, however, for when he saw her lights on every night and knew she never went anywhere, he was smitten with a sense of letting her down. Or perhaps it was more a sense of letting a fellow law enforcement officer down. She was pregnant and alone, no one to talk to, no one to confide in.

According to Alma Maybry over at Los Abuelos, Janey never volunteered any information about herself, and if anyone did ask her direct questions, she would answer but not elaborate.

Mickey Hopkins, feisty owner of the little used-furniture store—euphemistically called Antiques and More—said Janey had come in one afternoon and purchased all the furnishings for a two-bedroom house, including a crib that used to belong to the Jeffries. Mickey couldn't believe that anyone with that kind of knowledge of furniture would have up and sold all her own things.

"Why," Mickey said, "she even bought things like salt and pepper shakers and old fruit jars for canisters. And a set of dinner dishes. That poor girl didn't have a thing to her name. I'd have thought the state police would take better care of her than that."

Dave knew they would have, and most likely already had. But he also knew why she must have sold everything: she wanted to lay the memories to rest. It wasn't enough to simply give away her husband's clothes; she had cleaned out the entire house, lock, stock and canisters. He'd done the same thing after Patty died.

Jason Todd, from Todd Realty, made it a point to tell everyone in town how the little lady drove a hard bargain on the Meeks place, whittling the price down another ten thousand because she was paying in cash, and finally "walking away from the closing with a house that cost less than most cars nowadays."

Elton Stennis, over at the bank, was closemouthed about the amount of money she deposited, but did say she was pretty savvy about her financial affairs. He didn't know where all her money had come from, Elton said repeatedly, shaking his balding head.

Dave could have told him if he'd asked specifically. He'd had to break bad news to too many widows over the years. The money had come from the life-insurance policy and probably the pension, as well. One widow had bitterly called it blood money. Dave didn't know about that, but he did know that dollars and cents didn't warm a lonely bed in the long hours of the dark night, nor did it swing kids up on a broad shoulder on a hot summer afternoon at the county fair.

Not that Janey Anderson looked the sort of woman who would wile away lonely hours pining for anyone. She looked more the type who might freeze an unwelcome offer with a disdainful stare, or who might say two or three simple words and walk away, leaving a man crawling on his knees. Especially if he'd looked into those eyes and read the vulnerability there.

Jewel Lyon, Janey's nearest neighbor to the north, said she'd asked Janey to join the Women's Club, or at least participate in the bridge games there. Janey had thanked her but "turned me down flat. And she hasn't come to any of the church socials she bought tickets for, either," Mrs. Lyon said. But she'd said it with a note of rough pity, not condemnation. A woman in her mid-nineties, Jewel Lyon had buried two husbands and one of her children. She knew about the vagaries of life. And she knew about death.

Gavin Newsom, owner of the Home and Appliance store, said he felt sorry for "the poor little thing. Strikes me as she's just plain scared. Bone-deep scared. Cold, mind you, but scared."

But whatever she was or wasn't, friendly or standoffish, frightened or simply cold, nothing she did discouraged any-

one talking about her, and everyone did. How was she doing? What new repair had she done on the Meeks place? Did
anyone reckon she was here to stay?

And possibly because he was sheriff, or maybe because he
was single, or perhaps because he was the neighbor closest
to her in age, which everyone knew from the newspapers
was twenty-seven years old in her case and thirty-six in his,
they looked to him for answers.

At first he told himself it was only neighborly interest on
his part. Then he'd tried telling himself that as the town
sheriff, it fell to him to watch out for a woman living alone.
Then, after she'd nodded at him one evening, her reluctance to even grant him that small gesture, her withdrawal
from human contact so poignantly etched on her delicate
features, Dave realized he was keeping an eye on her for
many more reasons than simple altruism.

But he wanted to do more than just keep an eye on her.
He wanted to talk to her, to hear her unusually deep voice,
to have her talk to him. He'd called out to her just a week
earlier. Her blue eyes had flashed to his, as guileless as a
child's but as fearful. She'd nodded to him then, as before,
a slow acknowledgment, but her lips didn't curve to a smile.
Still, before she'd glanced away, he'd caught a glimpse of
something in her clear gaze, something that might have been
a longing of sorts.

And for just a moment, a split second of infinite understanding, he'd known her as well as he knew himself. For
he'd seen that look a hundred times in the past three
years...in his own mirror. It was a look comprised of
withdrawal, of loneliness, but mostly of shattered trust.

Having recognized it, suspecting what kept her lips from
smiling, what kept her locked behind her doors with her
curtains drawn, he couldn't let it go. Instead of an object of
pity, she became a challenge.

He had been luckier than Janey Anderson. He knew from
the news accounts that she had no family, no one to stand

as support for her. He'd had an entire town that had wanted him to come home after the disaster in L.A. He'd had a whole lifetime of knowing people who loved him, who cared for him, who eventually had urged him to run for sheriff. He didn't believe there was a person in town he didn't know by face or name, and everyone knew him, some better than others.

Because of this, because he understood, he felt he had to reach her somehow, if only to make her smile, to see her shoulders relax for one minute.

He felt he had to do this, if only to make her see what living in this town was really all about, the sharing of one's life with a group of people that really cared. The notion of trying to reach her was rapidly obsessing him. He'd lain awake all that night, that long week ago, trying to think of things that would make her speak to him, something that would make her smile. Instead, all he'd done was make himself tired.

Then, finally, two nights ago, he'd really spoken to her. Nothing special, nothing earth-shattering, and certainly nothing threatening.

"Evening, Ms. Anderson," he'd said, but the words had come out too suddenly, too loudly, his voice harsher than he'd intended, partially from not having spoken in several minutes, partially from a curious dryness in his throat. "When's the baby due?"

He'd had to control a wince as she flinched, and her eyes had darted to his in a mixture of apprehension and, strangely, relief. Had she been anticipating him saying something, and now that he had, she'd felt relief that she had survived it? The thought was leveling.

"I beg your pardon?" she'd asked. Her voice was pitched lower than he'd expected, deeper than her fragile looks had implied. There was no *r* in her pardon, and the lack of the hard eastern-plains consonant played on his ears and caused his heartbeat to accelerate. Or had it been the way she tilted her head, waiting for his answer, her lips parted as though half expecting something from him? Whether she had anticipated positive or negative, he couldn't have said.

"Your baby," he'd said and even now, in memory, his voice had sounded graveled, rasped. "When's it due? Soon, it looks like." As soon as the words had left his lips he'd wished he could snatch them back. That's the way to get her to talk to you, Dave, he'd thought with disgust: make personal remarks that could be taken either way.

To his relief she hadn't appeared offended. "In four weeks."

"An April baby," he'd said, and shifted uncomfortably. It wasn't his unnecessary words that had made him feel uneasy, it was the vision of a no-longer pregnant Janey Anderson holding her baby on her front porch, daffodils in bloom, lilacs scattering their scent on the spring breezes, blossoms tangling in her dark hair. And her blue, guileless eyes meeting his, her lips soft with smile, that sorrow-filled tension gone from her shoulders.

"Yes," she'd said then, as if answering his fantasy. Her gaze had slid from his, and he remembered flushing, half-afraid she'd been able to read his thoughts.

"Are you hoping for a girl or a boy?" he'd asked, more to keep her there than any real interest in the sex of her unborn child.

Her eyes had met his again, causing his lungs to catch. "Either," she'd said. She said it with a long *i,* and again the difference in speech pattern did odd things to Dave's chest. It had been he who looked away that time, as if by maintaining eye contact she would see too much. Then he hadn't stopped to ask himself *too much what?;* now, he wasn't sure he wanted to know.

"Are you all settled in?" he'd continued, knowing that she was, merely wanting to keep her talking.

"Mostly," she'd answered, and turned as if to leave. Her back had been rigid with the same tension that squared her shoulders. Again that wave of pity had swept over Dave. Pity and something else. She had raised one of her slender hands to her swollen belly and Dave had realized the gesture was instinctive, the mother protecting the child within.

His heart had performed an odd little fillip then, and for a second he had wondered what it would feel like to place his hand on her rounded stomach and feel the baby moving beneath it. Or to raise his hand to the full breasts rising and falling rapidly. He remembered having to drag his gaze back to her face, his own cheeks stained with embarrassed color.

And amazingly, with simple understanding, she had smiled. The change in her was as dramatic as the difference between cloudy and sunny skies, or as subtle as the contrast between sunrise and sunset. She had been a lovely woman, but with that smile, she had become breathtakingly beautiful.

The smile had faded almost as it had blossomed, but not quickly enough that Dave had missed the potential, the possibility inherent in the natural demonstration of amusement. Mischief, a wary sympathy and a hint of summer had seemed to linger on her face.

It was at that moment, that specific instant that Dave knew he had to make her laugh. He had to see it, hear it. Most of all, he had to know that *he* had caused the transformation from winter to summer.

Dave paused in the act of raising his sandwich to his mouth as Janey Anderson opened her front door. Tension froze every muscle in his body. Think of something to say, he commanded his brain, but all he could think of was that she was going to step in that door any second.

Janey Anderson opened the front door and stepped outside, pulling the door quietly closed behind her. She carefully locked it, a habit as ingrained in her as that of brushing her teeth, learned early in her foster-home life back East and reinforced following the death of her husband.

She wanted to glance over her shoulder to see if the tall sheriff was on his front porch. He had been there every night for the past two weeks. She had told herself that he pulled his unit into his driveway every night and rushed out to the porch to enjoy the first warm evenings of spring. But when he'd spoken to her two nights ago and had become tongue-tied, and his face had flushed a ruddy hue, she had known he'd been waiting to talk to her.

Janey sighed. She wanted to talk to him, too. But only as a friend to a friend, a neighbor to a neighbor, the widow of a uniform to another uniform. She just wanted to talk, and something about the tall sheriff with his crooked grin and his smiling eyes and his host of friends who dropped by his house without warning and always left laughing, held a lure to her that no one else in this town had managed.

All too clearly she remembered the evenings spent with friends dropping by, everyone welcome at Bill and Janey's house, men with guns unconcernedly hauling sticky-handed children onto their muscled thighs, and laughter everywhere. It had been the life she'd always dreamed of having, the home she'd wanted every single day of her childhood.

This small-town sheriff projected the same tolerance, the same respect for life.

But the very fact that he wore a gun and carried a badge deterred her, as well. Those days of believing in the invulnerability of the good guys were gone; the part of her heart that had guarded all the safe dreams of an old age and grandchildren romping in a yard was buried along with Bill.

Still she wished the combination of strength and honesty on the sheriff's face could be trusted. But the time for trusting was over, that too buried with the loving part of her heart.

She could feel his eyes on her now, and paused, drawing a deep breath before turning to face the scantily tree-lined street, the winter-yellowed lawns and scraggly hedges and root-cracked sidewalks that comprised the downtown housing district in Portales. If she met his gaze tonight, if she smiled at him, she knew his face would stain the color of the setting sun, the deep red of the earth on the flats south of town.

But that rise and fall of his color was part of the charm about him, a portion of the reason he made her guard slip a little when she thought of him. When she noticed his lights on long after the eastern-plains television station had gone to bed for the night, or when she saw him bending his tall frame over to see eye-to-eye with some neighborhood child, large hand resting easily and confidently on narrow, un-afraid shoulders, she felt the pull, knew the urge to talk with him, too.

She drew another deep breath, a process made more difficult with each passing day of her pregnancy, and wrinkled her nose at the strong smell of sour yeast rising from the nearby ethanol plant. She knew that the farmers in the area relied on the ethanol industry for consumption of the acres and acres of milo, a stubby, stunted-growth corn-looking hybrid that she'd never heard of before moving to southeastern New Mexico. But she was also distressingly aware that her pregnancy had enhanced her sense of smell and that the overripe bakery scent was getting to her more and more with each passing day.

The pregnancy itself was getting to her. As far as it went, she'd had an easy time carrying this baby. The early stages of morning sickness had faded before she'd left Taos, the small northern New Mexico town where she'd never felt a stranger, had built a life with Bill. That time seemed ages ago now, as though it had happened to someone else. It felt as if she'd been pregnant forever.

And she felt as if Bill had been dead for years and she'd been cast adrift all her life. She was a stranger in a sea of half-familiar faces, pregnant and alone in a town where Tropicana roses bloomed in October, tulips bobbed their waxy heads and the iris were already up, and people were playing golf and tennis in spite of the ground hog's forecast of six more weeks of winter.

Working with the terminally ill, she knew all the stages of grief, the nuances of despair. But knowing the stages and living them were two entirely different things, she thought. Waking up one day and discovering that hope has died changes your life. The only way she could get through each day, each night, was to hold herself away from that fragile trust of another human being.

And there was so much not to trust. When Bill had died, a flood of cards, letters and phone calls had come pouring in. People had surrounded her with concerned, caring offers of this and that. Then as time went on and the days stretched into weeks and the weeks into a month, the cards and letters stopped coming, and the flowers disappeared into wastebaskets and garbage pails. And one by one the people also disappeared.

At first, she'd been grateful for the solitude, blanketing herself in memories and the silence of her suddenly too-large house. But the news accounts never ceased, and as the preliminary hearing for her husband's murderer got underway, she found the walls beginning to close in.

She tried working off her grief at the hospice where she'd worked for several years, but while it was effective, it did nothing to assuage the loneliness, the unrelenting anguish or despair.

That was about the time she knew for certain she was pregnant with the baby Bill had always wanted, with the baby he would never see. And that was about the time the other letters started arriving.

She'd opened the first one without thought, assuming it to be an expression of sympathy, and automatically her eyes had dropped to the signature, only to find it curiously absent. The body of the letter had been rank with vitriol, fetid in its viciousness.

More letters followed, not all written in the same hand. Some spouted vague obscenities, others congratulated her on the death of her husband. Still others launched into a diatribe against police officers of all types. A few, like the first, threatened her own life if she didn't leave town.

She had taken them all to the state police and turned them in. But there were no return addresses and nothing her husband's brotherhood could do to stop them.

"Why don't you sell the place and clear out of here?" a friend of Bill's had asked her. "Leave all this crap behind, Janey. You don't need any of this, now."

And looking into his eyes, she'd seen the truth of his words, and so much more. He was right, she had to get on with her life, and she had to leave his friends, as grief stricken and curiously guilt ridden as she, to get on with theirs. She was a constant reminder of their own mortality, of the risks inherent with their careers, of the possibility—and probability—of personal tragedy touching their lives.

So she'd sold nearly everything and, after locating another hospice where she could work, moved to Portales. And things had been better. She had enjoyed—as nearly as she could enjoy anything anymore—working on her house, had found a peace in the bright hallways of the new hospice and in working with the cheerful and friendly staff. And she had relished the respite from the nasty letters.

But the letters had begun again; she'd had four in the past two weeks. They'd come here, to her current address, a location she hadn't given to anyone except the state police office. And these weren't the consolation cards nor the notes of sympathy, these were the threatening variety.

These made her want to talk to this tall sheriff more than ever. But she knew she wanted much more than just passing this weight from her shoulders to his. And she didn't dare, for he was another peace officer. As far as the sheriff went, as a lawman, he was another of those people who would always be desperately and terribly vulnerable to violence. She might be getting stronger, and her emotions were no longer roiling in that cloudy limbo, but she knew, without question or doubt, that she could never go through it again. Not even for a friend.

She turned then, scarcely aware of the dry, cooling air, concentrating on her footing on the weathered and pockmarked porch planking, willing the active child within her to subside the contrapuntal rhythm against her rib cage. She had only two more weeks to go and her baby would be with her.

And then she'd have two people to look after instead of just one. Two alone against an uncertain world. It sounded like one of the country-western songs played on the radio stations here, she thought.

Again she resisted an urge to turn and look at the man on his front porch. If only she could confide in him. If only she knew him well enough to tell him that she was scared of going through this alone, scared of the threats, frightened of the dark sometimes, and all too often so desperately lonely she would turn on the radio to talk shows just to hear other voices.

She raised her eyes then and, across the expanse of houses, lawns and pavement, met Dave Reynolds's gaze. He might as well have touched her.

Even from the distance of three houses down the block, Dave could see the rich blue of her eyes and the fullness of her unsmiling lips and felt a knot gather in his chest. She had the most expressive eyes, the most vulnerable face he'd ever seen. In his experience, people with vulnerable faces usually possessed loquacious tongues as well, vulnerability and volubility often went hand in hand. But not with Janey Anderson. And maybe this was why he'd been knocking off at quitting time instead of hanging around the office, dreaming up busywork that would keep him away from his empty, cheerless house.

All he could think about was the way the red from the waning sunlight was reflected in her black hair as she hesitated on her porch. As fine spun as silk, and as filled with flame as a ranch campfire, the dark, softly curling mass shifted in the early March breeze, as though the wind were a lover and the touch a caress. Dave's fingers actually twitched in response.

She held on to the cement pillar with a delicate, slender hand and carefully stepped down onto what had been, until yesterday, the somewhat rickety wooden steps of her house. Again she looked right and left. She hesitated when she saw him sitting on his porch, staring at her, and he wished he knew what she was thinking.

For a moment her face was stunningly defenseless, a wistfulness crossing the fine features; then as if she sensed she might be opening a door she preferred closed, she glanced away, her lips thinning not in disgust but in rigidly controlled emotion. When she looked back, all traces of vulnerability were gone.

Dave could feel the "stay back" message clear across the street. With a casual air he was far from feeling, he lifted his beer in a friendly salute then deliberately turned his gaze to the red-stained western sky, as if studying the oranges and pinks rippling across the thin clouds hovering on the horizon. Instinctively he knew that if he did anything else she would turn and walk the other way, not cross the street, not walk by his porch at all.

But he couldn't resist looking again. She stepped down a single stair, her hand still on the cement pillar. He wanted to call out to her, to ask her to sit with him awhile, to relax her evening ritual long enough to watch the sun go the rest of the way down, the reds blurring to purple and orange, to share the daily light show. To spend a few quiet moments with *him*.

He was ten kinds of a fool, he told himself, fiercely polishing off his tasteless sandwich. He was actually racing home every night so he could sit on the front porch and give a pregnant widow the eye. He felt devoid of decency as a randy teenager and as lacking in conversation as a fifth offender upon arrest. But he couldn't take his eyes off her, and he gave her his arm as support in nothing but spirit.

And then she fell.

One moment she was stepping down, her head raised, her eyes forward, her hand turning loose of the pillar. The next, she jerked forward, arms flailing, fingers scrabbling futilely at the pillar. She was like some graceful golden bird taking wing.

Her downward slump was matched exactly by Dave's thrusting upward. As she plummeted toward the ground, Dave hurdled the scanty railing on his own porch. Before she ever touched the ground, he was leaping over hedges and racing across the street.

As he ran, his mind screamed a protest at the possibility of her being hurt, at the unfairness of anything happening to Janey. How could something like this happen to one who had been through so much, to a woman who was pregnant? How could it have happened with him just sitting there watching it?

These thoughts tumbled around his mind, taking no more time than nanoseconds, and as his imagination pictured the result of her fall, he found he had triggered the reminders of the dreadful past he thought he'd left far behind him. As he ran, as his mind scrambled to assimilate the nightmare in front of him, his eyes sought reassurance, his heart clamored for relief.

Janey cried out as she hit the cement sidewalk leading to her house, seizing with even fiercer hold, the grip on his heart. Until then he hadn't realized that what he was witnessing had been in slow motion, that he had moved instantly, had run before she ever really fell. If he had been a second faster, she might never have hit the ground at all.

But with a sickening crack, her head contacted with the pavement and, as though seeing from eyes other than his own, Dave saw Janey's body jerk violently then seemingly go perfectly still.

"No!" Dave yelled, forging across her lawn in a single lunge, clearing the last of the stretch separating them. He murmured the denial a second time as he saw her limp hands and her twisted body. She was a golden eddy in a sea of gray-blue shadows.

"Janey...?" he asked, dropping to the ground beside her. *Don't let her be hurt,* he pleaded silently, reaching for her shoulders. She was so pale. So still. And unbidden to his heart came a harsher plea, *Don't let her be dead!*

"Janey," he said shakily, lightly running his hands over her face, her shoulders, over her swollen belly. "Are you hurt, honey?"

A shudder worked through him as his mind grappled with the past, trying to expel the memories that intruded. Shadows covered Janey's body, just as they had obscured Patty Donahue's body in that raid in L.A. And just like Janey, Patty had lain so still, so pale, so lifeless.

He'd been helpless then, also. And too late. The only difference between them was, he'd sent Patty to her death, sent her in as bait for a serial killer, never suspecting the killer was already there, never dreaming that Patty would be tortured and murdered while he and too many other cops waited outside not twenty yards away.

"Don't be hurt," he muttered, his hands reaching to pat Janey's legs, his lips twisting bitterly when he noticed that one of her low pumps was absent from her foot. A wave of revulsion and horror so reminiscent of that terrible night in L.A. swept over him at the sight of Janey's other leg, scraped and bleeding, still trapped in a section of the step that had given way.

She'd had the porch worked on only the day before. Hadn't the fool fixed the steps? Carefully he worked the leg free, frowning over the straight-lined cut on her leg, and edged her down from her sprawled twist on the steps. He cupped her head in his hands. "Janey. Honey, wake up."

He felt like screaming and crying. Was she alive? If she was, would she be all right?

But she moaned then, and her swollen stomach heaved mightily.

The memory of Patty abruptly departed, as did the memory of his race across the street trying to beat Janey's fall. These receded to another plane of existence, almost as though the earlier events had never transpired. And a new fear settled in on Dave's heart. For as he saw her body buck in response to the stomach rippling, he realized with chill terror that the nightmare was far from over, because Janey Anderson was in full-fledged labor. That was why she had jerked, perhaps was even why she had lain still afterward.

He looked away from her, first to the empty, dark house behind him, then up at the Lyon house, willing ninety-two-year-old Jewel Lyon to come out and rescue him. And for just a moment, despite his training and overriding his desire to help Janey, he wished he was anywhere on earth but on the chipped cement sidewalk leading out of her house, one knee in her Johnny-jump-ups, her hair a silky halo in his hands.

"Mrs. Lyon!" he yelled. "Call an ambulance, *right now!*" He saw the older woman's curtain twitch open then closed.

"Help me," Janey murmured, her voice huskier than ever with pain, and probably with shock.

"I'm here," Dave said, taking her hand, calling on every ounce of will in him to soothe her, to remain clam. This was a far cry from those childish lessons back in L.A. or the quickie-thriller course they put the deputies through at the department. And Janey looked a great deal different than the fat old L.A. sergeant with a pillow stuffed under his belt, a rubber doll in his gnarled fist.

"Mrs. Lyon!" he called again.

But even as he heard Mrs. Lyon's front door opening, Janey's eyes opened, as well. Her blue eyes met his more calmly than he would ever have imagined someone could do in such circumstances.

"Did I fall?" she asked.

For a split second, totally wrapped up in the awareness of that heaving belly, Dave couldn't think what she meant. Then his gaze flicked to the caved-in step and he nodded. "Yes," he said, not bothering to elaborate. He heard Mrs. Lyon's door close again and swore inwardly.

"My leg hurts. Is it broken?" she asked. Again he marveled at how calm she sounded.

"I don't think so," he said. "But you've got a pretty mean scrape."

"You came," she murmured.

"Of course," he said. "We'll get some help, now."

As she sighed and closed her eyes, Dave wished he'd paid more attention to those childbirth classes, even to those first aid classes. At the very least, however, he could wrap her leg with his handkerchief; that wouldn't take a genius at medicine. Still, most of the top layer of skin was gone along her calf. Almost in a broad square. As he placed the handkerchief against her leg, he turned to see the hole in the step. Janey drew in her breath on a sharp hiss as the soft cotton brushed her open wound, and he turned back to her swiftly. "Sorry," he said.

She sighed as he lowered her leg, resting it against his thigh, then she said again, "You came."

"Yes, honey. I'm here. It's all right, now."

To his surprise, her lips curved to a relaxed smile. They compressed so swiftly into a tight moue of pain that Dave decided he must have been mistaken.

Her hand clamped down on Dave's with enough force to have caused anyone else pain. Her breath whistled in and exhaled in short puffs of air, and a moan gurgled in the back of her throat. Dave forgot to look at his watch, but some dim memory of the training spurred him into encouraging her breathing, telling her it would pass soon.

As the pain peaked and began to ebb, he brushed the hair from her brow. "You're doing fine, Janey. You'll be all right."

"I'm having the baby now," she said, her voice dreamy and distant.

He felt like yelling a negation, but he kept it in, knowing it not only wouldn't do her any good, it would also have been patently untrue.

"I think so, honey," he muttered. He'd never felt quite this inadequate in his entire adult life. Except for that single agonizing moment when they'd found Patty Donahue's body.

"And you'll stay with me," she said. It wasn't a question, and the pressure of her fingers brooked no denial.

"Of course," he said. "An ambulance should be coming any minute."

"Oh, God," she murmured. "Here's another one. It hurts."

"Breathe like you were doing a minute ago. That's good."

Dave held her hand tightly and locked his gaze with hers, making her look at him, making her focus on him even as he wondered what the hell was taking Mrs. Lyon so damned long.

As the contraction subsided and Janey's shoulders slumped to the dusk-darkened pavement, Mrs. Lyon's porch light flicked on, her front door opened and the older woman stepped outside. From her expression, Dave could tell that the ordeal of the night was only just beginning.

She nodded at his questioning frown and called out to him, "There was a wreck out on the Lovington highway, almost to Dora, and all the ambulances have been sent out there. They told me it'll be at least forty minutes before they can get one here. And at least that long before we could have one from over at Clovis.''

Every swearword Dave had ever heard flitted through his mind, but he clamped his jaw tightly against loosing them.

"Did you tell them what had happened?" he asked, grimacing at the notion of having to do this himself.

Mrs. Lyon said she had, then asked if he didn't think the "little girl" wouldn't be better off inside. "You can carry her right on in the house. I'll unlock her door. She always locks it, you know."

Achingly slowly, as he scrambled to find the key, Mrs. Lyon crossed the lawn. She mounted the steps carefully, using her walking stick like a third leg. Avoiding the gaping hole, Mrs. Lyon took the key from Dave's almost nerveless hand and proceeded to unlock Janey's door. When she had flicked on the porch light, Dave told Janey he was going to pick her up and carry her inside.

Dimly he worried about a back or neck injury, but as she arched against yet another labor pain, he realized her back was probably fine and she had to be moved in any case.

Janey's sharp squeeze on his hand told him this wasn't the best moment to move her, however, and he looked back down in alarm. The contractions were too close together. There was no way, if the labor was already this far advanced, that she would be able to wait any forty minutes. It was one thing to deliver a baby overdue and ready for the world, and an entirely different thing to assist in a premature birth. What if something went wrong?

"It's okay, honey. Everything's under control," he said, and wondered if she could read the lie in his voice.

Her blue eyes, clouded with pain, seemed to bore into his, and clung to his as fiercely as her hand pulled at him. As he unflinchingly met her gaze, some primal instinct for protection washed through him.

As though she were exhaling his fears instead of her own pained breaths, he felt his fears of helplessness to handle the situation recede, then fade altogether. She needed him to be strong. She needed him period.

And come hell or high water, he was going to be there for her.

Chapter 2

"We've got to get you in out of this chill," the sheriff said, bending over her.

He was close enough that Janey could feel the warmth emanating from his body. His face seemed to swim in and out of her pain, a life raft, a buoy just for her. "I'm going to lift you up, now. Just hang on to me, honey. I'll have you inside in no time."

She liked the way he sounded as though he did this sort of thing every day. She liked the way his broad-shouldered body blocked her view of the darkening sky, of the shadows that seemed to linger on the edges of her porch, and suspected it was deliberate on the part of this man. She liked the calm confidence in his rich voice, the soft vowels, the blurred consonants that took her back to her childhood days and western television shows.

Most of all, however, she liked the sense of companionship, the feeling of not being alone. It was so unique and so foreign that she found herself clutching his hand more tightly than she needed to, wanting him to stay, needing him to remain with her now.

"It'll be all right, Janey. I promise you."

Through all the terror of the past nine months, through the long lonely hours between dinner and dawn, she'd been plagued by fears of going through this birthing alone. But now *he* was here, and even if she couldn't remember his last name, he'd told her he would be there for her, assured her it would be all right, and she believed him. His warm hand had only left hers to brush the hair from her eyes or to gently stroke her cheek. And in this painful, blissful moment she could relax. She could believe his words, listen to the message in his hands, the promise in his eyes.

"Up we go," he said, lifting her seemingly effortlessly.

It felt strangely natural to wrap her hands around his neck, and all too easy to rest her brow against the stiff collar of his khaki uniform. If only she could feel this way every day, all the time, she thought bemusedly, then tried to remember the last time she had felt so safe.

Nine months ago almost to the day. Bill had been alive then, and she hadn't even known she was pregnant.

Another spasm grabbed her before she could focus on the past, and despite the severity of the contraction, she was grateful for the respite in her thoughts.

"That's just fine, Mrs. Lyon."

She heard him speaking as though from a great distance. She bit down on her lip to keep from whimpering with the shuddering pain. Somehow, with their eyes locked, the pain didn't seem as strong, as though the link created a wall between the pain and her consciousness.

He laid her down gently, and, thankfully, as though reading her mind, swiftly bent over her, taking her hands from where she'd been digging into his shoulders. He gripped her fingers tightly and then drew her arms down, against her sides.

"Please," she whispered, unable to expel more than this one word. All she wanted were his eyes, those fathomless eyes locking with hers. His gaze captured hers as though he knew what she'd been pleading for. And gratefully she sank into the depths of smoky gray.

They were the color of the eastern New Mexico sky in January, the color of a fog on a winter's morning, or the mist that sometimes settled in the arroyos east of town to cool or moisten but never threaten.

Just the right color, she thought dimly, and clung to the awareness.

"Focus on me," he said, and his voice seemed to come from some other part of the universe, so thoroughly was she wrapped up in his eyes. She suspected they held that clouded color that would appear blue in certain lights, charcoal in others. Eyes she could trust.

And this trust, and the pain, and the pair of smoky eyes became the center of her universe.

"Breathe," he said.

The very steadiness in his manner, the confidence and certainty in his voice cut through the pain like a lifeline in a sea of agony. She gratefully did as he suggested.

"That's good, Janey," he said. His voice was deep, soothing. Comforting. "Concentrate on the breathing as the contraction ebbs." It was difficult to do as he asked, but because he had requested it, because he was there for her, she did it, all the while wishing she knew him better, wishing she had stopped and talked to him all those times she had passed his house.

She liked the way he called her by her name, easily, as though he'd used it a million times before. And she liked the way he called her "honey." The simple word conjured notions of warmth, tenderness, lent a personal air to a casual endearment, made her feel connected with him. And now, of all times, she so desperately needed to feel connected with someone.

When the pain abruptly ceased, as if some fairy god-
mother had waved a magic wand somewhere, she realized
that his breathing technique didn't lessen the pain, but it
served to still the fear in her and give her scattered thoughts
a focus. That and the warmth of his broad hands. And the
faith in his gray eyes.

He loosened his hands and she clutched at them in sharp
panic. "Don't leave," she begged, ashamed of the pleading, desperate for him to stay with her.

He smiled fleetingly. "No, honey. I won't leave. Don't
worry now."

His words entered her heart like a vow, and though she
knew that as soon as the baby was born, the feeling of trust,
the sense of belonging, would disappear, for this brief moment she felt she could rely upon it, revel in it, let it envelope her and keep her safe.

He brushed her hair back from her damp forehead and
lightly caressed her cheek with the back of his knuckles. The
touch was surprisingly gentle and intimate.

"Who's your doctor?" he asked softly.

"McCall," she whispered, never taking her eyes from his.

"Mrs. Lyon?" he asked someone, not turning away from
her.

"I've called both Drs. McCall and Heythrop. They're already at the hospital with patients. Probably with the accident on the highway," a voice quavered, presumably that of
the invisible Mrs. Lyon. "And Dave? I don't think I'll be
able to help."

That was right. His name was Dave. David Reynolds.
And he was the sheriff. A strong name. A strong profession. She relaxed into the thought of his name. It was a good
one, a name that meant strength, a name that meant the
world to her at this minute.

"Well," he said, smiling easily enough, "looks like we're
going to have us just a small party."

Despite the dreadful events of the night, despite the baby's imminent arrival, and regardless of the pain and fear, she found herself smiling back. "An intimate affair," she said, and flushed as the reality of her statement impacted.

He chuckled then. It was as if she could feel the relief in him through her fingertips. His face lightened, and she suddenly understood that he was as frightened as she. Instead of making her feel more scared, this brought back some of her flagging courage.

She drew a deep, steadying breath. Dave had said he was going to be there for her . . . she wasn't going to make it difficult for him.

But as if her body wanted to betray this, another contraction seized her and shook her in its mindless grasp.

"Ohhh . . ." she moaned. "I think the baby's coming!"

"Breathe," he said calmly. "The baby can't be coming quite yet. Slow down, take it easy. It'll be all right. I'm right here. You can do this, honey. Look at me, now. You're doing just fine. Breathe. That's good. That's it. This one's almost over. See? It's already ebbing. Look at me, honey. Stay with me, now."

Yes, she wanted to say. I'll stay with you. But she was too tired to speak, too drained by the need to hold back the pain for his sake. To be good, to be strong for his sake. A sudden rush of warm liquid soaked the bed beneath her and coated her legs. Tears of embarrassment gathered in her eyes.

"What is it, honey?" he asked, lifting a hand to her face, his thumb gently erasing a stray tear.

"I . . . my water . . . broke," she mumbled, choking back a full flow of anguish. It wasn't fair to feel so undignified, so out of control of her own body. Not now, not in front of him, not when she felt safe and protected for the first time in months.

He looked utterly nonplussed for a moment, then his face took on that ruddy, sunset hue that had drawn her from her first glimpse of him. "Oh. Well, that's to be expected, isn't it?"

It was meant as a reassurance, but it sounded much to her as if he were seeking it for himself. "Yes," she mumbled.

"Well, then. There we have it."

Suddenly, quite unexpectedly, she was no longer afraid at all. He hadn't run, he hadn't even flinched. He had blushed to the very depths of his epidural layers, but he wasn't going to walk out on her. And by staying he was granting her the dignity that her body had stripped away; he was giving her himself as a bulwark against the fear, a guard against the pain. *And a moment's respite from the nightmare of trusting no one.*

A giddy, almost buoyant euphoria swept through her and, to her own amazement, she chuckled. "Yes," she said. "There we have it."

Another pain tore all semblance of rational thought away. This was the worst one yet. This time, no amount of clinging to his hands or sinking into his gaze could mask the determination of the child within her to see the world. Dimly, over her short, locomotive-type breathing, she heard Mrs. Lyon ask something and heard him reply, but she had no idea what they said.

As the pain subsided, and before she had an opportunity to do more than sigh in relief, he released her hands and rose to his feet.

"No," she murmured, protesting his departure.

"I'm not leaving," he said clearly. "But we have to get you ready for this baby of yours. I think you're probably right—this young 'un is aching for freedom."

He spoke slowly, his voice like the honey he called her, sticking on consonants, smoothing the vowels to a blurred sweetness. He pulled back the blankets beneath her, talking to her all the while, his drawling, east-plains accent strangely soothing, like a melody gently strummed on an old guitar, his words inconsequential, his actions tranquilizing, neutralizing the fear.

With Mrs. Lyon's help, he soon had her stripped and lying on a fresh set of dry towels, her own down comforter draped around her shoulders. Between the rapidly converging contractions and his eyes, and following every command of his rich voice, she wasn't allowed to feel embarrassed, wasn't given time to dwell on the complete and utter indignity of the moment.

If anything, he made her feel that in some special way she was granting him the best gift of his entire life, that of permitting him to help her through the birth of her baby. Had he said this, or had she read it in his incredible eyes?

With his hands scrubbed and his sleeves rolled up, he looked ready to go to work, and when his eyes met hers, she felt ready too. Lying propped against a bank of pillows, she could see him clearly through the vee of her upraised knees and felt the warmth of his arms encircling her legs. What was it about him that made her feel so secure, so protected, so tenderly cared for, so much so that she didn't feel any more than the slightest awkwardness at this stark intimacy?

He was close enough that his body served as a barrier to the remainder of the room, to the doorway beyond from whence she could occasionally hear Mrs. Lyon's autumn-leaved voice. He was close enough that the scent of his after-shave's tang cut through the coppery scent of perspiration and labor.

He had been there for her, had appeared almost magically from the shadows on his front porch to sweep her from fear and pain, and was now sharing in the single most important moment of her life. It was as if at her lowest ebb she'd been granted a sight of goodness again, been given a present of man's true humanity toward his fellow in need. And there was something more, something that made her feel oddly feminine in this moment of complete lack of control.

"I'm so glad you're—" she began, but broke off with a hiss as her entire body seemed to convulse and shudder. All thoughts of the past few terror-filled months, memories of Bill, disappeared from her mind. All she could think about was the steady eyes before her, the firm grip on her shaking fingers.

"Good girl. You're wonderful, honey. Just keep breathing like that. That's great! Hey! I see the baby's head!" He laughed, an exulted, triumphant roar. She had to smile with him, and her heart pounded in fear and anticipation.

"Hang in there, darling, we're about to have us a baby!"

Even through the pain, she wondered if he realized how connected his words made them sound, as if it were their baby, made together, that was pushing his way into the world. And if he did, wondered if he would have any idea how strongly that idea appealed to her, how much it moved her.

The wonder of the moment held Dave in thrall, and he almost called out when the contraction ended and the brief glimpse of the baby disappeared. For the first time since this had begun—and it seemed like a thousand years ago that he'd sat on his front porch, a beer in one hand, a half-eaten sandwich in the other—he was glad that Mrs. Lyon had looked at him in total denial, that the doctors had been tied up, that the ambulances had been on call elsewhere.

In the back of his mind he'd been halfheartedly cursing the good people of Portales for not rescuing him from this duty. Now he was grateful they hadn't.

He was perfectly content to be exactly where he was. It felt so good, so right. He'd never felt so vitally alive in his whole life. It seemed as if everything he'd ever said or done had led to this moment in time, to this single, shockingly simplistic example of what life was really all about.

He looked up and met Janey's tired, almost glazed eyes. A frown marred the smooth line of her brow, but her lips were slightly curved upward. He smiled back at her, not

trying to hide the awe he felt, not dodging the surge of su-
preme protectiveness he felt for her and the child that was
soon to make its way into his waiting hands.

He hadn't been really curious about the child when he'd
asked her if she wanted a girl or a boy. But now, he felt
consumed with the need to know…to see. He actually held
his breath in sharp anticipation.

As she breathed out, so did he, and his fingers trembled
with the adrenaline rush, with the prospect of holding this
newborn infant in his big, rough hands.

"This is it, honey. When the next contraction hits, if you
feel the urge to push, I want you to go right ahead and push
with everything you've got." The words felt right, he
thought, they sounded correct…even knowledgeable. He
didn't stop to wonder where they'd come from. As if he did
this sort of thing every day of the week, he settled her knees
against his broad shoulders and reached around her legs,
taking her hands firmly in his. He hoped like hell he was
giving the proper instructions.

She had scarcely drawn the deep breath he commanded
she take before Dave saw her stomach ripple violently. He
barked at Mrs. Lyon to get behind her shoulders and help
prop her, even as he drew her upward to aid her pushing.

"Now push, honey. *Push!*"

For a split second, as Janey gripped his hands in fierce
obedience, closed her eyes and bore down, Dave knew a
stark terror that something would go wrong, that something he did or said would make things go awry, that she
would be hurt, that the baby wouldn't be all right.

But the baby's head appeared then, and swiftly transferring her hands to the back of her legs, he gently touched the
newborn infant's damp head, aching to assist the baby's
passage into the world.

"Don't stop now, darling, our baby's almost here. Keep
pushing. One, two, three…"

She cried out then, scaring him, making him feel guilty for his urging her to push, making him afraid this was hurting her too much, but his fear that the baby would be crushed frightened him more.

"One more, darling. One more."

And miraculously, she somehow found the strength to give him just one more violent push and as simply as that, a baby boy rested in his hands, tiny arms flailing, face contorted, damp body scarcely filling Dave's broad hands.

"He's here," he murmured to an absolutely silent room. "It's a boy, honey. And he's fine. So very fine." Relief and wonder shook him and something deep inside him exploded, as though this tiny baby had detonated a fuse on a locked door he'd never even known existed in his heart.

As if from a great distance, he heard Janey's sob of utter relief escape her lips, but he didn't look up. He couldn't seem to take his eyes from the tiny living wonder in his hands. He'd never felt so completely humbled and yet so thoroughly exultant as he did at that moment, holding this newborn baby that he'd helped usher into life.

Without knowing where the knowledge came from, or without thinking about anything but the next step in this tiny human's introduction to the universe of breathing and living, he gently swabbed the baby's face with the folded edge of a soft moist towel, and moved lower, cleansing the baby and his own hands while encouraging a breath with tender, cautious strokes.

Dimly he wondered how doctors of yesteryear could have swatted life into a newborn, when at the touch of his hand the baby gasped and pulled his first sharp breath of air into unaccustomed lungs. And without a cry, the baby exhaled, then drew another mewling breath.

Janey could hear the note of wonder in this amazing man's voice as he drew breath from her newborn son. "He's so beautiful, honey. So very beautiful," he said.

She tried raising her head, and Mrs. Lyon aided her to see what their efforts had wrought.

Dave's face was a study of concentration and tenderness. His rich brown hair was tousled from his exertions, and sweat ran down his temple, disappearing back into his hair. His mouth was parted and his lips were dry. His dark lashes shadowed his cheek as he gazed at the baby.

Two tiny, clenched-fisted hands reached upward as if to touch him. He looked up finally and met her eyes. It seemed, in the diffused lights of the bedroom, in the haze of spent strength, that his eyes were filled with tears. So slowly that her heart ached, he smiled.

"We have a son, honey," he said, not even aware, she thought, that he'd used the plural pronoun.

Her heart constricted at the note of pride in his voice, at the distinct relief. He shifted slightly, and with one hand beneath the baby's head, and another under her son's small bottom, he held the baby up in the air, above her knees, allowing her to see her baby better, but appearing as if he were introducing him to the gods of the night.

Then, with an obvious reluctance, he gently lowered the baby to her bare stomach. His hands were warm and damp and remained touching the baby, and softly stroking the tiny brow at the same time, they gently kneaded her pliant flesh. She raised her own hands to touch her baby, to pause for a moment to cover her rescuer's hand with her own.

Looking at her new baby for the first time as his mother, feeling a powerful surge of some new emotion, some hitherto untapped well of love and protectiveness, she felt tears of gratitude, of joy, of peace sting her eyes.

She looked up to a smoky gaze. There were no words anywhere, anytime, that could ever say enough to this man. She was alive, her baby was alive, they were together because of this man, because of his touch, because of his voice, because he'd stayed with her, giving her everything as surely and as generously as a lover, as a husband.

That he was as moved as she, there was no doubt, she thought. When she'd seen him before, all those evenings during her walk, there had been no denying his attractiveness, for he was handsome in a rugged, powerful way. But now, with his face suffused with awe, as though he'd just experienced a great enlightenment, he was beyond mere attraction, he was at one with her, as though he belonged with her, was attached to her by some mystical thread of life.

A soft whimper caused her to look back down, and she knew what that mystical thread was: a tiny newborn, downy and damp, small fist pressed to smaller mouth. His introduction to the world had been abrupt and early, starting in fear but ending in love. And what more could any mother want for her baby?

An unfamiliar sting and twinge stirred in her breasts, and instinctively she drew the baby upward where he automatically and equally instinctively began to suckle. As the letdown reflex kicked in with full tingling glory, she sighed and leaned back against the pillows.

Another shudder, a final contraction snared her and she heard her rescuer's murmur of encouragement. "It's over honey. You're all done. All we have to do is wait for the ambulance now," he said. His tone was a mixture of regret and relief. The relief made her smile, the regret lent a note of poignancy to their brief time together.

She knew regret as well; for a shining moment she had felt bonded with another human being. For a glittering, shattering half an hour she had given in to that connectedness, had grasped the opportunity to let someone else shoulder responsibility for her safety as surely as she had grabbed hold of his hands. And now it must end.

The pain was gone, but so was that halcyon respite from the darkness she'd been living in for nine months.

And all she knew of him was that he was a sheriff, his name was Dave, and that he'd saved her. She desperately wished she knew more, and felt a real sorrow in knowing that whatever she learned, it wouldn't change the fact that he was a law enforcement officer and that she couldn't open herself to that kind of torture again.

It distressed her enormously that in this moment of rare bonding he didn't know that she was only half a woman, only half a person, and that if he knew anything about her, it was comprised of the things he'd heard on the news, or the small details of her new life in Portales. In terms of real living she was as much a newborn as the baby at her breast.

"You were wonderful, Janey," he said, covering her with a warm, soft blanket handed him by Mrs. Lyon.

"So were you," she murmured in response, wanting to correct him, needing to let him know that it was due to him that the baby was born safely, that she felt fine, even happy for the first time in nine months. She had trusted him with her life and the life of her baby.

There aren't any words..." she began, then trailed off as the doorbell rang and Mrs. Lyon limped from the room to answer it.

"Janey," he said softly, forcing her to look up. He studied her intently for a few minutes, as if sensing the withdrawal in her but not understanding the reason for it, not after what they'd been through together. She couldn't explain.

"Thank you," she said finally, the only words she could possibly utter. The gratitude came from her heart, from her very soul.

In answer he patted her still-upraised knee, his long fingers gripping her for a moment of acceptance and reassurance. He didn't say anything and neither did she; everything that could be said had already been spoken, and the silence between them now was oddly peaceful, strangely filled with nostalgia. It was as if, not knowing the reasons why, he understood that the woman he'd taken care of was gone, that this was someone else altogether, someone who couldn't share anything with anyone, because sharing meant trust and trust was out of the question.

Over the sound of Mrs. Lyon's voice in the other room came the screeching whine of the ambulance's arrival.

There were no words to give him, nothing that could be said now to halt the cessation of the bond that had grown between them, no platitude that could stop the coldness, the despair from resuming. The hiatus was over.

"What are you going to call him?" Dave asked over the commotion just outside the house, the racket in her brain.

She looked from her nursing child to the man who had delivered him. There might be no words she could offer this man, but there was a single gift she could grant him.

"David," she said softly, a smile curving her lips at the rightness, the appropriateness. And tears stung her eyes at the flush of pleasure, of shock, that stained Dave's tanned cheeks.

"You don't have to do that," he murmured, his pleased, stunned face telling her that she did.

"I know," she answered slowly, meaning much more than the simple two words could express. She had intended, if the baby was a boy, to call him Bill. But somehow, calling him David was more appropriate, more suited toward new lives, bright futures. "I want to call him David. It fits him already."

"It makes me feel a part of him," he said softly, almost reverently, laying a large and very gentle hand upon her baby's back.

"You are," she said. "If it hadn't been for you—"

A bang at the doorway interrupted her, and a young paramedic burst into the room. "Stand back, sir. I'll take it from here."

Whatever the young paramedic thought he'd be taking, to Janey it seemed it could only be her moment of peace. Now, for the first time in what seemed like hours, she was conscious of her spent body, her nudity, of the indignity. The ever-present darkness that accompanied her nowadays crept close once again. She wanted to cry out against this intrusion.

"Right," Dave said quietly, absently, a flush on his face. He pushed to his feet, shaking his pants over his boots. His mouth worked as though he would say more, and his eyes met Janey's for a long, emotionally filled moment, though she couldn't read his thoughts, she knew he felt loss, for she felt it as well.

"So, are you in any pain?" the paramedic asked.

Yes, Janey thought, even as she shook her head in the negative. Her eyes were on the tall cowboy who stood away from the bed, his ruddy face averted. *More pain than I would have thought possible.*

Chapter 3

Janey watched Dave leave the room soon after the young paramedics crowded it with their instructions, their gurney and their confused babble. It seemed like some of the warmth against the chill of the desert's March night went with him.

As the medics carried the baby and her to the ambulance she caught a glimpse of him across the street, talking with three of the closest neighbors beneath the spilled light of the corner street lamp.

"Wait," she said before the youngest paramedic closed the doors, not wanting a mere glimpse of Dave in the dark to be her last look at the man who had saved her life, who had brought her baby into the world. It didn't seem right. Not fair.

As though he'd heard her thoughts, he suddenly appeared in the doorway of the ambulance, holding out a hand to her. His now dark eyes met hers solemnly.

She twisted to free one of her hands, touched his cool fingertips tentatively, then, as his fingers pressed against hers, raised his hand to her lips. She had no intention other than simple acknowledgment when she reached for him, but as she traced a rough knuckle with her mouth, a purely sensual reaction shook her to her core. It was as though the soft kiss came from a part of her soul, not merely her body.

His face went curiously blank, while his eyes darkened even more. As she drew his broad palm against her cheek, a muscle worked in his jaw and his lips tightened as though he were in pain.

He cupped her face almost as if he'd done it a thousand times, tenderly, gently, imbuing some emotions far greater than anything she'd ever known before. His lips were parted, and again, he looked as if he wanted to say something to her, and she knew instinctively it was something important.

She knew, equally instinctively, that if he said it, if she allowed his words to form, she would be forced to come to a crossroads of sorts. His words, his vulnerability, were all tangled up in their moment of connectedness, and if he spoke the words aloud, she would drown in their warm buoyancy. And she wasn't ready for that.

He shifted and the ambulance's whirling lights reflected off the star-shaped silver badge at his chest. She inhaled with a hiss. No, she wasn't ready, especially not with someone who would always be so terribly and desperately vulnerable to the kind of violence that had already ripped her world apart.

She raised her hand to his lips swiftly, gently. The quick frown of hurt on his brow caused her far more pain than her gesture could have caused him, she thought sadly.

To her mingled relief and dismay, another siren's scream pierced the still of the night and was followed by red-and-blue lights strafing the dark street. It seemed as if the quiet little street exploded with confusion: people shouted, feet pounded pavement, doors opened and closed resoundingly.

It all sounded too much like a night nine months ago, though there'd been no sirens then. Just the unmistakable sound of a police unit, two doors slamming instead of one, too many faces, too many words...too many changes to be borne.

Janey clung to Dave's hand a moment longer. There was so much to say to him, so much to thank him for, and so very much to explain, but she couldn't seem to get the words past her throat. Habit, carefully ingrained over the past nine months, wouldn't allow explanations, wouldn't permit truths and confessions.

"It'll be okay now," he said, lifting his hand from her face, leaving her suddenly cold both from the loss of his warmth and from his seemingly complete nonunderstanding of the reasons she must withdraw from him.

He circled his hand around hers, pressing it against his mouth. She wondered then if it was nonunderstanding on his part, or the deepest of empathies. Perhaps, she thought, her gaze locked with his, he understood more than anyone else had even come close.

His lips moved against her sensitive fingertips in a kiss as gentle as it was promising. He lowered her hand to her own slightly parted mouth and pressed her own fingertips against her lips, as if transferring the kiss, imprinting her with his surprisingly quixotic gesture.

Without further word or change of expression, he tucked her hand back beneath the blanket and nodded for the paramedic to join her. Then with an oddly solemn look in her direction, as though communicating a silent vow on her behalf, closed the doors, shutting her in, shutting him out.

Janey had to bite her lip to keep from crying out against the barrier between them, against the knowledge that once again she was alone, and that it had to remain so, for his own sake, if not just for hers. For she had seen the want in his eyes, had felt the communication in his touch. He deserved far more than half a person. His kiss had held promise and she was a person who didn't—couldn't—believe in promises anymore. No more midnight rides and pretty dreams. Not for her.

Her baby stirred and she lifted the blanket to see him. Little David, tiny and helpless, alive because of the east-plains-accented man who had smiled at her each night as she walked, who colored as easily as a teenager, who had somehow turned a terror-filled night into one of beauty and life. As she stroked her son's soft forehead, she knew she would always have a small part of her rescuer: her son would always bear the name of this man, would always carry a part of him. A permanent reminder of a single, shining moment of total trust, of complete faith.

Dave watched as the ambulance pulled away and felt as though it were taking away something precious, something—*someone*—he was meant to be with for the rest of his days. He had the odd feeling that he and Janey Anderson had connected on some primal level of existence, as though in those desperate few minutes of delivering her baby, they had joined destinies, had exchanged the basic components of their souls.

Someplace, sometime, they were supposed to be together, almost as if it were written down in starlight and rainbows. This was the beginning. Why did it already feel like the end?

Dave tried wrenching his thoughts from Janey Anderson and they turned, naturally, to her son. The baby. The tiny David, he thought, a child conceived by one cop, delivered by another. Oddly enough, the notion didn't bother him. And he wondered why it didn't, then he knew. For a long, seemingly endless moment, holding the newborn in his hands, the child had belonged to him.

It was the son his loins had never produced, the child of his dreams, maybe. But it had only been for that one moment, and now, standing in the darkened street, the chill

Portales night demanding he face reality, he had to acknowledge the truth: the child was not, nor would ever be his.

His insides twisted with a visceral pain at the thought and at the wonder of the memory of first holding him. And his heart constricted at the realization that the baby not only wasn't his, he belonged to a fellow officer killed in the line of duty.

Yet Janey had named her baby for him, giving the child a lasting memory of the night he was born, offering David a vicarious son, a living legacy of the most vital and resplendent night of his entire life.

"Quite a night, eh, Dave?" Charlie Dobson asked, dropping a hand on Dave's shoulder, making him start.

Dave dragged his gaze from the disappearing ambulance to look at Charlie's grizzled, leathery face. The black cowboy hat with the silver Portales Police emblem accentuated Charlie's white hair and pale blue eyes. Charlie had been on the Portales force as long as Dave could remember and now served as the town's police chief, one of the few chiefs they'd ever had who insisted on wearing a badge. It had been his unit that had arrived last on the scene, siren blazing, red-and-blue lights still whirling seemingly angrily, and as usual a good half an hour too late.

"It's been different," Dave said quietly, raising his eyes back up to the street, which was now empty of all but curious, low-voiced neighbors.

"Didn't know when we ran you for sheriff we was getting a midwife," Charlie said, and chuckled.

"It wasn't what I had in mind either," Dave answered, but his grin definitely felt awry. Somehow, delivering that baby wasn't something to joke about. It had done something to him, changed him some elemental way. He didn't think he'd ever be able to look at another baby and not remember that shocking explosion of emotion inside him.

"No, don't suppose it was, at that," Charlie acknowledged. "Serves you right for coming back home thinking you could lay low and not have any trouble beyond kids necking on some farmer's well road."

"Maybe," Dave said, his mind still on the baby and on the baby's mother. God, how had he ever thought of her as frightened? She was the bravest woman he knew.

"Well, the way I hear it, your reflexes is mighty quick. Mrs. Aragon—who, by the way, isn't any too happy about you throwing a bottle of beer in her flower bed—says you did the high jump over your porch rail and got to the Anderson girl's house before the little lady ever did hit the ground. What happened? She trip or something?"

Dave turned to look at Janey's house. Lights were still blazing and her front door stood wide open. Under the harsh lights from the porch overheads, the hole in her step gaped like a maw.

"No, porch step gave. She went right through."

"I thought I saw somebody working on that porch just yesterday," Charlie said.

"You did. So did I. Any idea who it was?"

"Nope. Don't think I'll hire him for my porch, though."

Dave chuckled at this and felt better for the small release of tension. "Me, either. But I think I'll get a few two-by-sixes and see what I can't rig up."

Charlie was silent, following Dave toward his garage. Grateful for the silence, Dave didn't try and reopen the conversation, content just to have companionship after such a night.

Charlie carried the hammer, nails and handsaw, while Dave hauled the lengths of two-by-six pine boards. When they reached the porch and Dave reached the nail-pull end of the hammer toward the hole in the porch, Charlie held up his hand.

"Look at that, will you?"

Dave didn't need Charlie's pointing finger. Now he knew
what had bothered him about Janey's scraped leg. Her
porch step hadn't given way, rotted boards hadn't finally
succumbed to age and crumbled beneath her slight weight.
These steps had been sawed clear through. A child's weight
would have snapped the remaining thread.

This wasn't any accident.

"Looks like it's a good thing you happened along,"
Charlie said.

Dave nodded absently, wondering what kind of mind
would do such a thing. This was no kid's prank. This could
have killed her; it was only a wonder that it hadn't. What if
she had fallen in the middle of the night? What if she hadn't
paused to look at him sitting there grinning at her? What if
he hadn't been there at all?

"Think dusting for prints would do any good?" Charlie
asked.

Dave shrugged. There had been so many people in and
out of Janey's house that night, and he and Charlie had just
put their hands all over the edges of the break. "No telling.
Couldn't hurt to try."

"I suppose that, like me, you didn't happen to get a good
look at whoever was working on her porch yesterday."

Dave shook his head ruefully. "To tell the truth, I didn't
even look at his face. I just figured it was somebody she
hired for the day. Kind of built like Jerry Thompson, but
heavier."

"Yeah, that's my thinking, too. Looks like we was wrong
about her fixing up the porch."

"Looks like it," Dave agreed, pushing to his feet. "You
want to call in somebody to dust, or want me to?"

"I'll do it. I'm city, you're county, remember?"

"You might have them look around for anything else that
might look suspicious."

"Yeah. This ain't nothing to laugh at."

Dave nodded and they fell silent a few minutes. Finally Charlie cleared his throat. "You going to the hospital?"

"I thought I would."

"Well, go ahead. I'll wait for the boys and make sure everything's locked up here. You better take the key, though, in case she's only got the one."

"Thanks, Charlie . . . and do me a favor, will you?"

"Ask me first, that way I don't have to go back on a promise."

Dave smiled but the grin felt forced. "Let's try to keep this quiet, okay? I think she's probably had enough news reports to sink a battleship."

Charlie nodded thoughtfully, pursing his lips together. "I'll do my best, Dave. But I can't promise anything."

"That's all anyone can do, Charlie," Dave said, stepping to the door for the key. He held it up to the light for Charlie to see, then waved, gave the hole in the steps a long look and lightly jumped to the pavement.

"Dave?"

He pivoted slowly. "Yeah?"

Charlie shuffled his feet a bit and shoved his big hands in his pants' pockets. The pants were slung so low on his hips Dave wondered how they stayed up. Charlie chewed on his lip for a minute, then shot Dave a sharp look.

"About thirty-five years ago, I helped a woman deliver a baby."

Dave waited, without speaking, for Charlie to continue, knowing this was leading somewhere.

"I'll never forget it."

Dave nodded.

"But Dave, the thing is, neither did she. I think in a funny sort of way she fell in love with me that night. Crazy, huh?"

Dave studied his old friend, a short, balding man with too many chili dogs beneath his belt and too many years showing on his face. "No," he said seriously, "I don't think that's crazy at all."

Charlie's face cracked into a rather wistful smile. "Just wanted to warn you, son. Women get real emotional about those sort of things."

"Not like hard-bitten old cops," Dave said gently.

"Yeah."

Dave raised his hand a second time. "See you, Charlie." He'd managed to take just two steps when he heard Charlie clear his throat.

"Dave . . . ?"

Dave turned around again.

"Just so as you won't be thinking there's somebody out there pining away for me, I should tell you that woman was my wife."

"I know," Dave said softly, and grinned when Charlie's concerned face registered shock. "Dorla told me last year."

"Well, I'll be darned. What in Sam Hill would she want to tell you about that for?"

"It was the night you were caught out in the blizzard and no one had heard from you for hours."

Charlie was silent for a while, obviously remembering. Then he cleared his throat again. "Yeah. Dorla thought I was a gonner. It wasn't the first time she had to sit with a bunch of nervous rookies and wonder if I was going to come walking back through that door."

"Yeah, I know," Dave said. He wondered who had held Janey's hand the night she heard about Bill and was both glad and sorry it hadn't been him.

"Cops' wives and women delivering babies, Dave. You gotta watch out for them."

Dave waved a third time and walked away thinking of the night's events. The enormity of cause and effect spiraled in his mind and he found himself almost grateful to the despicable person who had sawed her porch step, for having brought Janey so violently and thoroughly into Dave's life. Without that psycho as a catalyst, Dave might never have done more than exchange a few words with her, might never have known the overwhelming encounter with new life, nor discovered the well of courage and strength that lay just beneath Janey Anderson's vulnerable surface.

As he pulled his unit out of the driveway and onto the road, he turned to look at Charlie's short figure in the bright lights of Janey's porch. Charlie waggled a finger toward his head and then at Dave. The message was clear: *Use your noggin, Davey boy.*

Putting the patrol car in gear and heading toward the hospital, he found himself wishing Charlie was right. Janey Anderson had been the wife of a cop and now she'd had a baby. Unfortunately, it wasn't her wanting him that he'd have to worry about. It was *his* wanting *her.*

He rubbed the back of his neck, easing a crick. God, he felt tired. His shoulders ached and his back felt every one of his thirty-six years. With a sigh, he realized he hadn't carried a woman in his arms for years. Maybe not since he'd lifted Patty Donahue's battered body onto the gurney five years earlier. And he'd never delivered a baby before. Or was it that leap over the porch railing that did the trick?

Dave thought of seeing Janey again, and the baby and much of his tiredness eased away. The chaos on the four-hundred block of B Street didn't seem so terrible now; he'd managed to save a life—no, *two* lives—in the process.

And something had happened inside him that he hadn't believed was possible: he felt connected to someone again. He drew a deep breath and eased his white sheriff's department unit into the deserted parking lot of the hospital and cut the motor.

Sitting there in the dark, in the absolute quiet, he tried telling himself that the feeling of connectedness was all that snared him about Janey Anderson. Nothing more.

But even as he thought this, he understood that there was nothing simple about feeling connected to someone. It was as complex as all human emotions and as glaringly straightforward. The feeling was as pervasive as the clear

star-studded New Mexico sky, and as empty as the side
streets late at night in Portales.

All he really knew was that he had to see her again. Had
to hold her hand in his. And had to touch that baby's tiny
fingers with his own. He had to make contact.

Dave Reynolds, sheriff, and one-time big-city cop, sighed,
and got out of his department unit. Why would anticipating seeing Janey and her baby again make him feel so eager
and yet, at the same time so alone, so sad?

As he approached the brightly lit double glass doors
leading into the hospital, he knew why he felt ambivalent,
why he felt joined and alone at the same time. He didn't feel
as if he had anything to give the two of them. That giving,
easy part of him had died five years ago, when Patty, his
partner, his friend and his lover, had gone to her death at his
unwitting command. The part of him that could embrace
the connectedness with gratitude, with love, had died when
he saw Patty's tortured body inside that suburban house in
L.A.

He'd rescued Janey Anderson and her baby tonight. But
that had to be the end of the connection. Because there was
nothing else he could give her, nothing he could give the
baby. To think or assume anything else would be a false
promise, a promise he didn't dare trust. For their sakes.

As he pulled open the heavy glass doors of the hospital
entrance, he told himself that he couldn't let it matter that
he wanted things to be different. Because one look at Janey
Anderson's face before tonight had told him that she felt the
very same way: empty, alone, and sick to death at heart.

Striding into the foyer of the hospital, he fiercely cautioned his wayward heart that the part of him he thought
dead couldn't possibly come to life again. And as he walked
steadily down the hall to the maternity wing, his boot heels
clicking on the tiled floors, he told himself that he was a liar.
Because the fact that he wanted things to be different *did*
matter. He *did* feel something.

He quickly discovered her room number and, after a short conference with the night nurse, moved to her door. After sweeping his hat from his head and running a hand over his thick pelt of hair, he pushed the large wooden door ajar, his heart beating unsteadily. And as he took in the sight of Janey Anderson lying alone on the hospital bed, her dark hair spilled on the pillow, the yellow glow from the bed's lamp spreading a halo of light on her sleeping face, he knew the something he felt not only mattered, but mattered a lot.

Janey felt sleep drop from her as abruptly as it had come upon her and opened her eyes, taking in the room in a glance, the empty green armchair beside the bed, the nightstand holding only a telephone, and a broad-shouldered man silhouetted in the doorway.

For a shattering moment, a distortion in time and place rocked her and she saw the slim-hipped, obviously uniformed shadow as an echo of her dreams, as the past coming to life again for her and for their newborn baby.

"Bill?" she rasped, her heart beating raggedly, even as her mind told her it couldn't be so.

The silhouette in the doorway tilted his head toward the ground and the shadow of a cowboy hat came around his legs to be held in both hands. The sheriff. A wave of embarrassment swept over her and her body shook in reaction.

"No, ma'am. It's me, Dave Reynolds."

The hat turned in his hand like a wheel, and to Janey's sleep-fogged and exhausted mind the hat was a symbol of sorts. It seemed to represent the wheel of life, going around and around. But where would it stop, that wheel, and what did it mean? She raised her eyes from the hat to the shadowed face of the man.

"Sorry," he said, and his voice was almost a shadow of itself.

She didn't know whether he was apologizing for waking her or for not being her husband. Somehow she suspected it might be the latter.

"Don't be," she said. "I was dreaming."

"I figured," he mumbled.

He looked as if he was ready to bolt from the room. It seemed unfair that after all he had done for her that evening he should hang back in the doorway, feeling out of place, uncertain of his welcome. Was that her doing or his? she wondered.

"Please come in," she said, and shifted to a half-sitting position, questioning the rapid beating of her heart, the sudden feeling of breathlessness.

The silhouette moved forward, and in the light she could see Dave's solemn features. A frown marred his brow and his eyes were dark with some unspoken question. He stopped several feet away from her bed, his felt cowboy hat in his broad hand, his legs spread somewhat, as though he were ready to turn and leave at the slightest signal from her.

"Are you feeling all right?" he asked, his eyes raking her from head to blanket-covered toes and back again.

Something in his gaze made her acutely aware of her half-fastened hospital gown, of the way it was slipping off her shoulders. And something about the way he was looking at her, in a combination of plea and denial, made her heart beat in an irregular rhythm. She could feel his loneliness to her very core, recognizing it from having grown so acquainted with it herself. And it moved her like nothing else could have done.

"I didn't mean to scare you," he said finally.

He may not have meant it, but he did. He scared her beyond anything. Because simply by being there, by doing all that he had done, he made her want to trust him, and *that* she couldn't afford. Trusting anyone was an impossibility.

No one knew the dangers of trusting more surely than she. Bill, who had trusted no one, not even her, either before or after their marriage, was dead because of one moment of misplaced faith. And she, who had trusted everyone, had lost everything when Bill was killed.

"Are you all right?" Dave asked again, taking a cautious step closer.

"Yes," she said, and even to herself, her voice sounded huskier than usual, almost seductive in its throatiness.

"And the baby?"

His innocent question and her instinctive response to it, sparked the letdown reflex in her breasts and she crossed her arms to stay the instinctive flow. "He's fine. The doctor said that because he was early he'd have to spend most of his time in an incubator for a while."

Dave frowned heavily. "Is that normal?" he asked.

She smiled faintly. He sounded like a worried father. This thought sobered her instantly, but she answered easily enough. "Yes. Apparently with babies born premature like David was, there's a greater risk of jaundice. Something to do with their livers not being ready."

"I see," Dave said, but it was clear that he didn't. "But he'll be all right." It wasn't a question so much as a command.

"Yes."

"And you? The doctor said everything was okay?" Again that note of command.

Her smile broadened. "Yes, I'm fine." She added as if in an afterthought, though it was foremost in her mind, "Thanks to you."

He waved his hat at his side, as if brushing her statement away like so much dust. "How long are they going to keep you here?"

She frowned at that. She had already argued with the doctor over the need to be out of the hospital immediately. The doctor had adamantly refused. "The doctor said I'd have to stay in here at least a week."

Dr. McCall had run on about shock, about postpartum depression, common, he said, among women with unusual or difficult deliveries. And because she was alone, with no relatives at home to help her, he thought it best if she stayed at the hospital for a while. But it was depression he was most worried about. He had gone all around Bill's death without ever really mentioning it.

"What's all this stuff?" Dave asked, waving his hat at the intravenous monitor and the clear fluid dripping into her arm.

"Food, hospital style," Janey said, and smiled.

Much of the stiffness left Dave's face then, and he turned that crooked grin in her direction. He was the kind of man who looked easy to be around, but when he smiled, he looked the type of person one wanted to be with forever. It was a warm, fire-in-winter sort of smile, a rainy-day smile.

"Nothing like down-home cooking," he said.

"Just like Mama used to make," she answered. And for all of her, it could have been. She'd never known her mother.

"Probably better than my mama's was. She couldn't cook her way out of a paper bag," Dave said, nodding, his eyes bright with humor.

"Well, let's face it, if you made her cook in a paper bag, she was operating under a severe handicap."

It wasn't much of a joke, one produced primarily from nervousness, but it served to make him laugh, probably for the same reason. The rich rumble seemed to echo in the room and made her smile, pleased. Relaxed.

Janey couldn't remember the last time she'd felt so easy in someone's company. Nine months and a day ago? A lifetime ago. The thought sobered her. And she was sorry.

"Janey...?" Dave Reynolds was serious now. Please don't let him say anything special, she begged. If he did, she might cry. Her emotions felt too curiously close to the surface, too raw, almost new.

"Who was that guy working on your porch yesterday?"

"What?" she asked blankly. Whatever she'd expected him to ask, it hadn't been that.

"The fellow who worked on your porch, honey. Who was he?"

"What are you talking about? What guy?"

Dave frowned. "The worker on your front porch yest—" He broke off when it became obvious she had no idea what he was talking about. "You didn't hire anyone to do your porch, did you?" His voice was so flat that it acted like an alarm bell on Janey's oversensitive nerves.

She shook her head, a curious chill that had nothing to do with the fluid from the IV working through her veins.

"Why?" she asked.

He hesitated, looked at the dark window of the bedroom as though searching for an escape route, and turned back to her. "I saw somebody working on it yesterday. About mid-afternoon. After lunch, anyway. So did Charlie Dobson—"

"The police chief?" she asked, the chill deepening to a ripple of apprehension. What was he intimating?

"That's Charlie. He lives a couple of blocks down from us. From you." He paused, his cheeks staining, she suspected, at his inadvertent coupling of their lives. He shifted his hat, half apologetically. "Anyway, we both saw this guy sawing and hammering on your porch."

"What are you trying to tell me?" Janey asked. Even to herself, her voice sounded small. And cold.

"Your steps weren't rotted through," he answered reluctantly.

Janey couldn't think what he meant for a long moment, then the implications became obvious. "Someone sawed them through," she supplied slowly.

He nodded. "That's about the size of it."

"Why?" she asked, before she thought. Why did crazy people do anything? Why had Bill been murdered? Why did people beat children, kick dogs and hurt old people? She knew better than anyone that basic *unreason,* and not logic, was the constant in this uncertain world.

"I was hoping you might be able to tell me," Dave said, and his smoky eyes met hers.

She slowly shook her head, as much to deny her ability to tell him anything, as in answer to the unspoken question in his eyes, a question that had nothing whatsoever to do with the sawed steps and basic unreason.

The unspoken question had to do with county fairs and picnics on sunny May afternoons, and a bowl of popcorn in front of a winter fire. And reading these unspoken images made her heart beat more rapidly, warming her, sending a small ray of what almost felt like hope to dispel some of the chill clawing at her veins.

He broke the eye contact with her and took a few long pacing steps around her narrow room. He stopped by the dark window and stared at his own reflection in the window.

He said finally, "Charlie's going to have his boys dust for fingerprints, but neither of us think there's too much hope of getting anything concrete."

The letters, she thought. The threats, the warnings. "What did he look like?" she asked, and waved her hand as he turned and stared at her for a moment until her question registered.

"Short, maybe six foot or so."

Janey withheld a smile at the notion of someone six feet tall being considered "short." But by Dave's standards, that would be short. She wondered if he considered her "tiny" and thought that at five feet six inches, he probably did.

"And stocky. Kind of heavyset. Looked a little like Jerry Thompson only heavier."

Not knowing who Jerry Thompson was, Janey couldn't conjure an image of the man who had spent the afternoon before rigging her fall. She might have been killed. Before, when she only thought it was an accident, she had been chastising herself for not placing a higher priority on the porch and steps. It had been her fault, and therefore, within her control.

Now, an unknown menace was actually trying to harm her. She had been warned, not in specific, itemized threats, but in vague leave-or-else messages. Like the letters, like the calls. This wasn't something she had a handle on, and she had no control over it at all.

She was being victimized and tormented. She fleetingly wished for Bill and, when her weary heart sadly let her see the futility of that wish, she wondered when her inner strength would surface again. She seemed to have lost it sometime in the past six hours. She felt fragile and afraid, frightened beyond thought.

She'd been able to shove the letters and calls to some other part of her mind, ignoring them, at least on the surface. She had a new life, a new place. And even though whoever was sending them had managed to trace her, they hadn't shown themselves.

Until now. And now they'd tried to harm her.

This was real. Concrete. This was attempted murder. Sloppy, yes, but an attempt to harm her or kill her. What if Dave Reynolds hadn't been sitting on his front porch watching her? What if something had happened to the baby?

Some of what she was thinking must have showed on her face, for Dave moved to the edge of the bed and took her hand. "It'll be okay, honey," he said, squeezing her hand.

The unexpected bracing note in his voice, the endearment, and the pressure of his fingers against her palm brought tears to her eyes. She quickly looked away, lest he see the weakness.

Maybe the doctor had been right to worry about depression, she thought, fighting the threatening onslaught of tears. Why had someone done this? Why did there have to be more, now when she couldn't do anything to defend herself, when she felt so weak and alone?

She didn't dare cry, she thought. If she cried now, the flood might never stop. She couldn't let the dam break tonight, not when she'd been so frightened, had gone through so much, and especially not when this man had stood beside her, transferring his strengths to her, enabling her to arrive on the other side of fear and pain without loss of dignity and humanity.

Letting her guard slip now wouldn't be fair to him nor, she thought, ultimately to herself. She needed to be strong, all on her own right, not to rely on the solid strength of this giving man.

But it was so hard not to just fling herself into his warm arms and let him shoulder all her troubles. Because this added nightmare seemed too much. Like a wheel in a hamster's cage, the question of who was doing this circled around and around in her mind.

"It'll be okay," Dave said again, and this time she was able to meet his eyes without tears.

Her first instinct was to go get her baby and run. But where would she go? What would she do? How far was far enough? Wasn't she already there?

"I won't let anything happen to you," he said, his voice so low she could hardly hear it, the tone a vow she couldn't mistake. It shook the tears from her as effectively as tossing a rug free of dirt. She was already too aware of the thread between them, she couldn't allow it to grow any stronger. For her sake, and for his. She didn't have the wherewithal for more, and he deserved everything.

And she couldn't afford to lean on anyone, now more than ever. She knew from her hospice experience that dependency was one of the most invidious stages of grief. Thus far, she'd made it through without resorting to relying on others, especially when her heart kept telling her that this was the man to allow the shouldering of her troubles.

"I'm fine," she said, and gently but firmly pushed his hand away. The minute she had done so, she wanted to take the warm fingers back in hers, wanted to hold on as tight as she possibly could. And for the same reason, she couldn't tell him about the threatening letters. "It was probably just a prank of some kind."

"Probably," Dave said easily. Too easily, Janey thought. She risked a look at him and noted the dull color staining his cheeks. He was not a man who lied well. For some reason this steadied her and pleased her, as well. It meant that nothing he'd said or done with her prior to this moment had been a lie.

A year ago this man would have been welcomed in their home, treated like family, adopted as a brother, an uncle, a cousin. A year ago she might have confided in him, sought his advice, asked for his help. But that was before Bill had been killed, before she'd known for certain that life was no sinecure, that the bad guys win all too often.

So now she lay silent, knowing Dave's reassurance that things would be okay was an empty promise, that things were far from okay. Someone had violated her property, had proved they had access to her life, almost killed her, and now she had her baby to think about. He was orphaned by one parent, she couldn't allow anything to happen to her. Bill had no family, neither did she. And she refused, absolutely refused the concept of her son being raised as she was, one home to another, never belonging to a family, always an outcast.

"It will, you know," he said, and when she looked a question at him, added, "be all right. And remember, I'm only as far away as the telephone. You can call me anytime. About anything."

She smiled at him, then, trying to let him think his words had their desired effect. And when he patted her hand, she thought, with a pang of regret, that he had succeeded.

Dave carefully withheld a frown at the smile of disbelief on her wan face. She apparently knew he was lying, not about calling him, but about the person who had tried to hurt her. Yes, she knew he was lying, but, thank God, she didn't know what he was thinking.

She hadn't apparently, leapt to the same conclusions he had: that the family of Tony Aguilar, murderer of six people, and Bill Anderson, might be attempting some kind of revenge on Janey.

This notion wasn't farfetched. Dave had worked in L.A. and seen a hundred different cases of family feuds. And he knew that the feud mentality was alive and well in northern New Mexico. Tony Aguilar was in the penitentiary now, awaiting final sentence, and the most likely verdict for murdering a peace officer would be the death penalty. A family torn by grief, emotions running high and hot, might have decided that if the state was going to make an example of Tony because he'd killed a law enforcement officer, they would make their own example of the dead man's widow.

But this wasn't something he was going to tell Janey. If she was dismissing it as a prank, that was fine. In the meantime, he'd run a check on the family's whereabouts and put out the word to Charlie Dobson to have Janey's house patrolled as often as manpower would allow. Living so close to her, Dave could watch out for her the remainder of the time. He clamped his mind shut against the images this thought conjured.

"You need some rest," he said now. She glanced up at him. In relief, he thought.

"Thanks again, Dave Reynolds," she said quietly, and held out her hand.

He took her slender farewell far more easily than he felt inside. He wanted to draw her into his arms, to hold her for just a moment, assure her that tomorrow would dawn bright and fresh, that she wasn't alone, need never be alone again. But he couldn't.

"Be well, Janey Anderson," he answered, equally quietly. He turned loose her hand, then, unable to resist, lightly stroked her cheek, noting the swift rise of a blush. She was still pale but no longer looked as though the demons that haunted her had found her.

Her blue eyes met his. Her gaze was steady but fevered. A frantic appeal lay in the depths at the same time her face was distant and closed. It stirred him as nothing else could have.

"I'm fine," she said coolly, her voice at odds with her eyes. If he hadn't seen those eyes, hadn't fully read that silent appeal, he might have accepted the rebuff. But he had seen them.

"Yes," he said, meaning simply to agree with her. Instead, his single affirmative sounded like a wealth of half-uttered promises. "But as your quasi-doctor, I'd like to make sure for myself. I'll be back tomorrow," he added lightly, trying to dispel the haunted look in her eyes, hoping to lessen the feeling that he was making her a vow of sorts.

When she continued to look at him, half-beseechingly, half-stonily, and her lips parted as though she were about to negate his intention to return the next day, he couldn't restrain the impulse to lay his fingers against her lips, pressing lightly. He'd intended only to silence her refusal and was unprepared for the sensation the careless gesture roused in him. It was as if his lips, and not his fingers, touched her warm mouth. And he felt a return of the protectiveness, of a monumental awareness of their connectedness.

He reluctantly drew his fingers from her lips and shoved his hand into his pocket. He rubbed his fingertips together, still feeling the warmth of her lips, feeling as if he'd been branded, so hot did they burn.

He cleared his throat. "Things'll look better in the morning, honey. I promise."

She closed her eyes then, as though in pain. When she spoke, her lids remained down, not revealing any more to him. But her weary and wistful words said it all.

"You almost make me...believe the world...could be as simple...and as good...as you paint it. It isn't. But you almost make me believe it could be."

Chapter 4

When Dave finally broke away from the office and found his way to Janey's room the next day, she wasn't there. He felt a jolt of disappointment all out of proportion to the occasion.

"She's taking a shower," the day nurse told him, her voice clipped despite the drawling accent. Her eyes became speculative as she took in the two small, brightly wrapped packages he held in his hand. One was decorated in blue, the other in silver. One for the baby, the other for the mother. It shouldn't have aroused speculation, and probably wouldn't have if they'd been standing in any other hospital room in any other town in the world. Combined with the flowers he'd sent earlier with no card, these packages would spark *major* curiosity.

"She just left, so she'll probably be a few minutes. And we've had a few problems with the showers this morning, so it could take longer. You want me to put those somewhere for her?" she asked, nodding at the packages.

He didn't want anything of the kind. "Please," Dave said, depositing both of them into the nurse's outstretched hands. Again he felt that stab of disappointment. He'd been looking forward to watching Janey open them. The baby's was a miniature baseball glove made of some satiny—washable, the salesclerk had repeatedly told him—fabric. Janey's was a miniature as well, a hand-painted music box that played a single refrain of a haunting melody that Dave didn't recognize but that had seemed to embody Janey's personality.

"I'll leave a note," Dave said now.

"If you like," the nurse said, turning away from him to set the packages beside the telephone on the nightstand. "But these have got cards. She'll know you were here. Nothing you put in a note is going to say more than that." Her eyes slewed to his, half in that same speculation, half as though daring him.

The simple logic of this made Dave feel slightly foolish and added fuel to his frustration. But he said, "You're right. I'll just have to come back some other time."

"You can go have a look at the baby," she offered, as if finally taking pity on his dissatisfaction. "He's a treat."

The nurse was right, Dave decided: the baby was a treat. Asleep, tiny fist pressed to tinier mouth, body hidden by a blue blanket and face suffused in the incubator light's golden glow, the baby was all Dave remembered from the night before, and more.

A fine dusting of dark, downy hair capped the infant's head. No longer damp, the dark strands seemed like the pencil sketches of a portrait artist, delicate, wispy and ephemeral. *Janey's hair,* he thought with a pang. Little David's baby face seemed less wrinkled, and the tiny frown was absent from the small brow. He seemed content to bask beneath the false sunlight, as though storing energy for a later day, a day when battling the world would be necessary.

He'd looked up the baby's name—his own name—late in the night, in an obscure book of his mother's, struck when he found it underlined and a check mark beside it. For a moment, his hands on the old and much turned pages, it had almost seemed that his mother rested beside him on the worn sofa, her thin and careworn fingers pointing out names she had considered, choices she had rejected, choices she had made.

The name meant strength, implied courage. David, fragile boy against colossal odds, the weak versus the gigantically strong. Yet, in the tale of David and Goliath, David won. Would this child also fare so well? He'd had a rocky start; would things improve for this child, or would his life be plagued with one stumbling block after another?

The baby on the other side of the glass slept, unaware of the introspective man watching him, and Dave felt a moment's sharp awareness that he might not always be at hand to stay the weighty future. Like a father would be.

But this baby's father had been brutally killed and would never be there to look out for his son.

Dave wanted to tell the baby that he was there, however.

The thought rammed home with the precision and force of a bullet entering a shotgun's chamber. Like a loaded gun, he stood there, not knowing whether he would explode with these new, untested emotions or would misfire when he had to prove true.

All he really knew—*felt*—was that this fatherless child bearing his name could have all of him and more. This baby could take everything that comprised David Reynolds and set it to glorious flame. Because somehow, in the kindling of the emotions sparked by this infant's delivery, Dave knew the flame would last forever.

"I'll see you later, David," he whispered, holding his palm flat against the glass window. The glass was cool to the touch, but his hand felt scorched by the contact. Like his fingers had upon touching Janey's lips the night before.

During the time he'd been standing there, someone had joined him at the window and a small, bluish-haired woman turned now, startling him somewhat. "He's beautiful," she said.

"Yes," Dave agreed, and his heart constricted.

"Yours?"

"Mmm." He couldn't have said why he hadn't simply told the truth, why he'd allowed the noncommittal hum to leave a misapprehension uncorrected. And couldn't have said why knowing it was a lie hurt so much.

"Bonding...that's the important thing," the aide's voice intoned.

Janey heard the words, probably with greater impact than the other two mothers in the room, but her mind seemed elsewhere. She was listening, and yet her heart seemed crunched into the past.

Overriding the words of the aide was Bill's voice, *I don't know how, babe. I just don't know how to let you know how much you mean to me. I wish to God I did.* His voice had been filled with anguish, tight and rigid, the way it sounded when an explosive situation broke out in front of him. But when the explosions in his life occurred, he had his training and his badge to rely upon; when talking to her about their lives together, he had nothing. Or, at least, that was how he had felt.

And now, that *bonding* that the aide was so enthusiastically speaking about would never happen. Bill's son would grow up never knowing his father, never feeling his touch, never hearing the words that Bill might have learned how to say had he lived long enough to learn them.

"The first touch, the first hands to actually hold your child might impact her—or him—for the rest of their lives. We don't know. We can only..."

Dimly, as though from a great distance, the aide's words pierced the fog of the past, forcing Janey to focus on the present. *The first touch* had been *Dave's*. A stranger, and yet not a stranger. A man who wanted her, yet who had set aside any semblance of that want to stay beside her, to help her, uncertain of his own actions and abilities during the birth, yet willing to see it through just for her. And for David, his namesake.

And, as if burned on her retinas, she still could see Dave's face when he had held the baby above her. It had been flushed with triumph, joy and this awe-filled wonder. *Bonding.* That's what it had been. He had truly and absolutely bonded with her child, looking at young David as if he were *his* child, not Bill's, feeling everything, every emotion of a new father.

We're about to have a baby, he had said, and then had held the infant in his hands, coaxing life into the only viable thing she had to show from her marriage, a short lifetime with Bill, that span of time with someone else. And somehow, in that single shining moment, the sheriff had bridged the enormous gap between past and present.

Janey shook her head. She felt too raw, exposed, vulnerable. She felt too linked with this ruddy-faced cowboy, this man who, in many ways, seemed more vulnerable than she. It wasn't fair, she thought. It wasn't fair that she should meet him now, after the curtain had dropped, after the flag had been folded, after her heart had been buried.

But if she had met him before, Bill would have been there. And she couldn't wish that time away, not for anyone, anything.

"It's only natural," the aide continued, undoubtedly speaking of something else, but the words fell too aptly into Janey's consciousness, making memory shift and spiral.

For a moment, Janey felt released from the past, released from thoughts of the future. She felt she was stretched flat on a brief segment of the time continuum, able to see in all directions, as if she herself were the undefinable splice of a Möbius strip—a bandage on the never-ending circle-eight of time, thought and space.

In this moment she saw Bill clearly, concisely, understood him for what he was, what he had been to her. He was husband and police officer all at once, indivisible, with laughter and tears for all. A real man, a real life, but now, sadly, tragically, only a memory.

And she saw Dave Reynolds, achingly lonely and intensely giving, and perhaps more afraid of the future than she. She saw Bill's eyes closed, his hands folded across his chest for all time, saw Dave's eyes filled with wonder, his large hands holding up her newborn son. She saw the uniforms, different yet similar. She saw the badges, the imprints of peace officers, and wished she could see the link that held them together.

She didn't feel, in this endless moment of realization, that Bill held the baton out to Dave. If anything, she felt the reverse. Bill would have fought tooth and nail for what was his, and he would, in all likelihood, have simply and gruffly thanked the sheriff then blandly ignored him.

And in remembering Bill, in thinking about him, in reviewing the events of the day before, she knew an uncertain guilt. The moment that Dave had impinged upon her life, delivering her child—their child, hers and Bill's—was something that should have been reserved for Bill, and if not for him, by impersonal doctors who wouldn't remember her name a week later.

But Dave had been there. And she had named Bill's child for her rescuer. And there had been something else, something greater than gratitude that she had felt. That she felt even now.

"Are there any questions?" the aide asked. She folded her file closed and shifted it to her lap. It was the first time that Janey had noticed the manila folder. For some reason this lessened the woman's caring speech, as though having notes and statistics made the information more a mental exercise than a pronouncement from the heart.

Janey had a million questions but none that she cared to voice. Who had taken a saw to her front porch? Which one of the many threatening letters was penned by a potential murderer? Should she tell someone about the letters? Was the logical person to tell the same man who had rescued her and delivered her baby?

And what should she do about her confused feelings for Dave Reynolds?

She shook her head. She had questions, yes, but none that this woman could answer. None that anyone could answer.

"Well, then, ladies, let's have the nurses bring in your babies so you can start the rest of your lives together."

"Not a single decent print," Charlie Dobson said, shaking his head. "Might as well go ahead and fix that hole. Unless the guy shows up at the station, confession in hand, I doubt we'll ever know who served that little lady such a trick."

Dave shook his head, too, his eyes not on Charlie's cluttered desk, but on the yawning hole in Janey Anderson's front porch steps. Charlie was right: they would probably never catch the guy. But what kind of madman would do such a thing? It could have killed her.

Trying to get a lead on that "who" had taken up most of his day. He'd already called Santa Fe to have them run a check on the whereabouts of the Aguilar family not already behind bars. Thus far, it appeared everyone was where they were supposed to be. There was still a sister unaccounted for, but as she had long since pulled away from her wilder relatives, it was doubtful she was involved.

He'd called the state police to see if they could offer any leads. After being shifted through two or three different desks, he hit upon a possible connection.

"What did Santa Fe have to say?" Charlie asked now.

"Not much," Dave answered, then added, "but one gal at the state police office told me that Janey had been getting some threatening letters before she moved down here."

"Abuse stuff or real threats?"

Dave shrugged. "She's going to send us some copies they made. Hard to say if there's any connection. The type of creep that sends those kinds of letters doesn't usually include a return address."

"Has she had any since she's been in Portales?" Charlie asked, his shrewd question, as always, belying his haphazard appearance.

"She wasn't in her room when I dropped by the hospital, so I haven't had a chance to ask her yet," Dave replied.

"She okay?"

"So they said."

"And the baby?"

Dave felt his features relax. "He's just fine. They have him in an incubator now, something to do with his liver, but they don't seem worried."

He hadn't realized he'd been looking for reassurance when he said the words, but Charlie knew him well. "Yeah, they did that with Lenora, too. I remember Dorla standing on the other side of the window they have there to let you view the babies, just a crying for all she was worth. 'What's wrong, Mama?' I asked her, knowing perfectly well why she was crying, but just to say something, you know?"

"I know," Dave said, smiling a little.

"I expected her to say something about little Lenora, but danged if she didn't floor me."

When Charlie didn't continue, his grizzled face arrested, his eyes obviously seeing that long-ago image of his crying wife, Dave supplied the question he knew Charlie was waiting for. This was part of the ritual of conversation in Portales.

"What did she say, Charlie?"

"She told me if I ever came home late again she'd put out an all points on me and tell her bridge club I was running around with Leta Gregory."

Dave chuckled. Leta Gregory was the town's fiercest proponent of censorship, rules and regulations, and also ninety if she was a day.

"Here I was all worried about little Lenora and whether or not I'd maybe done something the night before to hurt either of them, and she was still fixating on something that happened maybe six months earlier. Go figure."

Charlie shook his shaggy white head ruefully and held his rough hands in the air, but Dave wasn't deceived. He knew as well as Charlie did why Dorla had said what she did, cried like she had.

"Took your mind off it, did she?" Dave asked.

"Take your mind off it, son?" Charlie's shrewd glance connected with Dave's.

Dave smiled and shook his head.

"Never mind. Nothing ever will. The minute you see that young'un, the second you become a daddy, there isn't a damn thing that'll ever stop you worrying about 'em. They can say all they want about a mother's instincts, but trust me—I know what I'm talking about here—there's a powerful lot of father's instinct going on, too. You're just getting your first taste of it, Davey boy. By the time that baby gets to be Lenora's age, you'll think you done ate the whole blame cake."

Dave had let a lie slide by in the hospital, but that woman had been a stranger, a grandmother come in from out of town, someone he would, in all likelihood, never see again. And this was Charlie Dobson. Dave used to run tame in the Dobson home, young Johnny Dobson and he as inseparable as only two boys the same age in a small town can be. Like brothers, like family. And Charlie was the father he never really had.

"That baby isn't mine," Dave said slowly, reluctance dragging at his tongue.

"No? Well, you wish it was, makes the same difference." Before Dave could comment one way or the other, Charlie plucked a sheaf of papers, seemingly at random, from his desk. "Now what are we going to do about that ruckus last week out near the Jordan farm? Weldon's hopping mad about what they done to his tractors."

The simple melody emanating from the music box shifted from major to minor key and back again in smooth transition. If Janey closed her eyes she could imagine herself on a mountaintop, picnic spread, ready and waiting, upon a plaid blanket, the sounds of a river somewhere nearby. Haunting, the melody seemed to offer hope and convey sorrow all at the same time. A lonely picnic, with only the dappled sunshine and the whispering pines for company.

She opened her eyes to gaze down at her sleeping son. *Lonely no more.* The thought slipped unbidden but welcome into her mind, into her heart. She had this tiny, wholly trusting infant to care for, to watch over, to guard. Her heart twisted, gazing at his perfect face, his curled hands.

The melody wound down and Janey glanced at the music box, opened and seemingly waiting for another wind, another touch from her to set it alive again. Carefully not to disturb the baby, she reached for the box and awkwardly rewound it, grateful for the gift, thankful to the man who had given it to her, and relieved she hadn't been there when he brought it.

She felt too exposed, too vulnerable to talk with him today. It seemed too pat somehow. Now, when she was missing Bill the most, when his loss was made all the more poignant by the birth of their child, she kept seeing a pair of smoky-gray eyes and hearing that honeyed, consonant-blurred voice promising to be here for her.

She didn't need watching out for, she wanted to argue with that part of her that so eagerly responded. She didn't need someone in her life...especially someone who wore a badge. And yet, her heart pounded more forcefully and rapidly at the mere thought of the cowboy, and her hands seemed to ache for want of his curled around them.

"More flowers, Mrs. Anderson," one of the nurses said, setting down a cut-glass vase on the window ledge. She squeezed it in between the four other arrangements. She handed Janey the small announcement card that had been woven through a plastic prong thrust amongst the bright daffodils and forced gladiolus.

"And here's a card someone left at the front desk."

The flowers were from kindly Alma Maybry, who served as receptionist and aide at Los Abuelos, the hospice where Janey worked. The other flowers were from her neighbors, Mrs. Lyon, who had helped so much the night before, and from shy Mrs. Aragon, and that sweet but tart-tongued Mrs. Judson, who had brought her a loaf of melt-in-your-mouth banana bread the first week she'd moved into the house.

The fourth bouquet was unmarked, and the simplest of the quintet. Comprised only of a single yellow rose, it sat alone in simplicity, and Janey knew with a woman's sure instinct that it had come from the sheriff.

"You want me to open that card for you, dear? There's something inside it. You don't want it to fall out on the baby," the nurse offered as Janey struggled to shift the baby to a more convenient positions.

"Please," Janey said, giving up the struggle and handing the card back. Somehow, in the past twenty-four hours, it had become almost easy to give up the hard-won independence she'd fought for after Bill's death. Or was it simply that she'd been closing her eyes, her heart, to the intentions of the people in this town?

What she'd taken as curiosity and perhaps even nosiness might have been simple human kindness. What she'd been

ready to assume was interfering advice might easily have
been honest concern. Had she been so self-conscious, so
afraid of depending on others, that she'd gone the opposite
direction? Was she still doing that, this time with Dave
Reynolds, being so afraid to lean on him that she was actually shutting the door in his face? In her own?

The nurse expertly ripped the edge of the envelope free
and withdrew a folded card. With an unguarded look of
enthusiasm, she flipped the card open.

She gasped, and her expression altered dramatically from
one of pleasant anticipation to one of horror. Something
dark fell out of the card and down to the floor.

"What?" Janey asked sharply, torn between leaning over
to see what had fallen out and not being able to drag her
gaze from the nurse's suddenly ashen face.

The nurse looked up at her question, her face curiously
blank. When she focused on Janey, however, she drew a
ragged breath and transformed into the professional woman
she was. "It's nothing, dear."

"What was that? What fell out?"

The nurse waved her hand. "Nothing. A . . . *nothing.*"

"What does the card say? Who is it from?"

The nurse looked around the room, as though for help,
then, when it was obvious none was forthcoming, waved the
card with obvious distaste and said, "You know how it is,
sometimes. Some nut will listen to the radio and send . . ."

She trailed off, her wide eyes on whatever had fallen to the
floor.

Janey could stand it no longer and leaned forward, regardless of disturbing the baby.

A dead wasp, curled and brittle, lay not inches from the
nurse's white shoes.

A wasp. Just an insect. A dead one, at that. Yet the implications of someone having stuffed it into an envelope,
inside a card, knowing she would undoubtedly open it ea-

gerly, sent shivers down her spine. What if she, and not the nurse, had opened it? It would have fallen on David.

Unconsciously she pulled the still-sleeping infant tighter to her chest, bending over him, as though protecting him from seeing what lay upon the floor.

"What's going on in here?" a deep voice asked from the doorway.

Janey was aware that both she and the nurse turned to face the door at the same time and that both of them had identical, conflicting emotions stamped on their faces.

Dave Reynolds stood in the doorway, much as he'd done the night before, only now he was no mere silhouette. He was as concrete and solid as the walls. His hat again dangled from his fingertips, and his thick, dark hair was pushed back from his suntanned brow, leaving a band of white, unsunned skin exposed. His eyes shone ice blue and his expression shifted from pleasant raillery to hardened police officer.

"What's wrong?" he asked, his soft voice sharp with surety that something was amiss.

"She got a card . . . left at the desk . . . it had a wasp in it, and . . . *this,*" the nurse said, thrusting the card in Dave's direction.

Dave read the card aloud for the second time, "'You had your chance. This is your last warning. Leave town or else.'" He lowered the card to the nightstand. He didn't bother to look at Janey. She hadn't met his eyes since that initial agonized stare. For some reason, perhaps empathy, this didn't surprise him. She wasn't the kind of person who would want to talk about misfortune. He'd known that before last night.

He'd already sent the nurse to the front desk to ask if the receptionist could remember who had delivered the card, and had called Charlie, telling his old friend about the wasp, about the words on the card. Charlie was sending someone around to dust the card.

"Not that there's any hope of finding a print," he'd said. "The nurse touched it, you did. And the outside envelope we can just forget. Half the county probably had their hands on it, by now. How's the girl taking it?"

Dave looked at her averted profile now. Long lashes lay softly against the slightly blue smudges beneath her eyes. Her face seemed drawn and tight, and her lips were compressed with some rigidly withheld emotion. Fear? Anger?

"I talked with the state police in Santa Fe," Dave said finally. She looked up at that, but not at him. She gazed out the window or perhaps at the flowers on display. Dave saw his single rose wedged in between the other, fuller arrangements and was glad he hadn't included a card. It looked meager in contrast with the other. He'd intended it as a symbol of sorts, a promise, perhaps.

"They told you I'd had some threatening letters," she said, her contralto voice infinitely more calm than he'd imagined it would be. She continually amazed him. Last night, today. A woman of rare character.

"Yes. They're sending me some copies."

"They didn't have to bother. I can tell you that the handwriting on this card will match some of them."

"Janey...?"

She turned finally, her blue eyes as clear as a mirror, but a mirror reflecting only his own image, none of her thinking. "Yes?"

"Do you have any idea who is sending these to you?"

She smiled sadly and shook her head. "If I had, I would have reported it long ago. No, I don't have any idea." She sighed and turned her gaze to her sleeping infant. "Half the reason I moved to Portales was to get away from letters like that, and the phone calls."

"What phone calls?" Dave asked, his heart jumping in dual reaction: one, to her stark statement of harassment, and the second, more complex, that of the sight of her so tenderly holding the trusting baby. He shifted uncomfortably, too conscious of wanting to spread his full mantle of protection around this remarkable woman and her son.

"There weren't many of them, three or four, maybe. I had the number changed."

"What did they say? Was it male or female?"

"Male. I'd hazard a guess that he's in his thirties or early forties."

"Why?"

She shrugged then and looked back up at him. He read a measure of certainty in her eyes. "I don't know why, exactly, except that something in the way he put his words together sounded to me like he was a little older than I am, but not too much."

He didn't pursue this hunch on her part; hunches played too strong a role in a cop's life. And a cop's widow would certainly have a strong measure of that same ability.

Instead he asked, "What did he say, exactly?"

"It was different each time. In the first one, the guy only told me that if I liked living, I'd better keep my mouth shut."

"Go on," Dave said when she paused. His fingers curled into his palms, unconsciously forming a fist.

"The second one was about the same, except that the guy let me know he knew where I worked."

"It was the same person?"

"I thought so, yes. It sounded the same."

"What did you do? Did you say anything to him?"

She half smiled. "I pretended that he had the wrong number, that it wasn't the Anderson residence."

"He used your name, then?"

"Yes, he called me Mrs. Anderson. Like it was an insult."

Dave heard a note of sour incredulity in her voice but ignored it. "And the other calls?"

"Basically the same. A little more abuse."

"Such as?"

"Swear words, less vague threats."

"Tell me," he said, then added, "Please."

She leaned back against the pillows and shut her eyes. He didn't receive the impression of tiredness so much as a general weariness.

Without opening her eyes, she complied with his request, speaking in as near a monotone as her rich voice was capable of doing. "He told me he knew where I worked and that if I didn't want anything happening to those sweet little old people, I'd pack up and clear out of town."

Dave waited for the rest. he knew, instinctively, that there was more. There was.

"And he said that once the baby was born, I wouldn't be able to be with him . . . or her . . . all the time, every minute, and that one day, I'd come home and . . . and . . ."

"Never mind," Dave said harshly, reaching a hand to touch her shoulder, as if she were a tape player and he could depress the stop button by mere physical contact. "You don't need to tell me."

She drew a shuddering breath and looked up at him. He couldn't read her expression.

"I left right after that last call."

"And came down here," Dave said, not asking a question.

She answered anyway. "Yes," she said softly, her eyes never wavering from his.

"You had your number changed but the guy found you just the same?"

"Yes. It was unlisted and he still managed to get through."

"Who all had your unlisted number?"

"A few friends," she said quietly. "And the state police, of course."

"No one else?"

"No, I didn't even tell the hospice director. He might know by now, though. He's on the board for the hospice here, and might have seen that I was working here now."

Dave hesitated but then asked the question foremost on his mind. "Any chance any of the Aguilars could have gotten access to that number?" Dave hated the way her eyes dulled when he asked the question, hated himself for bringing that dullness to the surface.

But she only shook her head, her eyes remaining linked with his. "I don't see how. Or why, for that matter."

"Some kind of personal vendetta?"

She looked away then, and when she finally spoke, her voice was so soft and her words so poignant that Dave felt as though he'd been flayed with a hot poker.

"Tony Aguilar already took everything away from me that mattered in my life. His family couldn't do anything worse."

"Until now," Dave said quietly. He felt the words were torn directly from his heart, bypassing lungs and throat.

She looked up and met his eyes, a bittersweet smile curving her lips.

"Until now," she agreed.

Chapter 5

The room was melancholy in that half-lit, shadowed way that only unfamiliar hospital rooms can have, items looming in corners, large blank screens suspended from walls reflecting more shadows, an empty adjacent bed looking for all the world as if someone lay atop its surface.

Janey longed to be home, away from the noise, clatter and bustle of the hospital, away from nurses waking her only to check her blood pressure and temperature. She wished for her quiet, simple home where she could sleep, an ear already attuned for her baby, her weary body given momentary respite.

Her arm ached, cold and sore from the maddening IV still needled into her vein. Though she was being allowed regular food, the drip was still in place as a precaution. Her blood pressure was running too low, the doctor had pronounced before finally agreeing to let her eat something, and her blood sugar levels were off.

Knowing her system better than he, she had patiently tried explaining the abnormal readings were consistent with someone who hadn't eaten in twenty-four hours, who had fallen down a set of stairs and prematurely delivered all at the same time. But he had taken one look at her statistics and another at the mulish set of her jaw and told her the IV was staying in for the time being.

As she lay there, sleep tauntingly eluding her, a ridiculous fear of the night stealing through her veins, as though seeping from the plastic bag above her, she realized that until that moment she hadn't once thought of the old house she'd purchased in Portales as "home." Until tonight, until that precise longing for it, she had only considered it a project, something to take her mind off the past, something to build for the future.

Now she thought of the variety of plants hanging in her living room bay window, brightening the room emotionally even as the broad green leaves darkened the light, presenting a cool, calm effect. She thought of the baby's room, warm, soft peach, brush stroked with unfinished featherlight clouds, of the crib, ready and waiting, of the baby blankets that she'd found in a trunk of Bill's when clearing out his things. Had they been his as a baby? probably. She'd never know, but thinking about them now, she knew it didn't matter. They were the infant David's now.

She thought of the flower beds outside, rich with loam and peat, gladiolus and lily bulbs warming beneath the soil, waiting for the last winter frost to come and water to beckon them, before sprouting green and fresh. She thought of the iris corms Mrs. Aragon had given her, lovingly set in the cool, eastern flower bed. And she thought of Dave Reynolds's tangled mass of twigs that must have been a flower bed last summer.

Home, almost an alien concept now, and yet, one that was so tantalizing, so revitalizing. When she got there she would set Dave's gift of the miniature baseball glove in the crib for the baby to play with and cover young David with one of the plush blue blankets. A gift from the past to go with the gift from the present.

And all of these thoughts led naturally—too easily—to Dave Reynolds himself. She almost sighed with relief as his image coalesced in her mind. Now she could admit it: he, and not the quasi-noisy hospital, was the cause of her restless slumber. His smoky-gray eyes, his long fingers, and his look of utter guilelessness. Did he have any idea how alluring vulnerability was? Did he have any notion how his tenderness pierced her?

She hoped he didn't know. Hoped he would never see it. For Dave Reynolds, with all his soft and easy ways, was still a peace officer. He was as different from Bill as dusk from dawn, yet he was the same in two concrete ways: he was a lawman and he moved her.

She shifted uncomfortably, fighting this knowledge, resisting the stark truth of it. She didn't want to be moved by anyone, let alone this tall cowboy. But fight it though she tried, she couldn't deny it. He had somehow crossed the frozen steppes that surrounded her heart and had, seemingly effortlessly, sparked a thaw in her.

Unfortunately, the thaw couldn't have come at a worse time. She was well aware that she was too receptive to the comfort of his touch, to the warmth in his eyes at this particular time of her life. And it was coming from the very type of man she had sworn to avoid for the remainder of her days.

The hospital room door swung open, revealing the silhouetted figure of a man. Her heart gave an uncomfortable jolt, not this time because she'd thought it was Bill, but because she thought it wasn't. Her pulse rate settled back down almost immediately as she took in the loose shirt and baggy pants of the male night nurse.

"Can you take this IV out?" she asked when he approached the bed with his cart of nightly torture.

"Sorry," he said. "No can do."

She felt a chill running along the backside of her arms and rubbed her unrestricted hand over the goose-bumped flesh. "Did the doctor say when it could come out? It's dreadfully uncomfortable."

The nurse stepped to the end of the bed and lifted her chart from its resting place. He flashed a penlight on the page then replaced the clipboarded chart. "In the morning, it looks like. But until then, you're stuck with it."

Again Janey felt that shiver. The drip was room temperature as compared with her usual ninety-seven-degree body heat. Maybe that was making her cold.

The nurse fussed with the equipment on the roll cart, the thin plastic gloves he sported seeming to make the job more difficult, then slipped a thermometer beneath Janey's tongue and took her wrist. After a few seconds, he dropped her hand, wrapped the wide black band around her forearm and pumped it until it was painfully tight. He released it slowly and to Janey, it seemed her breath expelled at the same pace.

She didn't like him, she decided. It was nothing in his manner, per se. A little rougher, perhaps, slightly more callous. But, she thought, he acted similar to every nurse she'd ever encountered at two in the morning: cheerfully unconcerned, dreadfully behind schedule.

No, it was something else about him, something undefinable. She didn't like the touch of his hand on her skin, and actually pulled away from him as he reached across her to draw the IV stand closer to the bed so he could make adjustments.

He turned his back half to her, fiddling with something on his cart.

Janey shifted the thermometer in her mouth. "What are you doing?" she asked. Even to herself, her voice sounded only curious, giving no hint of the unreasonable fear this man roused in her. Her whole body seemed to be jangling with unnamed alarm bells.

"Your chart calls for a sedative. Don't worry, you won't feel a thing." He chuckled and to Janey's sensitized nerve endings, the laughter personified evil. "You won't feel it, because this shot will never even touch your pretty skin."

His manner was overfamiliar and his voice was, too, but in a different way: it was almost as if she knew him. She wished it wasn't so dark, wished she could penetrate the shadows hiding his features from her.

Something about him reminded her of the dark days surrounding Bill's death. But she couldn't pluck anything concrete out of that dim fog. However, the feeling of dread was enough. Years of living with a state police officer had taught her one very valuable lesson: trust your instincts. How many times had Bill told her that relying on instinct was often the difference between the living and the dead? Hundreds, thousands of times.

A syringe glittered in the dim light, and Janey's heart seemed to go into overdrive as her body jerked backward against the far guard railing of her bed.

"Relax, Mrs. Anderson. This isn't going to hurt at all."

The way he said her name was an insult, his assurance was made into a challenge. Again she shivered.

The nurse deftly inserted the syringe's needle into a small bead about halfway down the clear tube and pressed whatever liquid was contained in the slender vial into the liquid.

Janey expected to feel an immediate sensation of some kind and was half-dizzy with relief when it didn't happen. Had the doctor been right after all? Was she suffering the effects of shock to the point that her fears were getting out of hand, that she was seeing bogeymen where there were really only nighttime routines?

"There. See? No pain whatsoever. You'll soon be sleeping just like . . . your baby. Oh, I almost forgot." He pulled the thermometer from her lips and, with only a glance at the mercury, dropped the thin tube into a glass of alcohol. "Sleep well, Mrs. Anderson. You need it."

He left the room then, drawing the door closed behind him.

The relief at his departure was staggering. So much so that Janey's mind again considered her own seemingly irrational reaction to him. What was it about him? She'd felt it before the syringe, before he'd paused and referred to her sleeping like "her baby."

She'd had the goose bumps first, then the inner alarm system had gone off, and then he'd administered the painless sedative.

Again her alarm system jangled and this time she knew why. One reason was nebulous but definitive, the other was fact. The first was his voice, and his calling her "Mrs. Anderson" in just that way, insulting and derogatory. Like the man who threatened her on the telephone. It was the same man. She couldn't prove it, but she *knew* it.

The alarm that was justified was based on the simple fact that she was a nursing mother. It was highly unlikely that anyone would give a nursing mother a sedative. Any medication would be directly passed to the baby, and while this had often been done in the past, nowadays it was universally frowned upon.

Janey pushed herself to a sitting position, staring at the IV tube in mingled confusion and horror. What had the man put in there? Should she ring for another nurse? What if he came back? Could she accuse him of . . . of what? Trying to hurt her? Trying to hurt her baby? Or had he simply made a mistake?

Instinct again, that unpredictable soothsayer, told her the nurse's actions had been no mistake. She'd been given some kind of drug and even as she sat there staring at the clear liquid in the tube, it was making its slow way into her veins.

Without taking time to think out the ramifications of her action, Janey ripped free the tape holding the IV in place and, with a small cry of pain, jerked the tube from the back of her hand.

Holding a pillowcase pressed against the wound, she stared at the door, half-expecting the man to return, to come back and check on his handiwork. But the door remained closed.

Was she being paranoid or were her instincts correct? Was someone trying to harm her? Her accident the day before loomed in her mind. Someone had tried to hurt her, had sawed one of the steps on her front porch. It was a daring, bold attempt, one taken in broad daylight, in plain sight of both the sheriff and the police chief.

And the card with the wasp in it and the angry menace of the symbol, of the words contained inside. A wasp, dead or alive, was still dangerous if the stinger was touched. Whoever had sent it had brazenly carried it into the hospital, leaving it at the reception desk.

If this was another attempt to harm her, this had been done equally boldly, equally brazenly. The man had posed as a night nurse, had even made a show of taking her vital statistics.

Slowly, feeling as though she were wandering through some kind of maze filled with potential land mines, Janey lifted the slowly dripping IV tube and shoved it into her empty water glass on the nightstand. She felt dull, drained and so very confused as she watched a small puddle form in the base of the glass.

Was she going crazy? Was she being foolish? Or was her mind finally coming awake, allowing her to take action, take some modicum of control over her own destiny again?

She shook her head. She couldn't think about being crazy or foolish. And if her mind was coming awake again, she had to use it to figure out what was going on, to decide what to do next. She didn't dare study the negative sides of her personality now.

She drew a deep breath. If she was right, then she'd done the only thing possible. If she was wrong, she would have to live with that, too, the way she'd learned to live with so many things in the past nine months. Second-guessing was for those with the leisure for introspection. She had no time now.

This mind of hers that had stalled consideration of the future for so long was befuddled, however, out of practice with such rapid conclusions and thoughts. Should she wait for morning? Wait for something else to happen?

A terrible thought set a blast of adrenaline through her body. What if this man had done something to her baby, too?

She whipped her legs from beneath the covers, her eyes still on the pooling liquid contained in the see-through glass. As she stepped down from the bed, her eyes traveled to the little music box beside the glass, and from that to the telephone.

I'm only as far away as the telephone. She could hear his voice now, feel the depth of honesty in the simple statement much more at this moment than when he'd said it. *You can call me anytime. About anything.*

Wondering for a flashing instant about the cutting edge between instinct and desire, Janey reached for the phone and lifted the receiver. It was only after she had punched in the number Information gave her that she questioned her certainty that, in calling Dave Reynolds, she was doing the first really smart thing she'd done in months.

Dave came fully awake on the first ring, whipping the receiver to his ear and barking out a "Yes?" as though he'd been waiting for the call.

And when he heard Janey Anderson's contralto voice, he knew that's exactly what he had been doing: waiting for her.

As if he were in the same room as her, he listened to her brief description of the odd encounter at the hospital, fleshing out the details with his imagination's vivid eye. He could *see* the drinking glass filling with whatever fluid had been intended for Janey, he could *hear* the black stain of fear in her voice and had to fight the anger that welled in him.

Not anger toward Janey Anderson, never that. It was a mindless, directionless anger that seemed to leap through him, stretching for focus. How dare anyone come into her room and try to harm her?

It wasn't until he was dressed and urging his unit out of the driveway that he questioned the probability of someone having penetrated the hospital security—lax as it was in the small-town hospital—and trying to harm a patient by such a method.

Even as he wondered about it, his mind supplied the answer in the form of a memory of repairing her porch. That had been no accident, either. Some guy had, right under their noses, managed to damn near kill her. It didn't take a quantum leap of imagination to paint this guy as the same one to drop off a card at the hospital, a card containing a dead wasp and enough vitriol to fill a snake's fangs.

With the town so small, and virtually no traffic at two-fifteen in the morning, Dave was at the hospital emergency room entrance in less than three minutes.

He pushed his way past the hospital staff—none of whom matched Janey's vague description of her night nurse—and all but ran to the window displaying the sleeping infants.

Janey was standing on the outside of the viewing window, her shoulders slumped, her forehead against the glass. One hand had a pillowcase wrapped around it and the other was pressed flat to the window separating her from her child. Her entire demeanor was one of abject grief, and for a staggering, terrifying moment, Dave thought he'd arrived too late, that something had happened to the baby.

He made some strangled sound of protest and Janey whirled to face him, her eyes ferocious, her lips compressed in mother-bear anger. Her feet stood some two feet apart in fight-ready stance, and the hand with the pillowcase wrapping lifted martially, barring his coming any closer.

It took a full three seconds before she realized who he was, before she choked in a sob and slumped back against the glass, closing her eyes.

A shudder worked through him, an almost stunning relief.

"Are you all right?" he asked, his eyes traveling the length of her, from where her nightgown slipped from her shoulder, to her bare, slightly blue feet, and beyond her, to the incubator with the tiny life safely held inside.

"I was so afraid," she said.

"I'm here," he answered, not knowing what else to say but knowing he had to say something.

Slowly, as though relief were making her dizzy, she lowered her strangely bandaged arm to her side. Would she really have hit him? he wondered, then as he took in the dying hysteria in her eyes, in the awkwardness of her stance, he knew that she would have.

Her mouth opened to answer, then closed again, as did her eyes. When she opened them, they were awash with tears, making her eyes seem bluer, larger, making the blood all but boil in his veins. How dare someone put her through this?

"It's okay," he said, stepping forward, gently lifting her bandaged hand. "Everything's okay, now."

She half raised her other hand, but the effort seemed too great for her. She swayed slightly, her color dropping, and shivers shook her slender frame.

Without conscious thought, Dave swept her into his arms holding her tightly against his chest. "Shh, now. I'm here, honey. Shh." He pressed his lips to her hair.

And though she wasn't crying, her shivering abated after a few moments and he felt her relax in his arms. Unable to resist the impulse to stroke her hair, to nestle her even closer to him, he continued murmuring inconsequential nothings of comfort, of understanding.

Over her shoulder, he could see the baby, David, sleeping peacefully, looking as though he hadn't moved since that afternoon, despite his change of clothing. And in the reflection in the glass, he could see the reflection of Janey's and his bodies entwined, locked together, her delicate face pressed tight against his chest.

Also in the reflection he saw, some twenty feet behind him, the diminutive and stocky figure of Donna Greathouse, the head night nurse at Roosevelt General. She was standing with both hands over her mouth, her eyes wide with curiosity and something more. When she lowered her hands and might have spoken, Dave shook his head, his eyes meeting hers in the mirrorlike window.

Finally, much too soon for Dave, Janey straightened and pulled away from him a little. She met his gaze with that same steadiness she had exhibited the night before.

"I'm sorry," she said. "I don't usually fall apart so easily." Her voice was husky with unshed tears.

"You haven't exactly had an easy night," he answered, glad that her color was better, glad she would be all right but wishing nonetheless that she was still in his arms.

She shook her head and smiled, ruefully it seemed to Dave. And perhaps a little wistfully. "I could be crazy, you know."

"No," he said.

"No... what?"

"No, you're not crazy."

"How do you know that?" she asked, a frown marring her brow, but her eyes filled with a gratitude he neither expected nor particularly wanted.

"Because I know you," he said easily. He saw the surprise on her face and the quick denial that rose to her lips, and he spoke before she could say anything further. "Since we know the baby's safe, why don't we go back to your room and see if we can figure out what's going on?"

She didn't move for a moment, her eyes turned from him to the incubator beyond the window, reluctance evident in the rigid muscles of her jaw, the tight lines of her shoulders. She shifted slowly and nodded.

"I hate the man who is doing this to me," she said softly, almost melodically.

"So do I, Janey," Dave said, but his voice, he noticed, carried almost no melody at all. Only hot promise.

He turned her around and slowly steered her back down the hall to her room. She ignored Donna, he saw, as they passed, and Donna held up her hands in the "I don't know what's going on around here, but you can't blame me for it" gesture.

Dave threw open her hospital room door and took in the entire room at a glance.

The IV tube ran into a glass that contained little more than a couple of tablespoons of fluid. The empty, rumpled bed, exposed by the night light, seemed mute testimony of the turmoil that had gone on that night. The flowers on the window sill sat like mute witnesses, and the telephone receiver was off the hook.

"Is that the stuff?" he asked, pointing to the glass. He knew it was, he'd only wanted to forestall any more of her self-doubt and to completely evade the look of gratitude he'd seen on her face earlier. And to keep from drawing her into his arms again.

He wanted many things from Janey Anderson, but gratitude wasn't on the list. Holding her in his arms definitely was, however.

"I'm going to take this now, and have it tested," he said, pinching the tube off and lifting the glass. "Is there another glass in case none of whatever he put in here has come through yet?"

She silently handed him a replacement. He dropped the dripping tube inside it. He turned and wished he hadn't, for she was still standing right beside him, her gaze on the empty glass. He could smell baby powder and soap and maybe a hint of hand cream. Hardly erotic fragrances, he thought, yet somehow, coming from Janey, they mingled with her deeper, richer scent, and roused him like no expensive perfume had ever done before.

She turned to him then, raising her eyes to his. "What is it?" she asked. "What's wrong?"

He could feel the damning color sweep across his face, the curse of his childhood, the bane of his adult life. He shook his head, angry at himself for his thoughts, angry at his own betrayal of them. He averted his face and told her he'd go ask a nurse to bring the baby to her. That would make her feel better.

He stepped away before seeing the answering rise of color in Janey's cheeks. When she'd looked up at him, caught him half scowling, and then surprised the sudden hunger on his face, she'd felt for a moment as though she'd accidentally tripped and fallen into some hitherto unknown territory.

She'd known passion with Bill, the kind of bursting passion that threatened to consume her at times. But she'd never seen just that look of hunger on Bill's face. Never. And until she'd seen it on Dave Reynolds's, she hadn't ever imagined she'd been missing anything. But she knew it now. And the knowledge left her trembling with the desire to give him what he wanted, to stoke that hunger, to assuage that fierce need.

She started when the door opened and a nurse appeared carrying young David. Behind her stood a nurse's aide, and the baby's namesake, one hand propping the door open, the other holding his cowboy hat.

Dave met her eyes for just a brief second, and in that instant, she read apology, a touch of that raw longing and something else. Embarrassment? Self-disgust?

Why? Why would he feel embarrassment or disgust? She, possibly, but why would he? He hadn't said or done anything to feel awkward about. She had been the one to call him in the middle of the night, possibly for nothing more than a case of the nervous nellies. She had been the one to stand half-naked in his arms, too aware of him as a man to take comfort in his being a sheriff. She had been the one to want him, knowing that she was incapable of pursuing that want.

"Stay with her, okay, Donna? And let's get her checked out ASAP."

"I'm going home?" Janey asked, hope infusing her words with greater strength.

Dave looked at her, puzzled, she was sure.

"No...oh! No, I didn't mean checked out of the hospital, I meant have some blood work done so we can make sure you don't have any of that stuff, whatever it is, in your system."

"I see," she answered dully. That made sense, but she was so tired she couldn't seem to think straight. It was almost as though she were moving in slow motion.

"Okay, Donna?"

"Sure, Dave. Sure," the first nurse said, stepping closer to Janey. "Go on and get back in bed, honey, then I'll hand him to you." The nurse and the aide's eyes were wide with curiosity, and their lips were parted with unspoken questions as the door brushed silently closed after Dave. But the elder woman waited until Janey was in bed, covers over her legs and slowly rousing baby in her arms, before asking anything.

Her first question made Janey smile. "What happened to your hand?"

Over the tsking of Donna and the aide, and clanging of drawers as the professional women overrode their curiosity in order to locate a bandage and to take a sample of her blood, Janey told them why she'd removed the intravenous tube.

The aide had to be prompted to rush that test tube of blood to the lab, but when she was gone, a flood of questions followed. Janey told her story for the second time that night. The nurse interrupted a couple of times, protesting the lack of the impostor writing down the vital signs, and nodding vehemently when Janey said she hadn't felt right about a sedative being administered to a nursing mother. When the explanation was finished, the nurse dragged a chair over and plunked into the hard seat.

"And here was me, thinking things were getting pretty dull around this place. Goes to show you, doesn't it?" She leaned forward, plump arms on plumper knees, her pretty face concerned and avid all at once. "I'm Donna Greathouse, by the way, and I already know full well who you are. Well, I'll tell you this for nothing, we don't have anybody like you described around here. We have a couple of male nurses, George Treghorn and Billy Marlowe, but they're neither one on duty tonight. And Orlando, he's one of our orderlies, he only works weekends. Katie and me, that's all we've got tonight."

Janey was silent, the initial fear and reaction wearing off and the woman's voice acting on her like a soporific. She yawned, and it felt as if her jaw cracked with the size of it. The baby began to whimper and unconsciously Janey began fumbling with the gown to lower it for the meal young David was asking for.

"I don't know that's such a good idea, honey," the nurse said quietly. "We don't know if you got any of that stuff in your system. Let's wait for the blood work first. I'll ring for Katie. She'll get you some formula for him in the meantime."

Janey felt disappointment. This was her bonding, her total point of connection with David. Anger at the intruder's actions filled her. No matter that she'd acted quickly, no matter that she hadn't been harmed—or worse—by whatever drug he'd squeezed into the tube, he'd managed to force a wedge in that fragile bonding between mother and child.

"Don't look so sad, honey. As soon as it's out of your system, you'll be able to go right back to nursing again. Though, if it was me, I'd use this as a golden opportunity to get right to the bottle. I believe that the sooner you introduce your young'un to a baby-sitter at least once in a while, the happier you'll be."

"How soon will they know?" Janey asked, and hoped her voice didn't sound as petulant as she felt.

"We already know," a male voice said from the doorway.

Both women turned to the door, the nurse's face lighting with a wary relief, Janey feeling her own face color in memory of her earlier desire.

"Was there anything in the saline?" the nurse asked.

Dave nodded, stepping on into the room. His eyes were all for Janey and the baby fitfully wriggling in her arms. His face bore a staggering relief.

"You're okay," he said.

"What was in there?" the nurse asked, rephrasing her question, raising her voice.

Dave flicked her a glance and Janey saw in that look just how worried he'd been. She'd never seen him anything but unfailingly affable to everyone he came in contact with. The rigid control he had on himself now, the distancing, was a scarcely contained fury ready to spring out on the first person who crossed him.

"Enough pentobarbital to frizz a horse," he said dully.

"Pentobarbital!" the nurse exclaimed. "Why, Janey has low blood pressure. Too much pentobarb, and she'd have just gone right—"

"You haven't fed the baby, have you?" Dave asked, cutting off Donna Greathouse's indignant outburst, his eyes, fevered with worry, locking onto Janey's.

"I wouldn't let her, Sheriff," Donna answered for Janey.

Dave closed his eyes in relief.

Janey eyed him in half-wonder. In the heat of the moment, in the clamorous realization that she hadn't imagined anything that had transpired that night, that she'd been right to trust her instincts, she had missed the significance of the nurse's shift from calling him by his first name, then by his title. And realized that a dim part of her had never thought of him as anything but the *sheriff*.

Looking at him now, taking in the staggering relief on his shuttered face, she saw in his suddenly slumped shoulders the kind of relief that a parent must feel upon knowing his or her child is safe from harm—as she had felt when she saw David was all right, as she had—and he?—when he'd held the baby above her knees, showing her the living, breathing, minute-old newborn.

This man with his eyes closed and his knuckles white from gripping his hat too strongly wasn't the sheriff in act or deed at that moment. He was simply, and tremendously, a man. A man who cared beyond the confines of normal concern.

When he opened his eyes and the smoky gaze focused on her, she wished she'd never had such a thought, for it roused too many unanswerable questions in her heart, posed too many problems for her weary mind to wrestle with at the moment. "I'll get back to work now," the nurse said quietly, and though Janey heard her, she didn't see her leave.

"When John told me what the drug was, and what it could do, I think I was never so scared in all my born days," Dave said, and his smile quirked at one corner. As soon as the words left his lips, Janey saw a shadow enter Dave's eyes and knew, suddenly, that he'd been frightened before, scared and, as a result, somehow scarred. Perhaps badly.

"I'm fine," Janey said softly, unconsciously holding out her hand. It seemed oddly unjoined, no longer her own, something independent from her body.

"Yes," Dave said, equally softly, meaning something altogether different.

He took the single step to her side and, after a long look, as though he too saw something different about her, accepted her hand and slowly, gently, raised it to his lips.

"You *are* ... *fine*," he murmured, pressing a soft, healing kiss over the bandage on her hand, on the sensitive flesh beneath it.

Chapter 6

Dave watched the baby consume the formula in the small bottle. He almost asked Janey if he could feed his namesake, but held back when he saw the look of contentment on her face, a look mirrored in her infant son's tiny features. He wished that double expression would remain just so forever.

In the glow of the night lamp, Janey's hair took on an auburn hue, and her skin seemed a pale gold. The baby's dark hair glistened against the sharp white of his mother's hospital gown sleeve, and his blue, blue eyes so much like his mother's, stared unfocused but concentrated at Janey's beautiful face.

The scene was so peaceful, so filled with gentle purpose, that it was hard to believe that only a half an hour before the room had been filled with police, bustling hospital staff, and punctuated by the sound of a very agitated David Anderson.

The nightstand and IV monitor had been dusted for prints, as was the doorknob of the room and any other place anyone could think of that the intruder might have touched. This included, to Dave's amusement, the knob of the television, the door to the bathroom, the closet, the trash can and the telephone.

The rewards were small, only four clear prints from the lot, and three of those were easily identifiable as hospital staff. The fourth print was Janey Anderson's. Janey had said the assailant/nurse was wearing those thin plastic gloves most hospital staffers wore nowadays, so the lack of results came as no surprise. But it was disappointing.

Who was the guy who had tried to harm her? What did he want? And how had he managed to waltz right into her room without a single other person noticing him?

The emergency room doctor had pronounced Janey safe from any effects from the pentobarbital, though she had a trace in her system. He suggested she not nurse the baby overnight but go ahead and use the hand pump to both relieve the pressure and to allow the lab an opportunity to test the milk, though if there were any traces found the next day, he would advise that she abandon nursing the child and resort to the bottle full-time.

Dave had waited outside her room, an embarrassed curiosity stirring in him, his mind on the strange contraption the nurse had provided Janey, his heart with the young woman whose stormy eyes had bespoken her displeasure at the bizarre circumstances that prevented this elemental contact with her son.

But she hadn't complained, nor argued with the doctor. She had only frowned and, in an unguarded moment, shared a long look with Dave. It was a straightforward acknowledgment of frustration, he thought, and an underlying belief that he would not only understand what she was experiencing, but in some empathetic way, share it with her.

He had then. And now he was participating in the hiatus, the calm between the buffets of fate. Somehow it seemed significant that he share that with her, as well. He

wondered briefly, without any hope of an answer, where all
this was leading.

She looked up then, meeting his eyes, and he read the intense reserve in her, the carefully erected barrier against
trust, against hope. Seeing it, he was angry. Not at Janey—
he didn't think he could ever be angry at her—but directed
at whoever was adding mortar to the walls she'd raised inside her.

Whoever had sawed her steps, had injected pentobarbital into her IV, was not only a potential killer in the physical world, but was doing a fine job of damaging her
psychically.

He forced a smile, projecting a reassurance he was far
from truly feeling. When she smiled in return, with no hint
of the relaxing humor lighting her shadowed eyes, Dave
knew she was beyond simple homilies, beyond a white lie of
comfort.

"We'll find the guy that did this," he said giving voice to
the reassurance.

She smiled again, that same bittersweet smile that had
curved her lips the night before, and he realized she could
see right through him. There weren't any platitudes and assurances in the world that harbored cop killers and allowed
murder attempts on the widows of peace officers. At least,
none that Dave could offer with any truth.

He dropped his eyes back to the baby, unable to maintain eye contact with this woman whose gaze held more
knowledge of pain than anyone should have encountered in
a single lifetime. Unbidden came the memory of the days
after Patty's death, those lost, stumbling-in-the-dark
mornings when he'd reached his hand out and find a cold
pillow, not a warm, sleep-flushed familiar face.

"Why do you look like that sometimes?" she asked.

"Like what?" he questioned back, his eyes still on the
baby.

"Like you've been there, too. Like you've seen the other side of hell and can't forget it."

He looked up then and saw the understanding in her eyes. Unbidden came the certainty that Bill Anderson had been the luckiest man on the face of the earth.

He would never have dreamed it was possible to be jealous of a dead man, but he was. Bill Anderson had had it all. And Dave Reynolds could only sit in Bill's shadow, wanting his widow, but knowing it would, in all likelihood, never happen.

"Would you tell me about it?" she asked. When he shrugged and shook his head, she added softly, "I'm sleepy, but I'm afraid to be alone."

The simple confession almost unmanned him. Like everything else about her, her straightforwardness spoke of courage. She might admit to being afraid, but the admission took a rare strength. And her innate honesty demanded nothing but the same from him.

Besides, he had to admit, the connectedness he felt with her forbade him from not giving her anything, everything, she asked for. No matter how difficult.

"I lost someone once," he said. "About four years ago."

"Your wife?"

He shook his head, breaking eye contact again. "No. No, she wasn't my wife. We were living together, maybe even thinking about marriage. Who knows?"

"Only you," she said softly. Too knowingly.

He smiled wryly at that. "Yeah. I guess that's true. Only I could know." He was grateful when she didn't reply. "We had an argument the night before she died."

"About getting married," she said. Her voice was soft and filled with that uncanny knowledge.

"Yes," he said. In an odd sort of way, telling someone about this, even after all those years, he felt better. Confession was, he decided bitterly, good for the conscience, if not fully for the soul. "We argued about getting married. All I

could think about later was that I wished I'd said things
differently. Better. Kinder, maybe.''

"I know.''

He met her eyes then and saw that she did know. She
knew too much.

"I'm sorry,'' he said. "You've been through enough
without having to hear about my troubles.''

She smiled, and what with the sympathy in her eyes, the
dryness of her lips, he thought the smile was probably the
saddest one he'd ever seen.

She said, "I'm not sure I believe that misery loves company, but I do believe that sharing helps.''

"Tell me about your husband,'' Dave said. As curious as
he was about her past, he had to clench his jaw to keep from
retracting his words. He wanted to know yet didn't. He
wanted to see yet suspected he would prefer his blindness.

She didn't answer immediately, and for a moment, Dave
thought he would be granted a reprieve and she wouldn't
respond to his demand for additional information about a
man who had died a hero, who had loved Janey, who had
been loved by her.

But she sighed finally and waved a delicate hand, as
though not certain where to begin. Dave wanted to take her
hand in his, to warm it, perhaps, or maybe just to cling to it
for comfort himself. Before he could, however, her hand
dropped down to the baby's back.

"He was a big man, a little taller and heavier than you
are, I think, but close to your size. And he had brown eyes.''
She paused, her gaze as unfocused as her baby's, and as
blue.

When she continued, her voice was dreamy, lost. "He had
small feet for a man his size. He had to special order his
uniforms, but he could buy his shoes and boots at any shoe
store.''

Dave understood what she was saying and what she
wasn't. The measure of a marriage—or any solid relation-

ship, he supposed—wasn't the major moments, the huge obstacles and great joys, it was the small, seemingly insignificant elements of a daily life shared and, obviously in Janey's case, nurtured.

"We would talk while he shined his shoes," she said. "Not about anything important. How his day went, what I did while he was gone." She half smiled, and the crooked corner of her lips seemed to puncture a place in Dave's heart.

He wanted to stop her, to call a halt to this torture, but her dreamy voice, her softened, relaxed features stayed his tongue, stopped his selfish urge for release from this full disclosure, this answer to the question he wished he hadn't dreamed of asking.

"We came up with the most outrageous pipe dreams, things we'd do or places we'd go when we were rich and famous, knowing all the time that we'd never be either of those things. It was silly stuff, mainly. Big things, some little things." She sighed. "Impossible things."

A restlessness gripped Dave with fierce command. He wanted to urge her on, he wanted to scream at her to stop. Couldn't she see the torture this was for him? And at his own unspoken question, he drew a deep breath and forced himself to remain seated.

It could only be torture for one reason: he wanted that kind of intimacy with Janey Anderson. He'd shied from it with Patty Donahue, and it was only after she was gone that he'd realized that he'd been running from something he hadn't understood had existed all along.

He let the silence draw a comfortable circle around them, allowing the import of her words to form a bond, then he cleared his throat and looked down at his linked hands. "When Patty died, I found myself hanging around the house, doing all the things she asked me to do but I never made the time for when she was alive. Gardening, fixing cabinet doors, little things like that."

Like him, she paused, waiting, he was sure, to make certain he was finished. "I know," she said finally. "I did that, too. I ironed every one of his uniforms. I hate ironing. He always took them to the laundry and had the people there do them for him. But I did it. It took me all night. And the whole time I was making sure every one had the creases just the way he liked them, I knew he would never wear one of them again."

Dave smiled crookedly. This was agony, but it was cathartic torment. For both of them. The kindest thing he could do right now was to share her grief, give her a glimpse of himself, let her know that someone else had been there too.

He drew a deep breath, and to his shock, it seemed to shudder as it entered his constricted lungs. He said, "About two months after she died, I put the house on the market and gave all of her things to a sister who lives in Vermont."

She made some murmur of acknowledgment, then after a moment said, "I thought I would never want to part with anything that had been his. Ours."

"But you did," he said with certainty...and with knowledge.

"Bill had this big chair, one of those recliners, and it always squeaked, and one night, about a month after he was killed, I found myself sitting in that big old chair just crying for all I was worth. I always hated that chair when he was alive. It was ugly, and noisy, and, I don't know, it somehow represented something chauvinistic—like he could just lay back in it and command everything in the house from that big old thing as if it were some control center. But without him there, it seemed like the only place in the house I could run to, hide in, maybe."

A single tear strayed down her cheek and the sight of it made Dave's eyes sting, as well. She moistened her lips with the tip of her tongue but made no move to wipe the tear away.

She continued after a bit. "It smelled like him. Funny, to think of things like that."

"No, it's not funny," Dave said quietly. "It's not funny at all." Nothing had ever been less amusing.

She raised the back of her hand to her cheek then and swiped at her face, a brief, almost angry, gesture. "I sold the chair, and everything else in the house, too." She looked at him as though daring him to utter a negative.

"And moved here," he said.

A tremor worked through her at his words, and she expelled a sigh that could either have been relief or pure exhaustion. A smile once again appeared on her face, making Dave remember his desire to make her laugh, to hear that throaty voice in full-fledged humor.

"You're a nice man, Dave Reynolds," she said, turning her wide, guileless gaze upon him.

Her statement could be taken as innocuous, maybe even tepid by some, but Dave knew it was anything but mild. It was as if she had spoken directly from her heart. He could see the truth of her emotions in those amazing eyes and felt it to his core.

Keep it light, Davey boy, he cautioned himself. Keep it easy, don't let her see how much she moves you. Don't frighten her away.

"Ditto, Janey Anderson."

He resisted the urge to touch her, her cheek or her hand, anything to add physical demonstration of just how "nice" he though she was. "Why don't you let me take the baby now, and you get some sleep?"

"I don't want the baby to go back to the nursery," she said, not shifting. "If he needs an incubator, they can bring it in here." Her voice was still soft, still low, but her tone was implacable. Utterly determined. Again he was seeing the rock-hard strength beneath the surface vulnerability. And it was magnetic, drawing the steel in him to her.

"All right, I'll see what I can arrange. But you don't have to worry, after what happened tonight, nobody's going to get within ten feet of your room without a ten-alarm warning."

She didn't move, nor in any way acknowledge his seemingly lighthearted statement. And at her next words, he understood the lack of expression was only an indication of her disbelief in the rightness of things anymore.

"Warnings have a tendency to be too late," she said.

His mind flashed on Patty Donahue and Bill Anderson.

"You'll be safe here," he said quietly, as firmly as she had spoken only seconds earlier. "I'll stay, if you want."

"You can't do that," she said. "You must be exhausted."

He smiled. She was right, he was bone tired. But he wasn't about to leave her alone in this hospital where someone had simply cruised into the room and damn near killed her. No, he wouldn't leave her before he'd arranged for her safety.

"Don't worry about me," he said, pushing to his feet and reaching his hands out for the baby.

After the briefest of hesitations, she pulled her hands free of their loving grasp around her baby. His hands brushed her breasts as he sought a more secure grip on the baby.

Janey stifled the gasp that rose in her, and fought the strange electricity that seemed to course through her body at his careless touch. Everything in her wanted to lean into the hot, searing, and wholly accidental graze. But it was over almost as soon as it began, and the transfer of the baby from her arms to his was complete.

His face, as he gazed down at her sleeping son, at the infant he so gently escorted into the world, was solemn, oddly humbled and, at the same time, transmuted into raw power. Janey knew, in that instant, this man would give whatever he had, to offer young David a better life, to make the world a secure, safe place. He had looked at her in just that manner the night before, and for brief moments this night. He was a man for all seasons, she thought, and knew that meant forever.

And it wasn't fair to him to let him continue to cherish these thoughts, these half-formed dreams.

"Dave . . . ?"

He didn't look away from the baby. A long finger lightly stroked the tiny brow of her son, the living legacy, the only thing she really had left from her marriage. "Yes?" he asked. His voice was absent of curiosity.

He was so wrapped up in the child in his arms—her child—that she couldn't bring herself to say the words that would make him look up, make him listen to what she had to say. Words, she knew, that would rip the fabric of trust he'd woven around himself and the baby. And around her?

What could she really say to him, anyway? *I can't stay here any longer; we're all in danger here.* She had been in danger before and she had run to Portales. Now there were two of them, the danger was real, the urge to run was even stronger. She wanted to grab her infant son to her chest and run and run until she found some safe place.

But there wasn't any place to run. There wasn't any place to hide.

Watching him, seeing him as a man, as a real, solid man, she wanted to warn him, give him the clear understanding that she couldn't love anymore, couldn't offer what a man needed from a woman, what a woman needed from a man: totality. She wasn't whole, she probably would never be whole again.

Yes, seeing him standing there, large, tanned cowboy with a sleeping infant in his arms, his expression almost fierce with pride and longing, she couldn't speak. She couldn't break the bubble, and if truth be known, at that moment she didn't want to burst it.

In an odd way, she wanted it to go on forever, for every one of those seasons, just the three of them, orphans of the storm, banded together, peaceful in one anothers' company, strong in unity, forging, if just for that beautiful instant, a family unit.

"When he gets older," Dave said, "I'll take him to baseball games. They have them in Rotary Park all spring and summer. They start baseball practice early here, because the weather's so mild. And I'll buy him a hotdog. Nothing tastes so good as a baseball game hotdog on a summer's evening. And nothing ever sounds so good as when a seven- or eight-year-old smacks that ball like a clap of thunder. And nothing's ever so funny as seeing that little kid just standing there, mouth hanging open because he finally hit one."

This was a natural extension of her thoughts, *too natural, too easy,* but one that leaped so much further than she dared go.

"We can't stay here," she said. "In Portales."

He looked up at her then, as she'd known he would. But instead of confusion, or even anger, what she saw was only a guarded question. "Because of what's happened the last few days?"

"Because someone is after me, and maybe even after David."

He didn't patronize her by denying it or anger her by waving it aside. What he did say, however, took the wind out of her sails. "I won't let him get close enough to you to do anything, Janey. Not again."

He said it so calmly, he might have been talking about the stars in the night sky, but so definitively that it was obvious he spoke from deep-rooted faith, utter conviction. And reading his eyes, she saw that he truly believed what he said.

"You can't know that," she said softly, hoping her expression of sorrow would rob the words of contradiction.

"I do, though."

"How?" she asked. "How can you say that? You can't be with us twenty-four hours a day."

"Why not?" He asked the two words as though they were a statement and not a question, slowly and with the same ring of conviction. His smoky-gray eyes locked with hers and Janey had to drag her gaze away to keep from believing him, to gather her shattered defenses in order to stay the trust she wanted to place in him.

He couldn't be speaking with any degree of certainty. He, of all people, would know that there were more bad guys than good guys out there, that all it took was one moment, one madman, and life's strange little game was over. Finished forever.

"Be-because . . ." she stammered, then trailed off, sensing his gaze still upon her, his confidence as palpable as a touch, as real as his strong arm gently cradling her son.

He was wrong. She knew it. She felt it. She'd had to live with it for months. Why—*how*—didn't he understand this basic knowledge? Had things always been so tame in Portales, New Mexico, that he couldn't recognize a real bad guy when he ran across one? She looked up again and felt that shock of contact when their gazes locked.

His eyes never wavered from hers. And she could see that he knew something of what she was thinking but wasn't going to treat her to a long list of reasons why she should believe him. Or should she say, believe *in* him?

Oh, but how he made her want to believe.

Finally, he half smiled, his lips quirking sideways. He looked down at little David.

"Honey, did you think we would let you just go back home and worry about this all by yourself? Between Charlie Dobson, the guys from two departments, me, and even the good ladies of the neighborhood—Mrs. Lyon, Mrs. Aragon and Norma Judson—did you really think we'd abandon you?"

Janey had to close her eyes against the sudden sting of tears that threatened to spill free at his words.

"Because, if you did, it just shows you don't know us very well. Yet."

She looked up then, blinking the tears away. Through her watery gaze, she saw Dave's easy smile. Her lips trembled as she smiled in return. But still she shook her head. "It's just not possible," she said. "What about when I go back home?"

"How is being home so very different from being here? Except you'll probably be allowed a little more sleep at home."

"What about when I go back to work?"

"Well, now, that'd be what, four, five weeks?" At her nod, he continued, "Then I see no problems at all. We'll have the jerk by then, and on the off chance we don't, Alma Maybry over at Los Abuelos can keep an eye out in the daytime for you."

"What about David?"

"Mrs. Aragon's daughter is already itching to baby-sit little David here. Her momma's had to sit on her to keep her from coming around before now." Before Janey could voice any further objections, Dave continued. "Her name's Linda, and she's had kind of a rough time. She married too young and her husband took off with a gal from the bank. Left her with two young'uns, both less than four, and a passel of debts."

Janey felt completely silenced by this disclosure. By that girl's standards, Janey would be the luckier of the two. Neither of them had a husband any longer, but at least Janey wasn't left destitute, a mountain of debt on her shoulders.

Still she had to say something. "Wouldn't it be simpler if we just packed up and left?" she asked.

Dave didn't answer for a moment, busy with rearranging the baby on his right arm. "For whom?"

"What?"

"Who would it be simpler for, Janey? You? You're in no condition to go running around the country without a place to land. The baby's not in any shape, either."

"You," Janey said in a small voice.

The cowboy sheriff looked up at that, his expression hard, then at seeing the anguish clearly etched on her face, he sighed. "No, honey. That wouldn't be simpler for me. Not one whit."

Watching her, fighting the urge to beg her not to run, Dave felt as if the earth were spinning at a different rate than he was used to experiencing. Day before yesterday, it had spun normally, the ground solid beneath his boots, but now everything seemed a little off kilter, as though it were either going faster or slower, just enough to make him feel dizzy.

Before yesterday the closest he'd come to standing around holding a baby in his arms was spending Sunday afternoon at Mrs. Aragon's and picking up one of Linda's toddlers when they pitched down on the rocky patio, or taking one of Mrs. Lyon's great-grandkids for a few seconds while she handed out the door prizes at the annual turkey dinner over at the Methodist church.

Today it seemed the most natural thing in the world to be holding little David in his arms. As if he were the baby's father, as if Janey were . . . his wife?

He couldn't let her go. Couldn't let her run. Yet everything in him screamed for him to do just that. It was torture for him to ask her to stay, to tell her that he would ensure her safety. Because it might be a lie.

He'd promised Patty Donahue safety. *Promised.* And he'd sent her to a terrible death. While he and a few other officers waited outside in the dark, drinking coffee to ward off the cold, while he sat less than twenty yards from her, thinking about their cool parting that morning, the argument the night before, not dreaming he would never have the opportunity to say he was sorry, she'd been killed. Tortured and killed.

Asking Janey Anderson not to run, urging her to stay in Portales, to remain where she was obviously in danger, was like reaching inside him and scratching open that scarcely healed scar on his heart, or like turning a thousand-watt floodlight onto the mistakes of his past.

He'd told Patty the morning she was killed that there were no guarantees. No one knew for certain what would happen tomorrow or the next day; a stray bullet, an overturned car, anything, anytime could upset the best and most beautiful of plans. And he'd been right, but he'd also been so terribly wrong. He should have grabbed her to his chest and begged her to marry him then and there, to share whatever brief span of time they might have together, because they might not ever have another chance.

She had died, his refusal in her ears, his promise of guardianship playing her false.

And here he was again, offering guarantees.

He'd seen in Janey's eyes that she didn't believe in them anymore. Why should she? She, like he, knew all too well that every breath taken could be the last one, that danger waited just out of eyesight for a single chance to strike.

But if she ran, he wouldn't be able to watch out for her—not that he'd done all that bang-up a job of it so far, he thought bitterly. He would never know how she was, what she was doing, and how young David was faring.

At this thought, his mind skittered aside, trying to analyze why it would matter so much that he never know about them, never be able to see them again. But this was too great to consider. Her life was at stake, and so was little David's, and that was all that could be allowed to matter.

He saw from her face that he'd been silent for some time. He cleared his throat, ruthlessly shoving the past into the far reaches of his heart, trying to force the images of a fugitive Janey and David from his mind.

"The first thing we've got to do is make sure you're safe while you're in here," he said.

"How?"

In answer, he marched his fingers across the nightstand to the telephone and picked up the receiver as if he'd just discovered its existence. "Magic," he said, tucking the receiver between his shoulder and chin and punching in a number.

"You're not staying here all night," she said, over the ringing of the phone on the other end.

"No," he agreed. "If I'm going to be watching out for you I need some sleep, too."

The phone was answered on the other end, and, juggling the baby, he took the receiver in his left hand. As he'd expected, Dolores Petersham, the dispatcher at Portales Police Department, answered. He quickly told her what he needed—an officer to man Janey Anderson's hospital door for the remainder of the night—and, after asking for two shifts of replacements for subsequent days of her stay in the hospital, rang off.

"How will the officer know if the nurse or doctor is real or not?" Janey asked.

Dave had already thought of that. "Everyone here has hospital ID. They've just never needed to use it before. Anyone without proper ID can't be admitted to the room. Besides, anyone on the force is going to know everyone around here."

He saw the look of skepticism on her face and couldn't blame her for it. The man who had tried killing her—or at least caused her a great deal of fear—had walked right by everyone in the hospital without being noticed.

"What if it's someone they know?" she asked.

"It won't be," he said.

"Why not?" she asked. "Because bad guys don't live in Portales?"

He sighed, then smiled. "We're not perfect, Janey. Sure, there are some creeps, there's even a few crazies. But we pretty well know who they are, and how they'll react to a given situation. I can't see anyone from here pulling the kind of stunts this character's been pulling on you."

"Do you have any idea how naive that sounds?" she asked.

Dave didn't try to argue with that, he merely answered her with a simple, "Yes."

"But you believe it."

"I've got to, Janey," he said. And he was telling the truth. Faith in the rightness, in the inherent goodness of a small town like Portales was what had kept him from falling apart back in L.A. after Patty's death. People he'd known and loved all of his life had called him home, and after a couple of years of living there, seeing these folks day in, day out, he'd come to know he was right to have that kind of faith in them. By and large, they were a good people. They had their faults, their petty squabbles, and their hot-blooded feuds, but they cried at christenings, danced at wedding receptions, and stood by family and friends at funerals. They were real people, trusting, earthy and, for the most part, as honest as the day was long.

"I've got to believe in the people here," he repeated, as though by saying it twice he could convince her, as well.

"I'm afraid for you," she said.

"For me! Why?"

"Because one of these days you'll have to wake up and smell the coffee. And it might not smell so good."

"Don't feel sorry for me, Janey. I've been there. I've been exactly where you are, and I came to Portales because it was the only sane place I knew on earth. Sane and corny, wholesome and sometimes stagnant. But real."

"I hope you're right," she said softly, the disbelief still very much in evidence on her face.

He forced a smile to his lips. "Don't worry about it, now. You need some rest. They'll take care of you. They won't let anyone in who isn't absolutely authorized. And I'll take care of you, too. And we'll talk and talk and talk until we figure out who this guy is and why he's after you." He shifted his attention back to the telephone and punched another number, this time inside the hospital.

A few minutes later, Donna Greathouse, the same nurse who had tended Janey earlier, pushed the door open—revealing a uniformed police officer already stationed in the hallway—and wheeled a large, unwieldy incubator into the room.

"In all my years as a nurse, I've never once seen anyone get permission to keep their baby in an incubator right in the room—not that I blame you, mind, I'd do the very same thing if I was in your shoes—but, I mean to tell you, it's nothing short of a miracle."

Donna bustled around the room like a human whirlwind, plugging a cord in here, removing a cord there until the incubator lit up and began to glow. "Now let's put the little lamb inside this snugly warm house of a bed," she said, coming at Dave with hands outstretched.

Dave shifted to allow her to draw the baby from his arms. His chest felt curiously cold and his forearm strangely weightless. He glanced at Janey to see if she had felt this odd sensation of loss when he'd removed David from her arms, but she was watching Donna's gentle, expert handling of her son.

"There now, little one, everything is going to be all right. You've got your mommy right here, and the sheriff. What more could a little baby want, now tell me that?"

"Nothing," Janey said, and both Dave and Donna turned to look at her.

To Dave, Janey seemed nothing less than the epitome of weariness, the image of a woman stretched beyond her endurance, and yet, as she gazed at her sleeping son, he saw the kernel of resilience, the need to be stronger than mere strength. Again he wondered what she'd been like before all the tragedy in her life, and again he felt that pang of jealousy of Bill Anderson.

She'd been through so very much, he thought, and wished he really was able to perform magic, for he'd do it now. For Janey.

"What did you say, honey?" Donna asked.

Dave turned to look at her blankly, lost in his mind's torturous passages.

Janey said, "You said what more could a baby want...? I said 'nothing.' You're right, a baby could want for nothing more."

Dave shifted his gaze to Janey, wondering if she felt the impact of her statement as he had. In his heart he had already changed the phrase: what more could *anyone* want? But could Janey ever grow to want that, too? And if she did, and then he let her down, if she came to him with open trust and he allowed danger to rip her life apart for a second time...where would that want go? What direction would it take?

Even if he did manage to catch the bad guy, save the day, could she cast off the past and don the present? And if she could, was he the present she would choose?

And in her face he read the answer, even as she voiced it aloud. "For *now,* he couldn't ask for anything more."

The phrase was slightly different; so was the meaning. Dave had to swallow the protest that instinctively rose to his lips.

But Donna apparently missed the significance. "I'm off now, honey. You get some sleep. Nobody's gonna bother you tonight...not even to check your temperature. And the incubator's got an alarm that's rigged to the nurses' station, so we'll know if anything needs adjusting on it. That pentobarb in your system must be screaming for you to sleep. Why don't you just let it go ahead and do its thing?"

Donna opened the door and held it open, obviously waiting for him. "Sheriff?"

Ignoring her, he turned back to Janey, reaching for her hand. "I can stay," he said. While she let him take her fingers, he could sense the withdrawal in her.

"No," she said, "I'll be fine."

Did he have any idea how much she wanted to hold on to his hand, to cling to the warmth, to keep this man at her side? She suspected he did, and that notion acted like a splash of cold water on her too-tired soul. She *couldn't* rely on him; she couldn't rely on anyone. She knew that better than almost any person on earth.

And she knew that she was particularly susceptible to this tremendous longing for connection due to the birth of the baby, his presence during it, and because of the unknown danger threatening her.

She shook her head, as much to deny the feelings of longing as to tell him there was no need for him to stay. She pulled her fingers free from his grasp.

He reached across her and pulled the light's cord. In the half-light, the spill from the hallway and the golden glow of the incubator, he looked as insubstantial as a ghost. And like the ghost he resembled, he seemed to want to say more but didn't. But unlike in the past, she was glad for his reserve.

He paused at the doorway, once again Dave Reynolds, and with his hand against the doorjamb, raised two fingers in a farewell salute. The door closed behind him and Janey had the odd feeling that the room was larger, less corporeal than before.

She turned her gaze to her sleeping son and sighed, thinking of the past two days, the past two nights, the dangers and the joys, the fears and the few shining moments of total trust.

After lowering the bed to a prone position, she lay down upon the pillow and drew the covers up around her neck, turned to face the incubator's warm glow. She dozed, jerked awake, eyes raking the interior of the incubator, and dozed again.

When she had done this maybe six or seven times, she tried rolling over but found that without seeing her son's tiny body, seeing for herself that he was safe, she couldn't even drift off. She rolled back over and faced him, watching his baby chest rise and fall.

"What are we going to do?" she asked her sleeping baby.

As if in answer, the telephone rang.

Startled and hesitant, Janey picked it up on the second ring.

"Did I wake you?" Dave Reynolds's rough voice asked softly.

"No," she said, and even to herself her voice sounded breathless. "Where are you?"

"The house," he said.

"The house?" she asked, having forgotten that a person could get anywhere in Portales in less than five minutes, especially late at night and with no traffic.

A ghost of a chuckle escaped him. "Yes, honey, *the house.*"

"What are you doing?"

"Taking off my pants."

The words should not have caused the strong reaction they did. At the implication, at her mind's errant wanderings, Janey could picture him all too clearly, trousers off, well-muscled thighs exposed, light dusting of black hair running up the legs and disappearing...

"Oh," she said, her heart beating too rapidly for comfort, her palms suddenly moist, her mouth dry.

"You place is all locked up tight, no one having come or gone. Except the florist...there were a bunch of cards tucked in your door."

"Thank you," she said, even as she wondered why he'd called.

As though he could read her thoughts, he answered, "I just wanted to call and make sure you were all right..." He trailed off, as if aware it was a thin excuse for calling.

And she wondered if he was unbuttoning his uniform shirt. Unconsciously she raised the sheet to cover her own chest. She could feel the heat in her cheeks against the sudden cold in her fingers.

"Thank you," she said again, and felt the words were inadequate.

"Get some sleep, now, Janey," he said, and where his use of the word "honey" had stirred her before, his voice deepening at the use of her name caused a riot of reaction in her.

She had to clear her throat before she could answer. "I will...and Dave?"

"Yes?"

"When I said thank you, I meant for everything."

There was a long pause and Janey imagined him looking down at the ground, his shirt dangling from his long fingers, a ruddy stain suffusing his face, his bared chest.

To her surprise he chuckled. "Janey, honey, I haven't done anything yet."

She half smiled, but his next words ripped the smile away and started her heart pounding in a wild, unmatched rhythm.

"And when I do, a thank-you won't be what I'm after."

Chapter 7

To Janey, the next three weeks slipped by in a seeming whirlwind of activity, people and acquaintanceship with her baby. It was a busy time and a strangely peaceful period.

Only two things disturbed this unexpected peace: one was the midnight and two-in-the-morning phone calls during which someone whispered her name and issued sibilant threats of danger if she continued to stay in town; the other was Dave Reynolds's continued presence in her life. After three weeks of both, Janey couldn't have said which was disturbing her more.

Sitting in her living room, the baby in her arms, flowers all about her, signs of spring evident from her front bay window, she had the odd feeling she was part of a movie scene. Everything seemed so peaceful, so fresh. Mrs. Aragon's grandchildren gamboled on the lawns across the street, and the librarian walked by four times a day, a cheerful wave to anyone spying her.

If it really was a movie, it would be almost bucolic in its gentle small-town ease, and if there had been a lake nearby, she might have expected to see barefoot boys in ragged blue jeans, sporting homemade fishing poles, pigtailed girls tagging along asking what kind of bait they were using.

But there was no lake nearby and the air was strangely still, as if waiting for a tornado cloud to descend.

It was like watching a movie with the sound turned down, thinking it was some documentary of small-town America, then turning the sound up and realizing it was a horror film, with the background music sharp and discordant, building to a terrifying minor.

The stillness, the music, the very contrast of the beauty and the sense of waiting seemed to say bad things lay in wait, the dark would descend. And the children's laughter would fade as the crescendo of fear-rippling music increased in volume and intensity.

Things were too peaceful, the people around her too unconcerned, too complacent. Couldn't they hear the music? Didn't they feel the tenuous calm-before-a-storm pressure building, growing stronger, getting closer?

Dave Reynolds could. She could see it in his eyes every time he picked up her mail from the box across the street and thumbed through the stack of cards, looking for an unmarked white envelope filled with a dark message. And though no more dead insects fell from between white vellum, the pressure of anticipation was always present.

Yes, she thought, Dave knew about the danger and felt the air closing in. She could hear it each time he asked her about the resumed midnight phone calls, or each time he said her name as she opened the door to him. His voice would be relieved, and he would say her name as if he hadn't really expected to be able to speak it again in her presence.

But, like her, he never voiced his fear, as if to say he was worried aloud would end the brief hiatus, would call the tornado clouds to them to cast a pall on the halcyon days.

The phone calls were a constant reminder that she was still in danger, that the nightmare that began some ten months ago wasn't over yet.

A phone tap initiated by Dave hadn't borne results as yet, because, unlike the device in most detective novels, keeping the lines open wasn't possible in such a small town—that kind of technology was still years away from Portales, where people still only had to dial five numbers to reach anyone in town—and again, unlike the novels, even in a large city a tap wouldn't result in an immediate pinpointed origin of call. All she could do was write down the time of call, then once a week Dave would drive the list over to Clovis, home of the nearest phone company office, and attempt to match the calls with the incoming log sheet.

However, the calls could be monitored by a phone answering device, and the ringing ignored in the middle of the night. The fact that the ringing often woke the baby and left Janey staring across to Dave's lighted window, wanting company, aching for a physical presence to chase the blues away, was known only to Janey, though she suspected Dave was aware of her wakefulness.

Like his reaction to the letters and calls, she could read it in his eyes the next evening. And she could read other things there, as well. And it was these other things that both created the false sense of peace during this time and destroyed her fragile hold on equanimity.

He would accidentally brush her hand and she would feel the touch deep inside her. He would stand outside his door, waving goodbye to the seeming hordes of people that dropped by to visit him in the late night hours, and her heart would ache to join him, to stand at his side and hear his rich laughter.

Each time she saw him, and it was often during those three weeks, she felt the churning, roiling confusion that Dave Reynolds inspired in her. And somehow, sitting there now, rocking the baby and gazing out at the clear early April

HOW TO PLAY 421

GREAT FREE GAME WITHOUT OBLIGATION TO BUY

1 With a coin, scratch the 3 silver dice opposite and discover in an instant whether you will receive... 2, 3 or maybe 4 free books and perhaps 1 or 2 extra gifts.

   To claim the Jackpot, it is sufficient that your dice display 4, 2, 1 in any order.

2 When you return the card to us, you will receive as many free Silhouette Sensations as you have revealed and perhaps also a cuddly Teddy and a Mystery Gift.

3 If we don't hear from you within 10 days, we'll send you 4 brand new Silhouette Sensations for just £1.99 each every month. You will of course be under no obligation and may cancel or suspend your subscription at any time by simply dropping us a line.

Silhouette Reader Service, Freepost, PO Box 236, Croydon, Surrey. CR9 9EL.
Registered Office: 18-24 Paradise Road, Richmond, Surrey. TW9 1SR
Registered in England No. 100449

Here is the cuddly Teddy that you could receive if you hit the Jackpot!

If you claim your free books we'll also send you this appealing little Teddy absolutely FREE. Soft and cuddly, he's a favourite with everyone.

PLAY 421 WITH SILHOUETTE

Scratch the 3 silver dice and see instantly which gifts you will receive.

YES! Please send me all the free books and gifts to which I am entitled and reserve me a Reader Service subscription. I understand that I am under no obligation to purchase anything ever. If I do not wish to receive 4 brand new Silhouette Sensations every month for just £1.99 each, I simply write and let you know within 10 days. If I choose to subscribe to the Silhouette Reader Service I will receive 4 brand new Silhouette Sensations for just £7.96 every month. There is no charge for postage and packing. I may cancel or suspend my subscription at anytime simply by writing to you. The free books and gifts are mine to keep in anycase. *I am over 18 years of age.*

MS/MRS/MISS/MR _____

ADDRESS _____

_____

POSTCODE _____ SIGNATURE _____

2S4SS

**4 FREE BOOKS
+ A CUDDLY TEDDY
AND A MYSTERY GIFT.**

**4 FREE BOOKS
+ A CUDDLY TEDDY.**

3 FREE BOOKS.

2 FREE BOOKS.

<u>To claim</u>
<u>421 can be in any order</u>

THE SILHOUETTE GUARANTEE

- You will not have any obligation to buy.
- You have the right to cancel at any time.
- Your gifts remain for you to keep in any case.

◀ TEAR OFF AND POST THIS CARD TODAY! ◀

Silhouette Reader Service
FREEPOST
P.O. Box 236
Croydon
Surrey
CR9 9EL

NO
STAMP
NEEDED

afternoon, it was difficult to tell which frightened her more, the intangible warnings of a murderous coward, or the very tangible warmth of a gentle rescuer.

She saw his white sheriff's unit parked at the side of his house and wondered how long it would be before he knocked at her door. He'd been by every single night since her arrival at home. And sometimes more often than that. And except for the look in his eyes that occasionally caused a riot of sensation in her, and the words he'd uttered on the phone while she was still in the hospital, he hadn't said or done anything that could be taken as other than pure business or perhaps neighborly concern.

She smiled now, thinking about him, wondering when he'd made the transition in her mind from sheriff to friend. It was a gift he had, a rare talent, this ability to inspire friendship. It was one that most of the town obviously recognized and valued. And one Janey envied now. She'd been in seclusion so long she'd forgotten the simple rules of companionship. In these four weeks since David was born, she'd found herself almost surrounded by the citizens of Portales. She might have gone back into her self-enforced retirement but for Dave Reynolds, who smoothed the introductions, encouraged her participation in the social calls and small talk. And somewhere along the way he'd become her best friend.

Because of that friendship, because of the growing camaraderie, was she reading too much into his actions?

He'd taken her home from the hospital, escorting her as carefully as if she'd been fashioned of blown glass. The steps were already repaired and he had even painted them to match the trim of her house. Inside the house, he had arranged the many flowers she'd received in the hospital, placing them haphazardly yet aesthetically about the living room. Someone had tidied the house, as well, stripping the bed and remaking it, clearing the few dishes in the sink.

She might have assumed one of the neighborhood women had done these things for her, but at the rise of color in the tall cowboy's cheeks when her gaze fell on the turned-down covers and the clean, folded extra sheets on the end of the bed, she'd known it was he who had done all this.

The thought had both warmed and disturbed her…it still did. As empty of effects as her home was, it represented a privacy too hard won to be shared. And he had seen it all. He had to have seen the photograph of Bill on the narrow mantel, had to have seen, if not looked at, the album of pictures of their life together as man and wife. He had watered her plants, fixed her porch, opened kitchen cabinets and found homes for cups, saucers and plates.

It was like being laid bare to him. Again, and in a vastly different way. Would he have seen the glass half empty or half full? Would he have recognized the loneliness and see the signs of a new life forming? Or would he only have seen a house, partially furnished, largely barren of knickknacks and bric-a-brac?

In many ways it was this unwitting disclosure to him that bothered Janey. He had cushioned the indignity and embarrassment of delivering her child in his presence by offering her his strength, his confidence, his very being at a time when she needed it most. And then he had smoothed her return home by also breaching the wall of privacy she'd built around herself. He knew her body as intimately as any doctor, and now knew her personality as well.

And he hadn't stopped there.

He'd questioned her endlessly, mostly about the letters and calls she'd received, about her work at the hospice, about her life with Bill. She felt she was completely and wholly exposed to him, but he let none of his reaction to her life show in his eyes. But sometimes his eyes avoided hers or lingered for a second longer than could be construed as comfortable, a dull stain coloring his cheeks, and he often left her wondering where he drew the line between business and pleasure. And left her wondering where she did.

He brought dinner, as often as not, and sometimes stayed to share a glass of wine or a beer, telling her stories in his east-plains drawl, tales that made her smile or made her remember or made her drowsy, but never made her feel uncomfortable or wish that he would go.

Only the silences, those moments when he'd bury his hands in his pockets and look away, his glance falling on the picture on the mantel or when his face softened with tenderness while giving the baby his bottle, only these bothered her. And they bothered her partially because they seemed too easy, too familiar, and she didn't know him, nor was she certain that she dared knowing him better. And they bothered her because she was coming to rely on him, and this she didn't want.

Yesterday he'd brought her a huge bouquet of fresh-picked lilacs, their uniquely delicate spring scent brightening her home as it lightened her mood. She looked at them now, smelling their aroma even from where she sat across the room. He hadn't made anything of the gesture, only telling her that his hedge in the back was overloaded and he thought she might like some. But his hands had trembled slightly when he set the vase down, and his eyes avoided hers.

He was like a man from a history book, filled with small, seemingly inconsequential gallantries, but with such quiet consideration that he made her wish that time and circumstances were different, that *she* was different. That life was.

"Tell me more," he would say, then listen as she spoke. And when she would wind down, he would fix her another glass of iced tea or pour a glass of wine and bring it to her.

"Tell me more," he would ask again. "Who's the director of the hospice in Taos? Tell me the names of the people you worked with. How is the hospice funded? Did the

Aguilar family ever have any contact with you prior to Bill's death? Did any of them try and contact you later?''

And when she had complained that she had told him everything there was to tell about her entire life, he had smiled crookedly. ''You've only scratched the surface, honey. I want to know everything.''

Why? Why did he want to know every detail about her? Was it only for the investigation's purposes, or was it much more complex than that? She wasn't sure she wanted the answer to those inner questions of her own, because if she knew the answers, they would undoubtedly only serve to underscore the impossibility of pairing with Dave Reynolds.

She stirred restlessly. Last night, before leaving her house, he'd lingered in the doorway, the cool breeze that carried the scent of the first mowing in the neighborhood and the multitude of lilacs blooming everywhere ruffling his hair. His face had been shadowed, but his eyes caught the gleam of the interior lights and seemed to lend them a fire that had only occasionally risen to the surface before. *Where there's smoke . . .* , she'd thought then, and shivered.

''Call me if you need anything,'' he'd said, his voice as rich and deep as the night, black dark and velvet around them.

He'd said the same words in parting every night for three weeks. But last night they seemed to carry a different connotation, a variance of a theme. *Call me if you want anything.* And something in his tone, something in the difference, made her legs curiously weak, made her feel oddly languorous. She'd actually had to raise a hand to the doorjamb to remain fully erect.

The want in her seemed palpable. And it was a want he'd created, she didn't have it for anyone else, anywhere. And until a month ago she would have sworn she would never have it again in her life.

"I mean it, Janey. I can be here in less than thirty seconds."

"I know," she'd answered, remembering, agreeing. "I will," she'd promised. And it was this knowledge and this ill-considered vow that plagued her now, watching his house, smelling the lilacs he'd brought her, holding the son named for him. Waiting.

Dave rushed through his shower and quickly drew the razor across his jaw and lower cheeks. His reflection in the mirror seemed to mock him. Why are you hurrying, Davey boy? it seemed to taunt. You used to rush home just to watch her, now you're hightailing it over to her house every night, asking questions and probing deeper and deeper, and for what? Certainly no investigation ever warranted the amount of time he was spending with Janey Anderson.

The night before he'd been so restless after he'd come home, he'd pulled a book from his dusty shelves and flipped the pages open at random. As if guided by fate, his eyes fell on a passage in which a young man sees an unknown woman's face, and he falls instantly, irrevocably in love with her.

Was that what had happened to him? A lightning flash of awareness that in Janey Anderson he was being offered a second chance, another hope, an alternate future? Was that why he questioned her endlessly? So that he would know and understand every nuance of what made her what she was? Perhaps.

His reflection smiled. Perhaps, hell, Dave thought. There was no perhaps about it. He'd been intrigued with her at the beginning. Delivering her baby had served as a catalyst for a connectedness he'd never dreamed would happen to him again. Then slowly, over these past four weeks, both in and out of the hospital, he'd grown to know her, and the more he knew, the more he wanted.

There weren't any doubts left. He wanted Janey Anderson, for now, for always. And he was going over there every night because he couldn't stay away. It was that simple. And that terribly complicated.

As he completed his cleanup ritual, he tried telling himself that tonight was no different than any other night the past three weeks. He tried convincing his wayward heart that nothing had changed in the four weeks since the baby had been born.

But things had changed. *They never stop changing,* a voice inside him warned. Janey's body was lithe and slender again, her daily walks before the baby's birth and her assiduous attention to exercise afterward had molded her flesh to firm, taut planes. And Dave wondered if she'd still be as soft, still feel as ripe and ready for life as she had the night David was born.

And spring had finally arrived, the dry, dusty winds having subsided and the grass turning green and needing mowing.

But something else was different. Even the breeze had a slightly different scent about it tonight. Clear, crisp in the early April air, it seemed to hold a new odor this evening, a smell of promise, of futures.

He crossed the street, a bag of tacos and burritos tucked beneath his arm, and a six-pack of cola in his hand. And his heart beat rapidly and his chest constricted with anticipation. For this moment, he would ignore the danger signals, just as he intended to ignore the investigation.

Tonight he was simply good old Dave Reynolds, a man out to enjoy a woman's company, *her* company, and he was going to work on making her laugh. Tonight he would hold the baby, rock it to sleep, and for a couple of hours, just absorb Janey's presence.

That's what he was going to do. That's all.

He stooped and picked up her newspaper and wondered how she was going to react to a front-page newspaper article announcing the sheriff was leaving town at the end of the week for a conference in Colorado. He hoped she would miss him. Because he was going to miss her like hell.

The tacos were cold and the burritos tepid, but Janey didn't think she'd ever tasted anything so good before. Nor had she ever felt such an electricity in his company before. He neither acted differently nor said anything unusual, but somehow all three of them seemed more alive tonight, charged, eager. Something was altered, she thought, unable to put her finger on just what it was.

He smiled as he always did and told tales of Mrs. Lyon, Charlie Dobson, and a host of other names she half recognized and dimly remembered. He was loquacious yet not eloquent, funny but not witty. But through it all, as always, he was real.

Studying him, trying to define the difference in the air that night, Janey realized there was nothing false or strained about Dave Reynolds. And something about this understanding, this basic truth, made her look at him anew as a man. Not as a rescuer, not as a sheriff, not as a neighbor, but as a man, with a man's needs, wants and desires. A man who could answer a woman's innermost questions.

"Johnny Dobson—" Janey already knew from something Dave had said last week that Johnny was Charlie's son who was killed back in '79 in a tragic car wreck, the son Charlie seldom ever mentioned now "—came and got me in the middle of the night one time. We sneaked out, borrowing his daddy's unit, and we cruised all over town, and most of the county besides. I think we put close to two hundred miles on that thing before we were caught. I don't know who was in more trouble, Johnny or me."

She smiled, not so much at the story but at the contrasts that lay just beneath the surface of Dave Reynolds. He seemed to epitomize the entire town of Portales. His history was as interwoven with people who had lived and died there as were the trees that shaded the streets or the iris beds that bloomed so riotously in spring or the roses and trumpet vines in summer.

The people of this town were real, like Dave. And they all, because of their isolation and close proximity, lived life on a slightly different level than city folk, even sparsely populated states' city dwellers.

Dave Reynolds was intimate with every aspect of living, from watching babies being born to waiting at a friend's bedside for the final farewell. He, like the rest of them, knew what to do when someone died or when someone was hurt. Casseroles and pies magically materialized on kitchen counters and, without direct organization, people dropped in to check on bereaved or ailing families.

And when they came, these people like Dave Reynolds, and sat around tables or on seldom used living room furniture, they didn't talk philosophy or esoterica, unless it was an earthy, realistic acceptance of the vagaries of life. They talked what was planted in gardens, how prices on houses were rising or falling, and they talked easily and with no crippling difference of people they'd loved and known and lost. Like Dave talked. Like Dave was. The townspeople seemed, and perhaps Dave most of all, the sum total of what feeling and living do, to and for a person.

Janey wondered if it was this that made Dave Reynolds seem real to her. He was a total stranger, yet she felt she had known him all her life. But was he such a stranger? He had helped her deliver her child, a child he held and looked upon as casually and as fondly as though that child really were his own. He'd held her naked, spent body as tenderly as if she were the wife he'd impregnated and delivered. He'd seen every nuance of her new and solitary life and asked every question to fill in the past.

No, Dave Reynolds was no stranger.

The thought made her mouth curiously dry and her heart beat in an unsteady, too-rapid rhythm.

"The real irony is that Johnny was killed by a hit-and-run driver. He couldn't drive worth a damn, but it was someone else that got him," Dave said, unaware that to Janey it was Dave who represented the irony.

In the years she'd worked with hospice doctors and psychologists, she'd encountered theories and suppositions miles deep in complexity and subtlety. When Bill was killed, she had immersed herself in every known self-help book and had spent hours at the bedside of favorite patients, trying to help them and hoping they would help her understand the meaning behind death.

None of the books, doctors or psychologists had offered such a straightforward view of life...and its twin, death. But to Dave Reynolds, who had suffered deep personal loss, in addition to the loss of childhood friends and family, death was just another facet of life. The dark side, perhaps, but no menacing, terrifying monster that lay in wait for the unwary.

How Violet Deveroux would love him, she thought, thinking of one of her valiant patients at the hospice in Taos. She was one of the lucky patients, a woman who had made a rough peace with her life, and now that she had accepted death as the inevitable, had slipped into a beautiful remission. At the last prognosis, she might actually live to see the earth for several more years.

Yes, Violet Deveroux would like this man who didn't hide behind pseudo-intellectualism but could talk about any subject as easily as he drew breath. And she would like his kindnesses and his consideration. And she would have tried to play matchmaker.

In all but the last one, Janey would have agreed with her older friend. But it was the latter notion that gripped her and filled her with an odd sense of possibility. When was the last time that *possibility* had been a real word, that the concept had really touched her inner self? She knew the answer—ten months ago—and it made her sad and, for the first time, angry.

"What did I say?" Dave asked.

"What?"

"You look almost fierce. What did I say?"

"Nothing. You didn't say anything wrong."

"Why did you look angry then?"

"I didn't, or rather, I didn't mean to. I'm certainly not angry with you."

"What then?"

"It'll sound silly," she said.

"Tell me."

And somewhat to her surprise, Janey found herself telling him. About her friend, a little of what she was thinking and, finally, about her new found anger.

"And are you angry at…Bill, or at yourself?" he asked.

She noticed the hesitation before he'd said her husband's name and for the first time since she'd met him she saw a bit of the confusion *he* must be feeling. She tried not to show this empathy as she answered. "I'm not sure it's directed at either one. Maybe just at life in general."

"You can't be angry at life, Janey," he said and smiled. "Fate, maybe."

She smiled in return. "Okay. Fate. I'm angry at fate."

"After Patty died, I was mad, too. At fate. I felt cheated. I felt like I hadn't been given a chance to finish things the way I wanted them done. Like I'd been cheated of the opportunity to set things right."

"Because you argued," she hazarded.

"Because I had been too stupid to see what we had was real, too ignorant to understand that life is what you make it, not what you pretend it can be."

Janey was silent for some time following this. She didn't know whether it was an accusation directed at her—your life is running on empty, Janey—or if it was another of his oh-so-straightforward commentaries on the ups and downs of living.

Slowly, feeling her way through her thoughts, she answered, "What Bill and I had was real. And I knew it."

"All the more reason for being angry then."

"Why?"

"Because it got yanked away from you. Snatched right out of your hands."

Did he have some amazing kind of telescope that could see straight into her heart? "I felt that way for months," she said. "But hurt, not angry. Now it's different."

"Maybe that's because life is coming back again. Your baby's born, and he's fine...oh, so fine...and you're beginning to see and hear again. Feel again."

This was too close to the truth for comfort. She *was* feeling again. Was that what was making her angry? Was it a guilt that was writhingly surfacing as misplaced anger? How could she possibly let Bill go so soon, so quickly?

"It's been almost a year, honey," Dave said, displaying that amazing way he had of reading her thoughts. "That's no time at all, but it's a long while to stay in one gear. Sometime you're going to shift, like it or not."

Uncanny, that's what he was. Earthy, solid...and uncanny. He was everything Bill was not, open and easy, relaxed and friendly. A man who could see the blacks and whites in life but understand the shades of gray in between. But he was like Bill, also: he moved her in a way that she'd only touched on once before in her life...and he wore a badge.

"I'm not angry at fate any longer," he said now.

She looked a question at him.

"That night David was born, I went home and just sat on the porch. It was colder than hell. But I kept staring across at your dark porch and thinking about what might have happened to you if I hadn't been sitting there earlier. Every notch the temperature dropped, I could imagine you lying there, nobody even knowing you'd fallen.''

The depth of emotion in his voice made her feel ashamed. So many times she'd thought of his rescuing her, but for some reason she'd never imagined him pondering the what-ifs and feeling the shuddering could-have-beens.

"I've thought about that, too," she said. Her voice was low with unexpressed sympathy.

"Honey, that's fate. And if you don't like the word, you can call it a lucky bunch of circumstances that combine to bring people together.''

Janey felt fate at that moment. As if it were a real and separate presence in the room, she felt the long tendrils of fate's intention wrapping invisible coils around her, drawing her to this man.

Their eyes met and she saw his recognition of her feelings, of her thoughts. His face lost every vestige of expression, but was so studiously blank that she knew he was holding himself in rigid control. What was he thinking? What did he want from her? And why did she want to respond?

He pushed to his feet then, breaking the eye contact, and Janey saw a muscle jumping in his tightly clenched jaw. "I'd better be off," he said, and without waiting for her usual halfhearted protest, made for the front door.

She was grateful and relieved he was going, for tonight, she didn't think there would have been anything half-hearted about her request for him to stay.

He stopped just outside her door, his silhouette a solid block against the light from the corner street lamp.

"Call me if you need anything," he said, and his eyes locked with hers, and she felt she sank into the gray, limitless depths.

"I will," she said.

And again she felt the difference in the night. As subtle as the difference between dusk and dawn, and as striking, she felt something new and tremendous entering the space between them. Like a palpable presence—fate, again?—it seemed to draw her closer to him, making her want to reach out to him instead of backing away.

"You do that," he said, and his voice trembled with a command of sorts.

"I promise," she answered. But what exactly was she promising? The way her heart was pounding, it was some great thing, something earth-shattering in its raw force.

"I'll be here," he said, and still he didn't move.

God only knows where her question came from, and how she dredged the courage to utter it, but she spoke nonetheless, "What do you want from me?"

"Everything," he answered swiftly, as though he'd been expecting her question, had already formulated his answer. Or perhaps more accurately, she thought, as though it had come straight from his heart.

"Everything," she repeated.

He raised a hand to her hair and brushed a single strand from her forehead. "You didn't ask me what I expected, Janey. You asked what I wanted."

She was silent in the face of such an admission, in the total honesty of a confession of such magnitude. His hand lowered back to his waist, as if searching for the holster that usually rested there.

"Janey..."

"Yes?" Was her voice really as breathless as it sounded to her?

"I have to go out of town at the end of the week—"

She couldn't hide her instinctive moan of protest, though she immediately tried covering it up.

"I...you won't be left unguarded," he said.

"What?"

"Someone will still be watching your house, watching out for you," he said, and it seemed to Janey that he was searching her face for a clue to her feelings.

"I see," she said, and she didn't think she'd ever felt so cold inside. "Is that what you've been doing...every night? Watching out for me?

"No," he said so steadily that it served as a brake to her speeding thoughts, her too-rapidly rising anger or embarrassment.

"What then?" she asked, and wished she hadn't, because she wasn't really sure she wanted to have the answer spelled out for her.

"If you don't know that, Janey, I can't tell you."

Chapter 8

If you don't know... I can't tell you.

I want everything.

The phrases haunted her, echoing in her heart and in her soul. They kept her awake long after he'd gone. And though she lay in her darkened bedroom, it was Dave's face she saw, and it was Dave's lighted window she used as a compass to guide her thoughts.

Her curtains were slightly parted, ostensibly to allow the cool fresh air into the room, but Janey knew what the real reason was: it was so she could see his lighted window from where she lay upon her bed.

He could be there in less than a minute, he'd said, and she believed him. And if he came, he could wrap strong, warm arms around her, hold her close and press firm, cool lips to her heated throat and quench the fire that raged in her at the thought of him. Or start a conflagration.

I want everything.

And, dear Lord, she wanted to give it to him. And she wanted everything in return.

She stirred restlessly, her sheets too cloyingly close, her blankets too warm. And the heat had nothing to do with the cool night.

She told herself, based on knowledge of the grief-healing process, from the years spent in hospice work, that what she felt for him wasn't wrong; it was natural and healthy in all senses of the word. She knew and believed that absolutely. As he had intimated, life was too terribly short for self-flagellation over trumped-up guilts and petty worries.

No, she had nothing to feel bad about in wanting him. But each time she slipped into the trust of his presence, the faith he projected in his touch, in his consideration, the sun seemed to glint from his badge, or his hand would drop negligently to push his gun or his holster aside, and she would be reminded of his chosen career.

It was a career she honored, she perhaps more than most people, but one she could never be part of again, one that she could never allow to enter her life. Why did that seem so unfair now? What was it about him that gave her the desire to lower the barriers and trust again? If only he weren't a peace officer, if only he were really just a cowboy, with an unruly herd of steers and a battered pickup parked in front of some ramshackle ranch house. If only...

She lowered her hand from her face to her overheated chest, her fevered eyes on the lighted window across the street. Was he awake? Did he have any notion that she lay awake, hands trembling, thoughts in chaos, her heart pounding with a long-buried, tortured want?

He wanted *everything,* but that's exactly what she couldn't give, no matter how badly he made her want to. She didn't have *everything* anymore. And the gulf between everything and something was wider than the Grand Canyon, broader than the Pacific Ocean. She knew. And so did he.

Call me if you need anything.

She needed, all right. Wanted, needed, craved and feared.

I promise.

Her own words taunted her, acid dripping on fine steel. What could she promise? No hope for the future.

But if she did call . . . would he understand?

Would she?

Dave flipped through the pages of notes he'd compiled in the past few weeks. He had to do something. Sleep was so far away he felt as if he'd drunk a full pot of coffee not an hour ago. Every part of his body jangled with raw nerves, and his mind rang with a thousand different alarm bells all sounding at once.

He forced himself to read the pages in his thick file. If anything, the information was sketchier now than when he'd begun. There was absolutely nothing linking the Aguilar family to Janey Anderson, aside from the murder of her husband. And from all indications, that had been a clear case of rotten luck, Bill Anderson being in the wrong place at the wrong time.

He ran a hand through his hair and glanced at the window in the direction of her house. All he could see was his own reflection, and even to himself he looked harried, tired. Old. He was turning thirty-seven in a couple of months, but he felt sixty. And for a moment he wished he was older, because older automatically seemed to confer wisdom, and God knows he needed some of that right now.

He needed wisdom to solve this mystery. He needed some wise part of himself to know how to handle a situation that had suddenly and flagrantly gone wildly out of his control.

Because he'd told the truth. He did want everything from Janey. He wanted her, he wanted her child that bore his name. He wanted her past and her present and, most of all, he wanted her future.

He wanted her body dewy from his touch and her eyes glowing with love. For him. For a life they could have together. He wanted her laughter, warm and rich; he wanted her trust, faithful and compelling.

He wanted it all . . . *everything*.

He had tried telling himself a thousand times a day that he was only watching out for Janey Anderson because it was his duty, as both sheriff and neighbor in a small town. He had almost convinced himself that he was doing it out of loyalty to a fellow officer, shot and killed. But, as before, on the night her baby was born, he knew he was kidding himself.

And now she knew it, too. He'd blurted out the raw, unvarnished truth like a kid confessing some major misdemeanor. And it left him stripped of defenses, bare of shields. He was wholly and completely open to her now.

His hand clenched on the desk and he stared at it dully. Slowly he relaxed it, studying his own fingers, the rough calluses, the blunted fingertips, the lack of jewelry. And then he knew. He understood the scrutiny, understood the metaphoric symbolism of his action. Of all his actions.

What he was doing with Janey Anderson smacked of courtship. Pure, simple and old-fashioned, and probably as corny as all get-out. But that's what it looked like. And where was the wisdom in that?

There wasn't any, he decided. And there probably wasn't any truth in the notion of courtship, either. He swept his hand from sight, only to lift it again when his thoughts seemed to challenge the subterfuge. When was the last time he'd taken flowers to a woman? Not since Patty Donahue. And when was the last time he'd puttered around a house, picking up, tidying, preparing for a homecoming? Not since Patty, maybe not even since his mother had passed away. Hell, he didn't even pick up his own place.

But he'd done just that for Janey, and taken her flowers and dinner and some silly something he'd seen in Dodie Shoemacher's gift store down on Main Street. And he and Charlie Dobson had spent a cool March evening, a couple of beers waiting for them on the cement pillar, mending Janey's porch steps, swapping stories and talking over the mystery of Janey's assault. And the mystery that was no mystery to Charlie of Dave's affinity for her son.

If he was absolutely honest with himself—and this late at night, the rest of the town asleep and Janey Anderson's windows dark, he could be as deadly truthful as a man could be—he'd have to admit it wasn't altruism that motivated him to check on her every night.

And it sure wasn't gallantry that had him stopping by her place sometimes when he had a break around noon. And it wasn't any misplaced loyalty to a man he'd never even met that had made him shower and shave before striding across the street to knock on her door, some tidbit of gossip on his tongue, some specialty item in his hand.

It was Janey Anderson herself that drove him. And her baby, child of a dead man, namesake of his own.

When he'd taken it upon himself to ready her house for her homecoming, overriding both Norma Judson and Mrs. Lyon's offers and objections, he really hadn't given the matter any thought. It was just something he could do for her.

But when he'd stood in her living room, eyes locked on the photo portrait of Bill Anderson, he'd felt an intruder. And when he stripped the sheets from her bed, the bedroom still bearing all the evidence of David's hastened birth, he'd felt he was violating her privacy, though the night that birthing had occurred he'd felt more intimately joined to her than he'd ever felt with anyone in his entire life.

All around him were the contradictions and dichotomies that comprised Janey Anderson. The spare pillowcases were neatly folded in a small linen closet in the back room, but the extra sheets were clean, wrinkled wads, jammed in any which way. A photo album lay beside her bed, the cover worn from constant use, the tissue box beside it half-empty, while the trash can beneath the nightstand was full. Had she lain awake at night, photo album on her lap, wet tissue in her hand, tears marring her lovely face?

Everywhere he turned in her house he felt he stumbled on another aspect of her personality, her loneliness, and all too often and too sadly, her courage.

A half-finished book, turned open-spined, facedown upon the dining room table was a text that offered advice coping with grief, and another book, this one on the living room coffee table, also half-read, was on do-it-yourself home repair.

The baby's room was painted in fresh, pastel yellows and peach, the blankets already turned down and inviting, a mobile made up of giraffes bobbing over the crib. It played some cheerful tune he remembered from his childhood, and though he couldn't name it, it had made him smile when he cranked the music box. She'd started a mural of a cloud formation on the wall but hadn't completed it yet, and the half-finished clouds hung there, mute testimony to the manifold changes in Janey's life.

Everything in the house was a confirmation of a life-shattering experience and her attempts to create order from the chaos of her husband's untimely death. His heart ached for her even as his desire chafed at the evidence of her sorrow, for it was a cold reminder that while both of them seemed free, neither of them was truly independent of the past enough to pursue a future of any kind.

Worst of all, perhaps he'd felt then—and now, as well—that he was peeking at the most secret places of Janey's life. In each room, in each nook and cranny of the old Meeks place, now Janey's, he ran across the telltale signs of a life in transition.

And it made him think of his own place, still harboring the remnants of his mother's life, furniture where it had been before his return from L.A., towels and blankets on the same shelves where they'd been when he was a child, a house giving an entirely different message than Janey's, for his might announce his stagnation. Would she have read as much into his home as he was reading into hers? Would she have felt as much a Peeping Tom as he?

As a result of this feeling of violation of her private life, he'd done more than he intended, dusting, watering plants, clearing a half sinkful of dishes, as though erasing his intrusion. It was only later, when he saw her eyes taking in the small evidences of his handiwork, that he'd wondered if he hadn't been trying to erase but, rather, to implant. *Dave's been here,* was that the message he'd been unconsciously trying to convey?

He sighed, and the sound seemed to echo in his empty house. Like the phone tap that yielded no results other than a string of unmatched phone-booth numbers, he had no answers to any of the questions that seemed to spring up like April flowers around and about Janey Anderson. Except one, and it was perhaps the only answer he had that mattered: he wanted her.

He wanted to cup her delicate face in his hands, feel that satin warmth against his fingers, feel her silky dark hair brushing his wrists. He wanted to know that her parted lips were soft and ready for him alone. He craved seeing that unexpected glimpse of liquid heat change her eyes from blue to sapphire. He wanted to draw her trembling body against his, run his hands over her full curves, mold her to him and let her know how she moved him. He'd shared a starkly real moment of intimacy with her, now he wanted to show her another form of sharing, needed to share another medium of intimacy.

But he knew she wasn't ready for that, either emotionally or physically. And even if she had been, what would he be offering her, beyond one night—many nights, he thought, please let it be many nights—of touching, loving, sharing?

He'd been four years without a committed relationship, and the wound of Patty's death was only just beginning to heal. How could he expect her to be willing to give up the memories of a husband she'd been happy within less than a single year? Could he hope to accomplish that in less than a lifetime?

It was painfully clear that he shouldn't expect anything. He'd seen the shocked look on her face when he said he wanted everything from her. He shouldn't have said it, God knows, and wished he could turn back the clock and unsay it now.

But he couldn't take the words back any more than he could turn back time and have the day dawn cloudy instead of full of sun. And he couldn't erase the tragic past for her, nor would she want him to.

But in wanting everything, wasn't that what he was asking her to do? To give up the past? He couldn't ask her to give those memories up. They were hers, they were part of her. Like Patty was a very real part of him. It would be unfair to her son, her dead husband, and ultimately unfair to Janey, and if she ever accepted Dave, it would be unfair to him as well, for that would mean only receiving a portion of Janey. And, as he'd all too damningly told her, he wanted it all.

Unfortunately, knowing he couldn't or shouldn't expect anything from Janey, and wanting things to be different were two entirely separate issues. They were so entirely dissimilar they were like the difference between want and need. The trouble was the line between want and need was so indistinct that it was hard to tell where one began and the other ended.

Luckily, he thought—or was it unluckily?—a man couldn't be faulted for his fantasies. Her involuntarily moan of protest at his leaving at the end of the week had fueled those fantasies to a fever pitch. And if his imagination wasn't entirely clear about how deeply and how thoroughly he yearned for this woman, then no one need know but himself.

Except her. *I want everything.* She knew. She'd heard him, and, from her eyes, she'd fully understood. There was no taking the telling statement back, no stopping time. He'd flung the words at her like a medieval knight flinging down a gauntlet. Would she pick up the gauntlet or ignore it? Could someone ignore such a challenge?

He wouldn't have been able to, and, judging from her other evidences of courage, he didn't think she would be able to, either. He didn't know whether to smile or slam the desk in frustration.

He looked back down at the notes. Here, at least, his role, or would-be role, was definitive: he was the sheriff with an investigation at hand. So where was a single clue that could turn the scales and allow him to take at least one of the weights from Janey Anderson's fragile shoulders?

The only connections he could find between her life prior to Portales and now was the murder of Janey's husband and the fact that she'd worked in a hospice up north and one here. The first seemed a washout, but certainly no more so than the second.

The hospice connection was so loose it was like trying to secure a railroad tie with a tenpenny nail. For several years in the hospice up north and seven months in Portales, Janey had devoted at least six hours a day to offering final comfort to a group of people for whom hope had little meaning and future was a word belonging to another world.

She'd talked about it a little, and tonight she'd mentioned a friend there, one of the patients, who would like him. How few people, he thought, would take the time to call a terminally ill patient a friend.

He glanced at the telephone and looked away, daunted by its muteness. He knew she received calls at night; she told him about them the next day. He'd taken to driving some twenty miles to Clovis every other day to try to find a match between the calls and a repeated origin of the whisperer's calls, but so far, the guy had used only phone booths.

Whether he'd found anything or not, he thought, Janey shouldn't have to face those terrifying calls by herself. But short of staying with her...

He grabbed the sheaf of papers and held them up as a barrier between his eyes and the telephone.

According to the director of the hospice in northern New Mexico, and to Alma Maybry at Los Abuelos, Janey was not only an invaluable asset to the hospice facility, but well loved in addition. The staff adored her almost as much as the patients did.

When he'd first called the director of the hospice up north, he'd been told that it was inconceivable that anyone there could bear Janey a grudge.

"She sat with some of them throughout the day, and then, after her husband was killed, she stayed with a few of them through the night. She saw them through it, you know, holding their hands, telling them to believe, telling them it was okay to relax, it was okay to let go, and she'd sit there, waiting with them for the end. She has the kind of strength some people only dream about."

The notion of Janey doing that for someone, giving her own grief, her own pain, left Dave feeling cold and strangely lonely. If she could do all that for someone consumed with despair, without a single ray of faith in the future, what might such a woman offer a man whose hope was only bruised, whose notion of the future was only distorted, not tattered?

Such a woman would offer a hint of spring, a breath of something fresh in that man's life. She would offer him a whole new life altogether. That's what such a woman would offer.

But what could a man whose dreams were tarnished offer her?

The director had gone on to say, "I wish she'd been here with Violet Deveroux. At the end, I mean. Janey really seemed to love the old woman. And, I believe Violet truly loved Janey. Thought the sun rose and set on that girl. She was terminal, of course, like the others. But she held on and held on, waiting, I think, for Janey to come back. She passed on about a month ago."

Before going, the director had said, Mrs. Deveroux had written Janey. "She left the letter with me. I'm afraid I didn't have Janey's forwarding address, so I couldn't send it on before now."

Dave suspected the man had simply forgotten the letter, but didn't say as much when he'd been on the phone.

The director continued, "Do you think she would like it now? Or would it be better to wait? I've read the letter and think it might be slightly upsetting to Janey, given the facts. However, Mrs. Deveroux was in a state of remission right before she died, and was quite able to write for herself."

Dave told him to send it and gave the department address. On the off chance that Janey had deliberately neglected to provide a forwarding address, then he could hardly go about giving it out, even to her former boss. Although whoever was after Janey already knew where she lived.

Looking at the notes now, Dave felt as though a winter wind was blowing wildly inside him. Hadn't she said tonight that her friend in the hospice was in remission? Was it the same woman? His mind tossed a dozen unrelated thoughts into the tornado that seeing the words had created.

He wondered if he hadn't given his address as a possible stopgap for Janey, and he wondered if he'd done a good job on her porch, if she was sleeping now, and he wondered if he could face telling her about Violet Deveroux.

To his mind, she'd been through enough without having to hear that a favorite patient had died, especially when the elder woman had passed away missing Janey. What if she said something to that effect in her letter? Would that hurt Janey?

He dropped the file back to his desk and raised both hands to cover his tired eyes. Was there a moment in life that signaled the last straw, the breaking point beyond which all additional pain was too much to bear? Dave believed that there was and thought that surely Janey must have reached that point.

Then he remembered her courage the night she had fallen, the night young David was born. And he remembered her valor the night of the assault in her hospital room, her indomitability, her implacable strength. Maybe Janey had that rare capacity for constantly reaching for the good in life, the joy, no matter how much she might deny it even existed. Perhaps she was one who wouldn't ever encounter that breaking point.

But all of this was irrelevant, he thought with irritation, allowing his hands to fall back to the desk and opening his eyes to stare at the thick but useless file. None of her amazing qualities mattered if whoever was after her met with success. The only thing that mattered at the moment, the only question with any relevance right now was simple: who was trying to kill Janey Anderson? Or who was trying to warn her away from Portales?

And why?

Was it related to her husband's death or had Janey Anderson seen or done something that would spark someone to such desperate measures? The questions chased around in his mind, caught in that whirlwind of chaos.

If the offender was in the nuisance category, wanting more from her than she was willing to give, Dave could understand it; just one look at Janey Anderson was enough to make a man crazy. But nothing on this earth justified attempted murder and backhanded terrorism. Especially not of Janey.

He reached out and clicked off the light, staring through the now see-through glass at Janey's darkened bedroom window. Her curtain was ajar, he could tell that much in the dim light cast by the street lamp. Was she sleeping? Was she dreaming of her husband? Was she feeding the baby in another part of the house?

Or was she lying awake, as his fantasy desired, blue eyes turned his way, thinking of him, wishing he was there, drawing her into his arms, driving the nightmares away with his kisses, with his need?

I will, she'd promised. But he thought she wouldn't.

The phone rang shortly after 3:00 a.m. and Janey answered it before coming fully awake.

For some reason, her sleep-confused mind insisted it was Dave Reynolds on the other end and that he needed her. As she sat up in bed, covers pooled in her lap, receiver at her ear, her mind registered the whispering of her name. She jerked away from the plastic device, ready to hand up, when she heard another sound, an unfamiliar one, issuing from the phone.

The noise seemed a cross between a woman's scream and an animal's cry of pain. It sent shivers along her spine and spiraled gooseflesh from her shoulders to her hands. Whatever it was made the whisperer pause, as well, and swear...no longer disguising his voice.

And though Janey couldn't match a name to the voice, she could pair a face. This was the same man who had injected her IV with pentobarbital. This was the voice that had threatened her life and that of her unborn child while in the northern part of the state. And this was definitely the voice of her would-be killer.

Before she could shove the receiver back onto the phone, he said clearly, "Your watchdog is leaving town, Mrs. Anderson. If you're smart you'll do the same. If you don't—"

She hung up on him then, dropping the receiver with a loud clatter. She sat perfectly still, willing the shivers to subside, praying the fear would dissipate. Without turning on the light, she lifted the white log sheet with its too many

entries from the night table and, after a glance at the fluo-
rescent alarm clock, and using the diffused light from the
street lamp outside, noted the time of the call. For all the
good it would do, she thought bitterly. Fearfully.

Your watchdog is leaving town...

Dear God, how could he leave?

Because he had to, she told herself firmly.

"Get a grip on yourself, Janey," she said aloud. Dave was
leaving town for a few days, but he wasn't leaving her un-
protected. And she wasn't exactly a helpless nitwit. If need
be, she too would leave. She would go visit Violet Deveroux. She would take the baby and go visit friends in Taos.
Better yet, she'd go to some other state, some other place.

If you don't...

She dropped the pen back onto the nightstand and the
clatter made her start. What had she been dreaming of before the call? She would think about that, she decided, and
still sitting, she drew the covers even tighter, forcing herself
to remember, to think about anything else but that deadly
voice and that terrible scream.

Gratefully, memory came. She'd been dreaming of Bill,
and he had been calling her name, his voice deep and rich,
a smile in his velvet tone. *I'm here,* she'd called, but he
hadn't seemed to hear her. It was Bill, yet his face seemed
insubstantial. It was only his silhouette that she could see,
and his hand beckoning her from a doorway far across a
cavernous room. But she could clearly see his smoky-gray
eyes and the hunger in them.

Now, sitting awake, shaken from sleep, shaken from
safety, her mind reeling, all she could think about was that
Bill's eyes weren't gray, they'd been brown. Raising her
hand to cover her lips, a chill sweeping across her already
frightened soul, she understood. It hadn't been Bill at all. It
was a silhouette, yes, but one with long, blunted fingers and
smoke-filled eyes.

Without conscious thought, she reached for the phone again, quickly punching in the much-memorized number. *I can be there in thirty seconds,* he'd said.

It seemed to take less.

Chapter 9

When Janey opened the door to him, Dave felt as though some primal force reached inside and gripped his heart, squeezing it so tightly he could no longer breathe.

The entry hall light spilled over her dark hair like an aura of gold, turning her black hair to shimmering ebony. Her gown was of some filmy material as insubstantial as the night breeze, comprised of an indistinct color, iridescent like dragonfly wings and as transparent. Her blue eyes, wide and luminous, sparkled like sapphires and her full lips were moist and parted.

She seemed an extension of his dream-stirred thoughts, a beautiful phantasm that had come to life. His mind called a warning his heart ignored.

As though independent from his body, Dave's arms raised, his hands outstretched to draw her to him. Too many times he'd thought of holding her, pressing her cheek to his chest, pulling her tightly against his body.

There was no way he could possibly resist the urge to do so now. Once he had her in his arms, however, actually experiencing her yielding flesh molding to him, he could only stand perfectly still, savoring the moment, half-afraid of moving, because she might prove to be just another figment of a dream.

Her slender frame trembled against him and he drew her closer, threading a hand through her silken hair and, after the briefest hesitation, running his hand down her back to pull her even more firmly into his equally shaking body. She shuddered once and stiffened, then relaxed into the embrace, wrapping her arms around his waist and holding on as though for actual physical support.

Dave pulled at the lilac-scented air as though he were drowning, and he thought perhaps he was. He felt submerged in sensation, his nostrils filled with the scents of the night and the clean, lightly perfumed smell of her hair. He felt the chill of the April night, cold from the cooling desert sands, and he felt the warmth of her semi-roused body. His heart pounded so rapidly and so fiercely it seemed a roar in his ears, yet he heard Janey's soft, shallow breathing.

When he delivered David, he'd thought he'd never felt so alive before in his entire life, but this rush of absolute awareness, of total contact with contrasts both external and internal was even stronger. He felt he stood poised at the precipice of some great discovery, a new canyon, an unexplored mountaintop, and that if he made a single movement, took a single step, he would careen over the edge and plummet, spinning wildly and willingly into the vast unknown.

"Thank you for coming," Janey murmured, catching him as he began the mental fall, yanking him back to reality.

She had called him for a reason, a specific need, and here he was giving in to a need all his own.

He forced himself to relax his tight grip on her and hoped she would never know how reluctantly he allowed her body to separate from his. But when she looked up at him, her blue eyes meeting his gaze, he saw his reluctance mirrored there, and something else, something deeper, something almost frightening in its intensity.

She made no move to hide this from him, and the realization humbled him somehow and served to bank the fire that raged in him. She was in trouble and alone. He had no right to take advantage of her situation, no matter how much he wanted her.

What was it about her that moved him so? Was it that she stirred every protective instinct in him, or was it that she sparked a sense of kindred spirit, an atavistic recognition of souls?

Unable to resist succumbing to at least one fantasy, he released her only to raise his hands to her golden face, cupping it gently, lightly drawing his thumbs over the planes of her high cheekbones.

She tilted her head back somewhat and closed her eyes. Her lips parted and her tongue slipped between them to moisten and, though she may not have intended it, to invite. He felt completely mesmerized as he watched her, unable to stop his caress of her soft skin, unwilling to move away.

Her breath came and went rapidly, warming his hands. Her skin felt like velvet, like the underside of a rose petal, and he had never wanted to kiss anyone, anytime, as much as he wanted to kiss Janey Anderson at that moment.

An inward battle raged in him. To take this advantage, to give in to the demand to kiss her now would be morally wrong, no matter how right it might feel inside.

"It'll be all right," he said, and he didn't know if he was assuring her or telling himself. When she opened her eyes and he saw tears captured there, waiting to fall, he wondered if she saw through his lie.

Her mouth worked, and she shivered once before clamping her lips tightly. A moan escaped her and she blinked away the tears, ignoring a stray that fell upon her cheek.

Finally she spoke. "I want you, Dave Reynolds," she said softly, shocking him with her simple honesty even as her words filled him with exultation.

She continued, alternatingly buoying him and sending him plunging into uncertain waters, "No matter how much I've fought it, no matter how hard I've tried to tell myself that it couldn't be so, I still want you. I think I have almost from the first moment I saw you. But that's not enough. It's not fair."

"Not fair?" he asked, struggling to keep from dragging her into his arms and carrying her through the house to her bedroom. *I want you, Dave Reynolds.*

Dear Lord, he thought. He had said he wanted everything; she pinpointed the rough edge between want and need, cut neatly through the multitude of nuances like a surgeon wielding a freshly sharpened scalpel.

"It wouldn't be fair to you," she said. "You deserve someone with more than half a heart."

He had to close his eyes. He felt as if she had looked into the very deepest place in him and spied the sealed doors, old and much dented, complete with the rusted padlocks. One of the doors, one he hadn't even known had existed, had exploded open the night of young David's birth, but there were others, and it was these she could see.

As he could see hers, he told himself. The difference was, her padlocks were new, made of brightly polished steel, where his were old, rusty and ready to be broken, ready to fall free. One touch from her was all it would take.

"You have more heart than anyone I've ever known," he said, feeling his way through the pathways of her mind, not wanting to argue with her but needing to contradict her belief that she only possessed half a heart. "And more courage."

"I get by, Dave, that's all. It's not courage to simply survive." She stood still, the tears gone from her direct gaze.

"It takes courage to start over, it takes courage to begin again."

She closed her eyes and shook her head. He instinctively tightened his grip on her sorrow-etched face and said, "Look at me, Janey."

Slowly, with obvious reluctance, she did as he asked.

"I'm not going to rush you, honey. I want you, too. You know that. You probably even know how much. And if that doesn't scare you, I have to tell you, it scares me to death. But I want you to be happy with it, comfortable about it."

What he didn't add was that he wanted her wholly, not just her body, but her love as well. He'd already told her he wanted everything. He just hadn't realized until that moment what "everything" meant. Now he did. And he did want it all . . . And he wanted it to be right.

"I don't think I can ever give that," she answered quietly, as though he'd spoken his thoughts aloud. "The part of me that could . . . love . . . was buried with Bill."

He wanted to scream his denial, and he wanted to pull her back into his arms and comfort her. But he did neither, he only said, "That's not true, Janey." But wasn't that exactly how he had felt and had continued to feel for four solitary years following Patty's death?

"It is," she said. Her voice was sad.

"No. You already love David."

"That's different," she said.

"It can't be, honey. Not really. The capacity for love all comes from the same place." He lowered one hand, lightly tracing a line from her cheek to the valley between her full breasts. He stopped there, pressing his knuckles against her thudding heart. "It's all here. And I'll wait, Janey. I'll wait for you to see it, to feel it, too."

"Please don't," she said, shaking her head again.

"Don't what, Janey? Don't wait, or don't tell you the truth?" Or, he wondered, was she asking him to take his hand away? This he couldn't do, though he knew he should.

She covered his hand with her own, pressing it tightly against her chest. "If things were different, Dave..."

"If things were different, Janey," he continued for her when she trailed off, "I would be down on my knees. Probably begging you."

After a few seconds, unsuccessfully scrambling to gather his scattered thoughts in order, he said, "But they aren't different." Even to himself his voice was harsh with unspoken need.

A shudder worked through her, either at his words or perhaps at his tone. She closed her eyes and again tilted her head back. Her throat was bared to him, and he had to fight the urge to press his lips to the rapidly beating pulse she exposed to him.

"You make me feel so...confused," she said.

"You aren't alone."

Her eyes remained shut. "That's where you're wrong, Dave," she said, misinterpreting him. "That's the whole trouble. I am alone. We all are. So terribly, terribly alone."

"You don't have to be," he said, and wished he could swallow the words back. They smacked of pressure, of his wanting her compliance. He wanted that, yes, but he wanted more. And more than that even.

"I know I don't have to be alone," she said, and her voice was as dull as a February afternoon. "I know that."

"Tell me why you called," he said, and was startled when her eyes flew open and color suffused her cheeks. It was so swift a change that he actually felt the heat beneath his fingers.

"I didn't call you because I wanted you," she said.

He smiled, he couldn't help it. She was so sincere, so lacking in trust. And so touchingly embarrassed. "I know that, honey. If you had, there's not a damn thing on earth that would have stopped me."

She looked nonplussed, and her color deepened.

He knew so much about her, he thought, but she knew nothing of him at all. He shook her slightly, almost surprised by the easy flow of affection that passed form his fingertips to her.

"Did you get another call?" he asked. Would that tell her that he understood?

She nodded and drew a steadying breath. "Yes. Yes, that's why I called."

It wasn't why she had told him she wanted him, he thought, and it wasn't why she had shivered at his touch, but he was damned if he was going to press her.

Instead he dropped his hands to hers and said, "Why don't we go on inside and you can tell me about it?"

She looked around the entry hall as if just now realizing where they were. She half smiled, and the pressure in Dave's chest eased a notch. She might be as vulnerable as a kitten in a rainstorm, and as weighed down with woe, but she had a ready humor, a sharp hold on the funny side of reality, and it kept her on the solid road to full recovery.

He stepped past her, into the living room, and heard her close the door behind him. His glance fell on the portrait photo on the mantel. Bill's eyes seemed to meet his with reproach, or maybe it was with betrayal. Or more realistically, Dave thought wryly, it was only *he* who felt that way. He turned away from the photograph with a sigh.

Janey said, "I feel silly now, calling you. I should have waited till morning." Her hands clasped her arms tightly as if she were freezing despite the warmth of the room.

"I told you to call if you needed anything. Some nut calling you in the middle of the night definitely constitutes an *anything*," Dave said easily, smiling.

He never felt less like grinning in his whole life. First holding her, now just inches from her, he could only cling to what little vestiges of dignity his conscience allowed him. But it was difficult. She was standing in front of an end table lamp that turned her negligee into silken gauze, as see-through as a window in broad daylight. He was unable to move, incapable of looking away.

"It wasn't the telephone, exactly, that made me call you. I recognized the voice."

"What?" He gripped her shoulders fiercely, as much to ground himself as to make contact with her. "Who was it?"

"I don't know his name. But the caller *is* the same man who was in my hospital room. And the same man who was calling me in Taos."

"That's something, anyway," he said, releasing her. She would never know how fiercely he'd waged a battle not to let her go. "But you have no idea who that might be. You'd never seen him before, right?"

"No, I don't have any idea who he is, or what he wants. But the more I think about it, the more I believe I *have* seen him before, but I can't think where. And I can't think why he would want to kill me."

"There's nothing you've seen or witnessed that could shed some light on this?"

She sighed, and he stifled the urge to draw her into his arms again. He knew why she sighed: they had gone over this so many times in the past four weeks. Over and over, talking and talking, but never stumbling across a single thing—besides her husband's death and her choice of career, that seemed to coincide with the present attempts at murder.

"What did he say? You must have stayed on the line longer this time, to collar his voice like that."

She told him what the man had said and was almost sorry she had when the color drained from Dave's face.

"I won't go," he said.

"Dave—"

"No. It's that simple, Janey. I'm not leaving when this guy is threatening you. Let him make his move when he thinks I'm out of town. He's already getting sloppy. What made you recognize his voice tonight?"

She said, "In the background of the call there was a terrible scream."

"A scream? A woman's scream?"

She shook her head.

"What then? Describe it."

"I thought at first it was a woman, that he was torturing someone else—" It struck him with a coppery flash of gut-wrenching anger that for all her daily insouciance about the calls, she used the word "torturing" now, when she was unwary, when she was *trusting* him. "But the scream startled him, too. I could tell. He swore out loud, and that's when I recognized the voice."

"Tell me about the scream," Dave said.

Janey did, ending with, "It sounded more like an animal, a crossbreed of some kind maybe." She added sotto voce "A poodle and an hyena."

Dave chuckled. "Sounds like a peacock, honey."

"A peacock?"

"Sure, they have the worst screams known. They make terrific watch birds for that very reason. In my grandfather's day the peacocks were the only burglar alarms. Lots of people on the fringe edge of town use them thataway now."

"But this was a scream, not a bird's call," she said.

"That's what they do. First time I heard one, I was about nine or ten and was out skeet shooting. Damn near shot my foot off and did wet my pants."

She looked at him for several seconds without saying anything, an arrested expression on her face, then she laughed.

Her laughter was everything he had dreamed it would be: full, rich, filled with a throaty power. It transformed her from merely lovely to exquisite. And it froze him in place.

Janey couldn't remember the last time she'd really laughed. She knew it had been a feeble joke, no different from a hundred stories he'd told, and one perhaps not even intended for more than a half smile. But looking at Dave

Reynolds and imagining the tall, utterly capable sheriff a stiff-legged nine-year-old who fired his weapon at his own foot and then wet his pants was more than her too-taut nerves were able to bear.

He didn't say anything or laugh with her. A crooked, pleased smile curved his lips and his jaw seemed to relax. His eyes grew dark with some unexpressed emotion, and the ready color was noticeably absent from his cheeks. How had she ever imagined him tongue-tied and reticent? He was eloquent even in his silence.

"You are so incredibly beautiful," he said softly.

No longer laughing, Janey felt as if she'd just run a two-mile course. Her breath seemed constrained and her throat constricted. She was both hot and cold at the same time. She hadn't realized until he paid the compliment that she hadn't heard anyone call her beautiful since Bill died. And she had missed it.

The words didn't change the world or alter her life, they were only words. And yet, hearing them, seeing the truth of them on Dave Reynolds's almost stunned face, she felt an affirmation of sorts. Looking into his eyes was like looking into a magical mirror and seeing someone else's reflection. Sleeping Beauty's image, perhaps.

How long had it been since she had considered her looks as anything other than "healthy"? How long had it been since she even wondered about how others perceived her? Weeks, months?

Maybe, she thought, someone else had to care about your looks before you noticed them yourself. And maybe, just maybe, you became as beautiful and as incredible as that person believed you to be. Looking at Dave's face now, she hoped that was true.

She felt a prick of something other than lust stir her. He was such a kind man. Such a very good man. If things were different, she would link her arm through his and walk off into the sunset with him, David against her chest, her sorrow and pain left behind.

"But things aren't different," she said aloud.

He blinked, then nodded, the stunned wonder gone from his face. "No, they aren't, are they? But trust me, Janey, they will be. They have to be."

"Why?"

"Because I believe, don't ask me how or why, but deep down inside me, I truly believe that things happen for a reason. And I don't think I could feel this strongly unless we were meant to be together." His eyes never wavered from hers during this amazing speech, but now he whirled and strode to the fireplace and stood with his back half turned to her, his gaze on the photo of Bill.

He said, after a few seconds, "I didn't know him. I don't know whether I wish I did, or I'm glad I didn't. It's hard enough wanting you and thinking about him having been a cop. It feels disloyal somehow, like wanting a brother's wife. Something like that, maybe. If I had known him . . . I don't know whether that would have made it easier or made it completely impossible. I'll never know."

He turned then and met her eyes. "But I do know this, Janey, I've come into your life. And I'm not leaving."

Janey couldn't have spoken if her very survival had depended upon it.

After a long, steady look, his expression lightened and he shrugged. "So, why don't you hop back to bed and we'll figure out who this character is in the morning."

On the night David was born it had been contact with his smoky-gray eyes that had forged a lifeline for her, had allowed her to escape the worst of the torturous pain. Now, his looking away from her let her breathe again, pulling at the warm air in her living room as if she had been suffocating.

Had anyone ever said anything like that to her before? No. Bill hadn't; he couldn't. He hadn't even been able to tell her he loved her. And here this man, this relative stranger, had told her point-blank he was in her life and wasn't leaving. He couldn't have known how rare the words were, how precious they would be to her.

He might know her body, might know her house, but he couldn't possibly have known the inner secrets of her soul.

"I'm going to stay here for the rest of the night," he said, leaving the fireplace and going to the front door. He flipped the dead bolt. "There's only three places I know of with peacocks that would be close enough to a phone booth that you would have heard one of them scream. We'll check it out first thing in the morning."

Janey felt as if she were moving in fog as she stepped around the coffee table and through the dining room. She stopped at the doorway to her dimly lit bedroom and turned back to find him watching her.

"I can't go through it again," she said, almost amazed at how softly the phrase came out when it was a roar inside her.

"You don't have to," he said.

"I meant . . . loving . . . someone . . . and losing them."

"I knew what you meant," he answered.

"You're a peace officer," she said. It came out like an accusation.

His jaw tensed, but his eyes never flickered. "Yes. I am that."

Couldn't he understand what she was saying? Did she have to spell it out for him?

He spoke before she had to. "I know people have told you that it's just as dangerous to ride a car as it is to be a cop. You and I both know that's hooey. Pure and simple baloney.

"Charlie Dobson told me once that putting on a badge was like pinning a target right on our chests. That could be true. But it's what I do. And I'm damn good at it. So was your husband."

He raised his hand, palm toward her, to forestall any comment from her. The gesture was unnecessary; she couldn't have spoken.

He continued, "I *know*. I know he got killed. And it ripped your life apart. I know because I went through it, too. Patty Donahue got killed, also. And she was a good cop. It happens, Janey. Lord, it happens."

Him, too? He hadn't told her that. He hadn't told her that his girlfriend had been a police officer. He didn't allow her the opportunity to ask questions, to pursue this thought.

"But you're alive, Janey. And so am I. And that's what has got to count. That's all that can count."

"No," she said. She was shaking all over. "There has to be more."

"Like what?" He took a step forward, his hand dropping to his side, then advanced. "Like what, Janey?"

He came toward her so slowly, so steadily, that she felt hypnotized by his approach. When he was close enough that she could smell his musky scent, feel the heat emanating from him, he stopped. He neither raised his hand to touch her nor leaned down to press his lips to hers. But he might as well have done both.

It was she who lifted a hand to his cheek, feeling the rough, unshaven planes of his face. He had run into the night, straight from his bed, at a single word from her, and he had reached deep into her soul and stirred the ashes of what she had thought were long-dead coals. And had started a blaze, a flicker of life.

It was she who leaned into him. He raised his arms to enfold her to his broad chest.

"I can't make any promises," she said, meeting his gaze, mesmerized by what she saw there but needing to tell him the truth.

"I'm not asking you to," he said. "There aren't any guarantees. There can't be. Life is too uncertain."

"Maybe I just need someone tonight," she offered, shaking at the implications of his words, of hers.

"Maybe I do, too. Maybe I need just you. Tonight. And tomorrow."

"There may not be tomorrows."

He smiled crookedly and raised his head to cup the sensitive skin at the base of her neck. His thumb traced an invisible circle, sending ripples of sensation throughout her. When she thought she would go insane from the arousing touch, he stopped, and the longing for its resumption made her weak. Her lips parted.

"There is always a tomorrow, Janey," he said. "Every...single...day...has a tomorrow."

At his words, her resistance crumbled, she had no defenses left to block him, to block her want for him. He was offering her a moment, accepting her limitations, acknowledging her freedom to be selfish.

"Be mine, then," she said, drawing him closer. "Tonight... *you* be my tomorrow."

He studied her for a long moment, not giving in to the pressure of her hand or, apparently, the force of his own want. She read all of that on his face before he closed his eyes and achingly slowly lowered his head.

The touch of his lips on hers was as subtle as a dream and as full of portent. Hot and slow, his mouth moved against hers, tasting, questing, promising. His breath fanned her cheeks, her closed eyelids, the sensitive hollow of her throat, as hot as a furnace blast and as irregular as a stallion's galloping, unsteady pace upon catching sight of the waiting mare.

His hand tangled in her hair and drew her closer, urging not demanding, gentle and yet firm. His other hand lightly stroked the soft material of her negligee, as delicate a touch as the gown itself, sending shivers of reaction up and over her shoulders, and down. She felt her body turning to liquid fire, molten and languid, fiercely desirous and aching for his touch.

Her breasts, no longer swollen with milk now that the baby relied solely upon a bottle, seemed full again, but this time with desire. Her nipples hardened at the rough contact with his shirt and the light touch of his fingers. She grasped and arched upward, wanting him more now than she had ever wanted anything in her life.

His hand trailed down her side, a single fingertip lightly tracing every curve, every line of her body, down over her hips and finally coming to rest on her upper thigh. There he paused, his kiss deepening, then the slow, delicate torture resumed in upward progression.

She sagged against him, clinging to his broad shoulders, held upright only by his hand at the small of her back.

"I want to make tonight last forever," he murmured against her collarbone. She couldn't let herself ponder the implications of his hope, and as his mouth trailed lower, and lower still, she forgot his words completely.

His hot breath played through the diaphanous material of her gown like a warm summer breeze, enticing, inciting, and she arched still further to allow him purchase. Dimly she was aware she was draped over his arm like a rag doll, as limp as only true desire can induce, and as filled with trust.

Here, at least, there was nothing to fear. His want was total, his need rock hard in evidence, but, as he'd been so many times in the past few weeks, he was there for her. Yes, with his teeth lightly grazing, instigating a riot in her but causing not an instant of pain.

He'd said he wouldn't leave her, and she knew he'd spoken the truth. In his arms, she could feel the ache building in him, growing in him, and she knew that he would hold it back for her, allow her to sink into that trust he inspired. He was allowing her to take the night and make it hers, make it theirs, and he wouldn't press for more but would wait, hoping maybe, not trusting but wishing, and take tomorrow as it came.

And because of that, and because she felt so thoroughly and completely in tune with him on this night of no future, she could forget that he wore a badge, forget that he would don his gun tomorrow and once again place himself in danger.

Chapter 10

Dave raised his head to look at her. Spilled across his forearm, her head thrown back, her breasts were thrusting upward, full and firm, her back arched like a gymnast's. He shuddered at the sharp ache in his loins.

She was all he had ever wanted and more. She talked about a lack of trust, about only having half a heart left, yet she was fully confident and open in his arms. She had let him share the birth of her child, and now she was letting him share her love, her warmth, the single most private element of Janey Anderson, the one thing that was solely and absolutely hers...herself. She trusted him to take the gift honorably and with caring.

He would take it with more than that, he vowed. He would take it with the gift of himself, as well. No barriers, no cautious holding back of emotion, no stepping away from total honesty. He would love her as only a man who could cherish the gift she was offering could love her.

He slid his free hand beneath her legs and swung her into his arms. He had carried her once before, filled with fear, rushed by anxiety. Now, though he felt the remorseless tapping of tomorrow and the what-ifs and maybes of the future clamoring in his ears, he felt invincible. He pulled her tightly against his chest, reveling in the feel of her arms stealing around his neck, her trembling fingers threading through his hair.

He wanted to say something to her, something important, something that would make her always remember that for one night, one time she had made someone—him—feel as mighty as Hercules, as strong as Achilles. He wanted her to know that in just holding her, his veins felt infused with an almost superhuman quality. He knew, and wanted her to know, as well, that he could carry her anywhere for any length of time.

But like the heroes of the past, he too possessed a fatal flaw, a heel, a mortal capacity: his awareness that tonight was a single fragment out of context, free from rhyme. He might be here tonight, but at the light of day, reckonings were due. And tomorrow the magic would be gone, as would her trust.

And so he contented himself with saying her name, murmuring it against the soft planes of her temple, against the beating pulse at her throat.

As he lowered her to the bed, he told himself that thoughts of reckonings and worries of the future couldn't be allowed to matter now. Her arms were entwined around his neck and her lips were parted and eager for his kiss. Now had to be enough. He lowered his mouth to hers and drank deeply, losing himself in her scent, in her taste, in her moment of absolute trust.

The bedside lamp sent rays of golden light across the rich brown of his hair, across his face, and seemed to linger in his eyes, warming them, turning them from smoke to flame. For a moment he seemed like someone else, someone from another lifetime, another plane of existence.

"Dave . . . ?"

"I'm here," he whispered, and whatever questions hovered on her lips were swallowed by his next kiss. She knew he spoke the truth: he was here for her. And that was all that could be allowed to carry any importance now. Her fears of the future and the sorrows of the past, both could be forgotten, ignored, abandoned if only for a short space of time. She clung to the promise in his words, in his touch.

His hands no longer skimmed delicately over her surface, but swept full-length from shoulder to ankle, gliding over the silky nightgown like an ice skater skims across a clear, frozen lake. But if he was like an ice skater, his skates were made of fire and the lake beneath his touch shivered and melted until all she could think about was absorbing him into her.

She said his name, more of a breath of scarcely held air, and her fingers, almost of their own volition, slid between his collar and his bared throat. Suddenly past patience, she tugged at the buttons that kept material from allowing her access to his broad shoulders.

His wide and callus-roughened palms massaged and exhorted her response, while his fingers plucked and pulled at the soft material, bunching here, smoothing there.

Shifting slightly, he slipped his hands to the hem of her twisted gown and raised it swiftly, baring her completely. He loosed the silky material, allowing it to puddle around her shoulders like a soft, full necklace.

She could feel his hot gaze upon her and felt he branded her with his eyes. And she saw in his ragged breathing and his flared nostrils the drive to take her then and there. She saw the battle raging in him and saw the reluctant acquiescence to his better nature.

"Yes," she said, as if he'd asked her permission, as if his supplication had been spoken aloud. "Now...please."

He shook his head slightly, and a tender smile curved his lips. "Not yet. Not for a while, yet, Janey."

He lowered his hands to her once again, but this time it was bare skin they stroked so softly, bare and wholly sensitized flesh. She wanted to cry out against this tender onslaught and wanted it to last for ever. As his large, warm hands circled her breasts, cupping them, molding them to his gentle grip, she couldn't control her restless want, and her body writhed at his touch.

When he bent to take a nipple into his hot, wet mouth, all thought fled, all rationality departed. She arched to meet him, her fingers threading through the soft waves of his thick hair, and involuntarily her legs parted to him.

Fully clothed, determined to remain so, Dave gave in to the sheer perfection of Janey. Tasting her made him ache for more, touching her left him both weak and strong all at the same time, longing for full taste, full texture.

Suckling, loving how her nipples grew turgid in his mouth, he lowered his hands, sending them roaming the rich curves and deep valleys that comprised her. He felt as if he really were some hero of old embarking on some fantastic quest, only the quest here was not for any giant or dragon, but for the love of one woman.

She gasped and bucked as his fingers met the entrance to her very core and he paused, fearing he'd hurt her. It was too soon after childbirth, he thought, starting to lift his hands from her. This was why he remained clothed. His mother's sister had died in childbirth . . . a result of getting pregnant again too soon after the birth of his cousin, his mother had always said.

Was this too soon also?

A hesitant, slender hand covered his and her murmured encouragement spurred him to continue. Again her honesty and trust humbled him and inspired him.

Honey sweet and molten, her inner core beckoned him, and he raised his head to watch her as he resumed his quest. Her eyes were closed and her lips parted. Her hands were loose on the bed, palm upward in trust, fingers splayed, arms spread wide. Her breasts rose and fell with her rapid breathing, and he again lowered his head to take a rock-hard nipple into his mouth, determined to give only and to give her what such absolute trust deserved.

She might not be there tomorrow, she'd said. He knew she meant emotionally and also understood this was probably the truth. But tonight, he could give her a night she would never forget, a night she could lock away in her heart and take out on rainy days like a treasure, a gift she would always have to remember.

Janey moaned as his tongue left her breast and laved the sensitive flesh beneath it. And she writhed as his fingers dipped into her and withdrew only to dip a second time and a third. As his mouth lowered, his cold-hot tongue igniting her skin, she raised her fingers to his shoulders, pulling at his shirt. But he brushed her hands aside, then pressed them to the bed as though telling her to wait, to hold off a while.

She felt exposed, utterly open to him, and she felt glorious. She felt she had conquered the tallest mountain on earth and lay upon it, eager and waiting for the elements to command her.

And they did in the form of Dave Reynolds's questing hands and tongue. Hot and moist, he kissed her as she had never before been kissed, and took her into the very sky to mingle among the stars and clouds with his sure and delicate caress.

Around her the world pulsed and shook, and a quaking began in her that threatened to rip the universe apart. Helpless in the wake of the furious storm that gripped her, she could only dig her fingers into the covers on the bed, clinging to them as though to an anchor.

When her back arched and her hips raised, Dave found himself shaking in response to her spasmodic convulsions. Had he ever wanted anyone this much? He didn't think so. He knew so.

When she cried out, his name on her lips caused a curious wrench in his middle, as if someone had hit him square in the stomach.

"Please..." she murmured, clutching at his shoulders, drawing him upward. "Please..." she said again. She plucked at his shirt, trying to remove it.

"No," he said, and it was the hardest thing he'd ever done in his life.

Her eyes opened and he could read her confusion. It was only slightly less than his resolve.

"I don't understand," she whispered.

He shook his head and ran a hand across his damp face. He could still smell her, could still taste her, and he had to close his eyes to subdue the raging need in him. How could he explain what his body was barely letting him understand himself?

"This night is for you. Not for me. I...I want you to have that tomorrow without any strings, without complications." In his mind's eyes, he saw his cousin, orphaned and forever bereft. No, he wouldn't take any chances with Janey, with little David.

She spread her arms in answer, inviting him, encouraging him. He shook with the need to give in to her welcome. He had to grip the covers on the bed to hold back.

"I'll wait, Janey," he said. "It's too soon for you. Both emotionally... and physically. I'll wait."

"I feel fine," she said, and he had to smile.

"Yes, you do," he answered. He raised a trembling hand to cup a breast. He let it lie in his palm, full and heavy, soft with languor, relaxed with her body's satiation.

"Was this what you meant when you said you wanted everything?" she asked quietly, covering his hand with her own.

"No. Yes. Hell, don't ask me to explain. I'm not sure I can right now. I just know this isn't the right time. I want you so badly that my whole body shakes with wanting. But I want it to be right for you, Janey. Perfect.''

"It was. It is."

He shook his head sadly. "I'm an old-fashioned kind of guy, Janey. I don't want to do anything that could hurt you, or cause you hurt later. Does that sound crazy?'

"A little," she answered, honestly, but her lips curved in a soft smile.

He smiled back crookedly. "It does to me, too. Right at this minute it seems about the craziest thing in the whole world."

"Well, then?"

He didn't answer, he merely lowered his head to the breast he was cupping and slowly, lovingly drew the again hardening nipple into his mouth. Finally he raised his head, meeting her eyes.

"I want this to be just for you, Janey. A gift from me, maybe. Something that's just yours. A night, a time, that I could shower everything on you without taking anything but your pleasure in return. Tell me you understand."

Looking into his eyes, seeing them dark with suppressed desire, with need for her understanding, she did know what he meant. But she also knew that without the sharing, without the final communication, it was an incomplete package, a rare gift, certainly, but one not finished.

"Are you afraid of getting me pregnant?" she asked.

"Yes," he said simply, but she could tell the admission was neither an easy one nor one he was comfortable with saying.

She smiled and ran a hand down the strong planes of his face. "So am I, to be perfectly honest."

"It's better this way," he said.

"No. There are other ways. Protection," she offered.

He colored slightly, and Janey could feel the heat in his face through her fingertips. "Would that be a problem?"

she asked, amazed that she was able to talk so easily with him about this.

"No, no it's not that."

"Then what?"

He smiled crookedly and the heat grew more intense in his face. "I didn't...expect anything...anticipate...well, I don't..." his voice trailed off from the jumble of half explanations.

She cut through his embarrassment. "The hospital provided me with whatever you might need," she said, pointing at her nightstand's drawer before kissing him soundly. "It's not as romantic, I'm sure—"

"That's where you're wrong," he said harshly, and pulled her upward, arching her into a kiss that seemed to last forever. When he released her, it was as if a measure of tension had eased, as if in the few words of reality, in the kiss, they had somehow crossed a barrier between strangers and lovers, between stumbling in the dark and coming into the light.

"You are so very remarkable," he said, cupping her face. His color was back to normal now, and his hands on her face were warm and tender.

"Because I want you?" she asked, knowing this wasn't the reason but saying it to make him smile.

He did. "That, too. But I meant because you're willing to say it. Because you're willing to talk about things most people sweep under a veil of mystery and obscurity."

"It's because I'm a coward," she said.

"It's because you're the most amazingly strong person I know. And the most courageous." He wasn't smiling now, and the warmth in his eyes seemed to inflame her, as well.

After several seconds passed, aeons in which he seemed to probe every secret in her soul, he reached his hand for the nightstand drawer. As if from other eyes, Janey watched as his now-steady hand disappeared into the drawer and reappeared, small round packet in his blunted fingertips. He gave her another long look, this one questioning, and at her solemn nod, shifted to sit on the side of the bed.

After a moment, he reached for the top button of his shirt, still not taking his eyes from her.

"Let me," she said, rolling to her side and sliding her arms beneath his, pulling his back to her and pressing her lips to the sensitive skin at the base of his neck. When he shuddered and she heard his sharp intake of air, she trailed her fingertips down his bared throat until they met his and she loosened the button for him.

"Janey..."

"Mmm?"

"Ohh...you drive me insane, honey." His head dropped back to her shoulder and his lips found hers.

When she had his clothing free, his broad shoulders and narrow hips exposed, muscled thighs quivering with her touch, he kicked the last of the barriers separating them away from the bed and turned to capture her in his arms.

"Tell me what you want. Tell me every secret wish or want you've ever had."

"I can't do that," she whispered into his bare chest, her cheek tickled by the dusting of dark hair there.

"Then I'll find out for myself," he said, trailing his hand up her body to her nightgown's fastening. Slowly, tenderly, he pulled the silky fabric from her shoulders, leaving her completely naked, completely open to him.

Slowly, without taking his eyes from her, he reached a hand for the light and doused it.

The dark was so startling and so complete that Janey was dazzled by its velvet deprivation. She couldn't see him at all, could only feel him moving toward her, could only hear his ragged breathing over the sound of wrapping being rent.

"Let me," she whispered.

"Too late," he chuckled, and pulled her into his arms. His touch was electric and his body hot and strong.

He whispered phrases of encouragement into her ear, mouthed them against her breasts, and his tongue sang a sweet melody to her body's rocking harmony. And he kept his promise, never leaving her, never losing her for an instant, and finding every secret wish she had ever dreamed. And when he had, over and over again, explored her body and brought her to the peak edge of that dizzying mountaintop, that doorway to other universes, he would hold her close, warming her, safely guiding her back down, soothing her body with touch, easing her scattered mind with words, spreading a balm on her wounded heart with his loving.

Finally, unable to withstand the onslaught any longer without full and complete union, Janey swung her legs over his, trapping him beneath her, and taking him deep inside her.

He cried out and clutched her almost frantically, but as they shifted into a slow, achingly sweet rhythm, he stroked and cajoled and murmured words of desire, of fulfillment.

Time lost all meaning and the past fused with the present. Everything in the world seemed grounded, centered on the meeting of their bodies, on the melding of their hearts. As she felt him quivering inside her and felt his body tense sharply and heard his breathing all but stop, she felt she was actually in tune with his very soul. Feeling him inside and out, shaking her with his need, she cried his name aloud and rode the wild storm clouds of the universe.

As if his name on her lips were the catalyst that released him, his head snapped sideways and his body bucked in tremendous power, driven by a wholly primal force.

"Janey!" he called once, and then again, only the second time it was more of a sob and his hands curled around the soft curves of her hips, drawing her closer and closer still. Whether it was feeling him inside her, his going wild beneath her, or the dizzying sensation of having blended with his soul, Janey couldn't have said, but perhaps all three combined to send her over that perilous edge once again, tumbling and spiraling, lost in the whirling clouds of repletion.

Dave caught her as she fell, holding her tightly to his heaving chest, cradling her, comforting her, soothing her back down to earth. And he held her there, gentle hand stroking her hair, her back, keeping her with him even as he stayed with her.

Finally, after what seemed like hours, he rolled her softly to her side and disappeared into the adjacent bathroom for a few minutes, returning with a warm, dampened towel that he used to further soothe her spent body. He tucked them both beneath the tousled blankets, smoothing them after drawing her into the crook of his arm.

Janey sighed and nestled there, content for the first time in months, replete for the first time in countless days and nights, and trusting, safe and *whole* for the first time since a stray bullet had claimed half her heart.

Before drifting into the first real and peaceful sleep she'd had in over ten months, cradled in his arms, feeling his warm breath playing against her hair, she realized that she had not only ignored the past and the future, she had ignored the present. When daylight dawned, he would once again pin the badge to his chest and take the gun to his hip.

But he wasn't wearing that deadly target now. Now he was safe, his long legs tangled with hers, his fingers linked through her own. And because he was safe, she felt safe, too. And because she felt safe, she could sleep and then dream.

Dave's heart constricted when he felt Janey's rhythmic slippage into sleep. He wished he could follow her there, see into her dreams, fathom the deepest reaches of her mind and understand them as he now understood her body, as he finally felt he understood her heavily guarded heart.

He held her close, her silken legs wrapped around him, her full breasts pressed to his chest, her hand curled confidently in his. He had never felt so good, so perfect in all of his long life. And Janey had done that for him. She had done it all. She had, though she may not have even recognized it herself, lowered that self-imposed guard on her heart and she had given him everything he had asked for. And more.

He felt a stir in his loins and had to smile. It was a mere spark of life, that was all. She had taken everything he had to give already. He couldn't give anything more.

She was such a fine woman. Alive and vibrant, wholly open and, in bed at least, totally trusting. She had been reticent about telling him her wants at first, but as the night had worn on, she had, hesitantly at first, let her wishes be known. And before she had finally collapsed into this deep sleep, she had been teaching, instructing, urging him to greater and better heights.

He wondered if she knew how proud she made him feel, giving him that confidence, giving him that capability. It was as if she had been telling him ''see how much I care for you? I want things right between us.'' Had she felt that way? Her sleepy smile and her hand tucked in his seemed answer enough.

The first rays of the sun's arrival crept through the slightly parted curtains and glinted off the window. Looking out, Dave saw that the curtains parted just enough to allow her a view of his front window. And for the first time since she had called and he had run across the street, buttoning his shirt as he ran, he began to relax.

She may have said she couldn't offer tomorrows, or that she only had half a heart, but looking out the window now, his head upon her pillow, her body nestled against his, he could see what she looked at during the nights, and he smiled.

While he had been watching her house, guarding her, she had been watching his. Guarding him, too? Or guarding these newfound feelings they inspired in each other.

She shifted against him and murmured his name in her sleep. Dave drew her closer, pressing his lips against her temple, soothing her back to a deeper slumber.

The baby woke them, David's lusty yell for early-morning attention shattering sleep and calling attention to the sun's advanced position in the morning sky.

Janey scrambled out of bed, feeling awkward and slow this morning. She didn't know how to meet his eyes and couldn't, for the life of her, think of anything to say to him. She was actually grateful for the baby's cries, as they gave her an excuse to flee the room without having to conjure a reason.

Dave watched her go, stunned by too little sleep and aroused at the sight of her nude figure slipping through the door, her tangled negligee in her hands. He waited until the baby stopped crying before swinging his legs from the bed. She didn't need young David screaming while Dave senior tried getting her to say good morning.

He ran a hand over his beard-roughened face, smiling as he caught a whiff of her scent still on him. Further aroused, he pushed himself from the bed, trying to force his mind to the day's order of business.

He would check the farmers' homes with peacocks, those near enough to a telephone to matter, anyway. Then he would run down to the nearby town of Clovis and pull the phone records to see if he couldn't match up the call. He wasn't sure how much good, if any, this would do, but they hadn't gotten anywhere so far and this was, at least, something he could do to fill in the time between morning and seeing her again.

Then he'd check his mail, and if the letter from Janey's former patient was there, he'd bring it over to her. Or he'd make the decision on whether or not to give it to her. Then maybe he'd tackle some neglected routine business and head home for a much-needed nap.

But first, he'd get Janey to look at him. Maybe even smile at him.

He'd felt her stiffen at the first sound of the baby. And he'd felt her stiffen even more at the awakening realization that she still lay intertwined in his arms. The time of trusting was over, and her guards were once again in place.

He found her in the living room, in the oak rocker by the bay window. Her hair was tousled and black as night, her face was averted, her eyes on little David's avid suckling. But he could tell she knew he was there, watching her.

"Janey," he said quietly.

"Yes?" she answered without looking up.

"Look at me. Please."

She did as he asked, but so slowly that her reluctance was like a scream.

"Nothing has changed between last night and this morning," he said.

Deep color flooded her cheeks as if contradicting him.

"It hasn't, honey. Not really. You're still Janey Anderson and I'm still Dave Reynolds."

"It . . . seems . . . different, then," Janey said finally.

Dave smiled. "I know. I feel that, too. But it isn't."

"But you . . . we . . ." she trailed off, her color so high it looked painful. She turned her face away to gaze out the window.

"We did what we wanted to, Janey," he said softly. "It was wonderful for both of us. Wasn't it? I know it was for me."

"It was," she mumbled. Her eyes met his again, and in them he could read a dozen questions. "I look at you and I try to see the man I knew yesterday, but you seem different to me now."

"Why?"

The color flared again then subsided, leaving her almost pale. "Because you made the present seem real again. Because today I feel like 'future' is a real word again."

"What are you saying, Janey?"

"That even though 'future' seems real, it doesn't hold anything for the two of us."

He couldn't say anything for a moment. "Why?" he asked finally.

"Because you're a peace officer."

"Because I'm a peace officer," he repeated dully. He felt dense, his brain fogged by the sensory overload of the night before, his heart battered by the hard sorrow on her face.

"I said I couldn't promise anything. I'm not sure there will ever be a right time, Dave."

"You're not sure of a lot of things now, Janey. Neither am I. But we will be."

"How can you say that?" she asked, and knew she sounded like a child who wanted reassurance that the dark couldn't harm her.

"I told you I believed in fate. I cursed fate once for taking someone away. I want to get down and kiss her feet now for bringing someone new."

"I can't be that someone, Dave," she said, and while he knew she meant to sound definite, she only sounded confused. He knew exactly how she felt; he was pretty confused himself.

"Why not?" he asked.

"Because you're a cop!" she said, and it sounded like a sob.

"What does my being a cop have to do with anything?"

"You said it yourself, you're a walking target for every bad guy with a case of the angries. I can't go through it again."

Dave stared at her for a long moment, wishing like hell he could think of something clever to say, something wise and comprehensive. "You're wrong, Janey," was all he could think of, and all he could say. "Not about me being a walking target, but to close the door on what we could have together."

"I just can't do it, that's all," she said, and her tone said that really was all there was to it. No arguments from him, nothing he could say would change her mind. He could hear it in her tone, in her voice, see it in her averted gaze.

"I can," he said quietly.

Her eyes darted to his and lingered there. "I don't understand," she said.

"I can do it for both of us. You opened that door to me last night, Janey. I'm damned if I'll let you slam it shut on me now."

"I told you there were no promises," she cried.

"You lied," he said. And for the life of him, he couldn't help smiling.

"What?"

"You lied. You gave me every promise that could ever be given. You gave me *everything*, Janey. You can't take that away now."

She continued to stare at him, her expression dazed, her lips parted. He wasn't sure whether she looked at him with hope or with doubt, but he wasn't sure it really mattered. What mattered was that she understood he wasn't going to walk out on her.

"I said last night that I wasn't leaving," he said now. "I meant it then, and I mean it now more than ever. One way or another, Janey, I mean to stay in your life. How rich you want that life to be, how intensely you want to live it, is up to you. But I'm staying."

Chapter 11

The narrow strip of pavement known as the Bethel Highway stretched in front of him like a silver ribbon into infinity. The fields flanking it seemed components of a massive patchwork quilt, some plowed under, red-brown earth exposed and choppy, others furrowed and fringed with the pale green shoots that would later become milo or peanuts or even potatoes. Still other patches were filled with tall, yellowed grass and weeds, a field no one plowed, a farm that had long since gone under the auction block.

Dave raised his fingers from the steering wheel each time he met someone on the not-so-lonely stretch of road. Some of the drivers he knew, many he didn't. But in a county where only twelve thousand people tried carving out a life, pitting themselves against the economy, the environment and the vagaries of the weather, every friendly gesture mattered.

Don Albright in his spanking new pickup might need a helping hand two miles down the way when a tire blew from hitting one of the many nails spilled during Andrew Deen's accident a month or so back. And Jerry Lou Dickerson, old grouch that he was, nonetheless always lifted his hand at every vehicle he met on the road. One time, back in '72, his daughter had overturned the family car and wouldn't have made it but for one of the Deen boys who was coming home from taking his girl to a dance over in Clovis.

Lonely stretches, lonely places, but, like the cactus that pocketed water against the privations of drought, they were filled with people, made rich with humanity, with man's recognition of man's need for one another, of lives interwoven and inextricably intertwined.

Like his and Janey's. From the first time he'd seen her, he'd felt the nudges of fate, the intertwining of two lives. Three lives, really, since it was David's birthing that had joined them, once and forever.

He lifted his fingers at someone else and thought of Janey, the baby and the reasons why people in lonely parts of the world waved at each other. And today, feeling a little bluer than usual, he was glad he was the sheriff, for everyone—except the travelers speeding through Roosevelt County without noticing the towns and people, without seeing the sandy soil, the clear blue skies, the kids growing like bean poles and marrying and having kids of their own—everyone but the passersby waved at the sheriff. It was like an unwritten law, an unnamed code of the West.

It had been hours since he'd left her house, but he could still seem to taste her, still feel her satin skin, dewy and soft beneath his fingers. And he could still see the deep, self-driven core of resistance in her, he could feel it with every fiber in his being, for he'd felt it melt away the night before.

He understood her so well. She had given him every piece of herself like a multidimensional jigsaw puzzle, and he knew the picture. She was looking for a fresh start. Difficult as it was, she was standing up to the vagaries of life and trying to forge her name in the rock-hard soil of a shattered existence.

She might be having difficulty in accepting what Dave wanted to offer her, and notwithstanding this nut who was plaguing her, she couldn't have picked a better place than this one to settle in, Dave thought.

In Portales, in the heart of Roosevelt County, in the largely unpopulated state of New Mexico, Janey could stand on a downtown corner, hold her arms straight out and turn around and around and never touch anything. She could look across the flat desert earth that wasn't a desert to the people who lived there, and she could see for miles.

In Portales, where time moved at a slower pace, she could let days, months, even years, heal the terrible wounds that had been dealt her. She could savor the scent of lilacs now, and later, the roses, and then, in the fall, stop and smell the pumpkin pies cooling all over town. She could let her son grow up with small schools, baseball games, tag football and summer nights spent playing kick-the-can.

She could, that was, if someone wasn't trying to kill her. Or rather, he corrected, she *would* do all these things if he could figure out who was after her and stop him before he could succeed in another scheme. Thanks to the article in the newspaper, the guy thought Dave was leaving town for a few days. He'd told Janey that might work to their advantage. And it might, if they could lay a trap of some kind.

A door in Dave's mind slammed shut, blocking his thoughts, telling him to leave this idea alone. The last time he'd set a trap... Patty had been killed.

Dave leaned forward in the seat, his anger compelling movement, his thoughts seething with the need for action, the need for resolution.

This was *his* town, damn it. Place of his birth, place of his growing up. This was the home he'd run to when there seemed no place else to run, no place willing to open arms and accept a man who'd left years earlier thinking anyplace was better than a two-horse town with only one movie house and a single restaurant where you couldn't get anything other than iced-tea and coffee.

It wasn't right, he thought, this kind of insane violence, this mysterious dogging of Janey's peace of mind. This was a town where—until now—no one had to lock their doors, where they left their cars running when they ran into the grocery store, where freedom was as dearly held as a family heirloom handed down generation to generation.

Until the attacks on Janey, this had been a town where the worst violence that had spewed forth was on a Saturday night at the local bar when Andy Trevors had a few too many and decided his momma was right after all and pool shooting just wasn't any good for nobody and he'd bust up the place with the bar's only decent pool cue. But Andy Trevors had spent four years in Vietnam, had a metal plate in his head and hadn't been the same since, so everybody understood, and the local bar never pressed charges.

Maybe that was the difference between Portales, or maybe any small town in America, and the large metropolitan areas. Here, it was small enough that everyone knew one another and, as a result, understood one another. They understood the ups and downs of living, of dying. They accepted without judgment, or judged and yet still accepted.

The quantum leap between the likes of Andy Trevors and this unknown would-be killer who was tormenting Janey Anderson was tremendous. There really wasn't any comparison and Dave found himself clenching the steering wheel as if it were the unknown assailant's neck. How dare this creep come into this town and do such a thing? How dare he do it to Janey?

Dave shifted on the car seat, relaxing his sudden lead foot on the accelerator. This case, the worry and the feelings of inadequacy over it, and the heartbeat steady want of Janey Anderson were all combining to drive him crazy.

So far he hadn't done a damn thing to halt this unknown menace that threatened Janey and her baby. He'd set up a few blocks, yes, like details checking out her house, like the guards outside her hospital room, like the phone taps.

Like spending the night with her?

But he didn't have any specific leads to follow, no clues to pursue. He'd confided his frustration to Charlie Dobson earlier, over a bowl of green chili at La Hacienda.

"Hell, son, seems to me you've got yourself a fine clue. All you have to do is scoot on out to the edge of town and listen to the birdies. What you got yourself is a classic peacock lead," Charlie said, and laughed so hard Dave had to stand up and bang on his back.

When the choking subsided, and Charlie's color had returned to almost normal, he'd continued, "Seriously, Dave, I don't think you've got much choice. It's them birdies or nothing." Again he laughed. And again he choked. This time the waitress pounded on Charlie's broad back and laughingly told Dave to quit funning the chief with bird stories while he was eating chili.

Unfortunately, Charlie was right. It truly was a case of investigating the birdies or nothing.

Dave had already checked out two of the farms with peacocks he'd thought close enough to a telephone for Janey to have heard one scream. In both cases, in order for a peacock to be heard the man would have to have been using the family phone. And both Mrs. Jordan and Mrs. Newcastle swore—with perfectly straight faces—there weren't any strangers about their kitchens in the middle of the night.

That only left the Buchanan place. And Dave had little hopes for it. If he remembered correctly, the nearest public telephone to the Buchanans was at the gas station on the corner of the Bethel Highway and the road leading back to Portales. And that station was at least two and a half miles from the Buchanans spread.

But he'd check it out anyway. In his quest to make sure Janey was all right, he couldn't afford to leave a single "birdie" unchecked.

When one of Dave's deputies brought by a letter for her, Janey was surprised but not unduly so; Dave hadn't been out of her mind for more than a minute all day.

"The sheriff said he was expecting this letter from Taos and to keep an eye out for it. I figured if it was that important, I'd better get it over here as soon as it came in. So, here I am. And here it is."

Janey thanked him, a little taken aback by the boy's extreme youth. He couldn't have been much more than eighteen. He didn't look as though he'd even begun to shave yet. But he was wearing a badge and, as Bill would have said, the boy was packing a piece.

The boy deputy hopped down the steps like a child playing hopscotch, jogged across her yellowed lawn and slid behind the wheel of his department unit. He seemed to transform into a man as he carefully eased the car onto the quiet street. On her porch he'd been young, off duty for half a second, now he was a man with a serious responsibility, holding the mike, giving his location and intention over the radio, on call and ready.

She knew that shift in personality so well, that flipping of an internal switch that changed someone from person to public servant, from boy to man, from lover to policeman. She knew it so well, so sadly.

She watched the car with the unlit strobe lights on top disappear down the street, wondering why Dave didn't seem to fit that mold she knew so well. He didn't change from officer to man and back again. That's how he was different. Why didn't he? Why did he always seem the same—friendly, easy, simple, and yet, sometimes so terribly complex?

And she wondered if that was part of the attraction he had for her, part of the reason she felt such confusion around him.

Involuntarily, remembering the complexities of the man who had delivered her child, who had, in many ways, delivered her the night before, her hand tightened, crumpling the letter the young deputy had delivered.

She looked down at it now, curious, more than a little reluctant. She'd received too many crank letters, too many threats in the past ten months to view any sort of mail with anticipation.

This letter was different, however. It had been sent through Dave's office and bore a return address of the hospice she'd worked for in Taos.

A thousand tender and sweet memories flooded her as she ripped open the letter only to find a lengthy memo from the director to Dave, explaining that this was the letter he'd spoken of on the telephone that afternoon. She didn't bother to read the rest, knowing how ponderous it was likely to be and anxious to see what the other envelope contained.

Still, she frowned. Why hadn't Dave told her about the letter? Why hadn't he told her about the call to the hospice? Or had he, in among the many things they'd talked about in the past five or six weeks, during that time of getting to know each other, during those many evenings of slowly building a fragile trust?

It didn't matter now; the letter did. She slipped the inside envelope free and for a moment simply held the small but thick package in her hand. She recognized the spiky handwriting, the deliberate lettering. Violet Deveroux.

Janey sighed, and smiled. Dear, and so very sweet Violet Deveroux. The woman was only seventy, but had been through enough in one lifetime to make anyone want to give up. But Violet couldn't or, more accurately, wouldn't. She clung to life with the tenacity of a young girl who had yet to dance at her first prom, and with the faith of a priest kneeling to take his vows.

She had cancer, and it had spread throughout her system. Doctors couldn't operate early on because Violet Deveroux also had a heart condition, and to try to cut the deadly cells free would endanger her life. She must have suffered intolerable pain, yet she always had a pleasant smile and a kind word for Janey. She had been one of the lucky ones. Just before Janey had left for Portales, Violet had received word from an outside doctor that her prognosis was excellent: almost complete remission. She could relax now, he'd told her, and if she continued as reports indicated she would, she could live another three, six, even ten years. If she remained stable for the next three months, she could actually leave the hospice altogether.

Just last evening Janey had talked about Violet Deveroux, telling Dave the older woman would have liked him. And now she had a letter from her.

She had a pleasurable feel of the rightness of things; the grass had been mowed two doors down and was being watered, giving off that fragrant scent so redolent of spring, Mrs. Aragon's grandchildren were playing on the older woman's front lawn, shrieking and splashing in the sprinkler, and she had a letter from Violet Deveroux.

Without going back into the house, savoring the sense of new life, happy for the connection with the past, Janey sat down on her newly repaired porch steps and opened the letter from her old friend.

Dearest Janey,

It seems like only yesterday that you were sitting here beside me, reading me the newspaper or telling me about your hopes and wishes for the future. I wish you were here, now. I miss you so much. And I'm so frightened. It's funny to me now. A year ago, when I knew I was going to die, I made peace with my life, and with my dying. When the doctor told me that I would, if everything went okay, live several more years, I felt as if I'd been given a second chance at living. You know about second chances, don't you, dear?

The only thing that grieved me was having to say goodbye to my friends here at the hospice and know that they weren't receiving such a beautiful gift also. And then Angela Martinez passed away. I was so shocked and so saddened, because only the day before we talked in her room for hours. We talked so much about so many things that Angela didn't even seem to mind that terrible spinal test they did on her once a month. She was feeling so good, she said, and so charitable, that she decided to make peace with her son. She was going to call him the next day and ask him to come for a visit. And she was going to change her will in his children's favor. When she died, during her sleep in the night, I felt it was such a waste that her son would never know how much she loved him.

I thought it was my duty to call him and tell him of her wishes. Before he could come, however, I began failing again, myself. The director here now tells me that what I had experienced was "false" remission and that the doctor from Albuquerque was known for his misdiagnosis.

Where I felt strong before, Janey, I now feel weak and afraid of the future. I wish I could see you again before I go. It would mean so very much to me.

There are so many things I would like to tell you. Things I didn't know before, things I should have guessed. You know you are like the child I was never able to bear. If this letter finds you well, Janey dear, please think about coming to visit me. I would cherish seeing your sweet face again.

My fondest wishes,
Violet Deveroux

As though in a nightmare, fighting her way through a foggy hallway, Janey read the letter a second time, her eyes filling with tears, her throat constricting with sorrow.

She would leave tonight, she decided. She would pack the baby, get in her car and go to Taos this very day. Listlessly, despite her mind's seething activity, she pulled the memo from the director into view and began reading his pompous and long-winded memo.

Halfway through, when she encountered the cold, stark words that told of Violet Deveroux's death, she cried out and buried her face in the crumpled page.

Violet had died weeks earlier. The night before her might-have-been grandchild was born. She had died without hearing from Janey, without response to her final plea for solace, without ever knowing that Janey cared, would have come no matter how difficult. She had died without knowing she was loved.

Tears, scalding and painful, burned rivulets down Janey's cheeks, stained the typed memo from Dr. Swanson, and fell onto the dropped vellum and spiky handwriting that represented Violet Deveroux's last message to her.

This was why the hospice director had sent the letter to Dave Reynolds. Dave had known of Violet's death. Why hadn't he told her? And she understood so much in that split second. He hadn't told her because he hadn't wanted to cause her any more pain. And he hadn't said anything the night before when she spoke of Violet, because she hadn't used Violet's name.

But how she wished he had told her, wished she hadn't had to find out like this, reading a letter from a woman already gone, a woman who had died with an unanswered letter, an unfulfilled request.

I am frightened, Violet had said. Dear God, Janey sobbed, let her be at peace now. If only she herself could be.

And as she cried, her tears seemingly coming from some desperate place deep inside her, she wished Dave Reynolds

was there. He would know what to say, he would know how
to unlock this pain's ferocious grip on her heart. And he
would understand her anguish and offer solace.

The Buchanan place was a total bust. They had gotten rid
of the last of their peacocks a little over three weeks ago,
selling them, Ed Buchanan said, at "one hell of a profit."

Dave felt like a tire with a three-week-old puncture in the
treads. But he hung around, chatting with Ed, talking over
the possibilities of rain, chewing over the pros and cons of
the coming mil-levy election slated for June, and finally, as
he was getting back into his unit, about the peacocks again.

"Since when you been so all-fired interested in peacocks,
Davey?" Ed asked, hefting his leg to the bumper of the department's finest.

"Since last night," Dave said. "Friend of mine's been
getting crank calls in the middle of the night. During the one
last night, she thought she heard somebody scream."

Ed grinned. "She's got that right."

"When she said it sounded like a cross between a poodle
and a hyena—" he had to wait for Ed's guffaw to subside
"—I guessed she might have heard a peacock."

"So naturally, you thought of me. I'll tell you what,
Davey, Veeta would skin me alive if I started making girlie
calls in the middle of the night."

It was Dave's turn to grin. "So would I, Ed."

"I'll tell you this, too, I'd rather have the both of you
skinning me alive than have to listen to those damned birds
one more day. Jumped right outta my coveralls every time
one of them got fired up."

"I'm with you there, pal," Dave said.

"Yeah. I wasn't going to argue with the fellow that laid
down a cool two hundred for those screaming idiots, but I
did think it was sort of funny."

"What was?"

''The fellow buying them was from that new old folks' home out on East Third. You know the place?''

Dave nodded slowly, feeling a numbness creep through his veins at almost the same time his heart started pumping a little faster, shooting adrenaline into his system.

''Los Abuelos?'' he asked, and was almost amazed to hear his voice sounding exactly the way it had only moments before.

''That's the place. A hospital or something.''

''A hospice,'' Dave corrected softly.

''That's it. A hospice. Seemed pretty peculiar that a place where they take old folks to be peaceful would have a bunch of screaming peahens and cocks running around.''

''Does, doesn't it?''

''Well, it's none of my business. They bought them, they can keep them. And if they drive the old folks crazy, they can roast them for supper for all I care. Veeta'd probably offer to go cook them up for them.''

Dave grinned, but the smile was definitely forced.

As he drove back to town, Ed's words rolled around and around in his mind like a ball bearing inside a hubcap, clattering, not letting him have any peace. *Seemed sort of funny to me . . .*

It wasn't anyone buying peacocks that seemed so funny to Dave, it was that the call had come from somewhere with peacocks. And the only phone near a bunch of peacocks seemed to be the hospice, and Janey Anderson had worked there until her son was born. *Until she fell down her rigged steps,* his mind corrected.

And Janey had worked at the hospice in Taos.

And the man who had assaulted her in her hospital room had a pretty handy knowledge of medicine.

And who would have that sort of knowledge?

Someone who worked in a hospice. Maybe even someone who had worked at both the hospice in Taos and the hospice here.

Dave stepped on the gas and his unit sped down the narrow strip of the Bethel Highway. He didn't notice the fields this time, or the other cars. He had one thought on his mind: seeing Janey.

He had to see Janey Anderson. Now.

Janey heard the car pull in at her curb and looked up to see Dave Reynolds charging out of his unit. How had he known? she wondered idly, dully.

"I think I've got someth—" he said as he rounded his car and took two swift strides up her walk, but he broke off the words and checked his gait as he took in her face.

There was no way she could hide her tears and she didn't try.

"What's wrong?" he asked. His tone was sharp, his lips compressed. He crossed to her side and, squatting down cowboy fashion, pulled her unresisting body into his arms. "What's wrong, honey?" he asked again, more softly this time.

Janey didn't answer, but held the crumpled, tearstained pages out for his inspection.

He drew her even closer before taking the pages in his free hand. "Bad news?"

She nodded against his chest. She flicked her finger at the pages, making them crackle.

Without asking any more questions, he turned his attention to the letters. She was grateful for his arm around her and for the rapid beating of his heart, a pounding that grew even faster as he read the contents of the two envelopes.

When he had finished, he wrapped his other arm around her, pressing the letters' pages against her hair.

"Honey, oh, honey... I'm so sorry. I wouldn't have had you find out this way for the world."

Janey shook her head, not denying his words but negating the need to shield her from the truth, from the harsh, terribly unpleasant truth.

"There wasn't anything you could have done, Janey. And there wasn't any way you could have known."

"I should have," she said.

"How?"

"I don't know, I just should have known. I should have given Dr. Swanson my address, then at least the letter would have reached me."

"You couldn't have known she would—" Dave broke off suddenly, so abruptly that Janey pulled away from him to see what had interrupted his train of thought.

"What?" she asked.

"Why didn't you?"

"Why didn't I what?"

"Why didn't you give Swanson your address?"

"I told you, I was getting so many crank letters and calls that I—"

He cut in with a wave of his hand. "Right, but you gave it to a few friends. And to the state police. Why not Dr. Swanson, director of the hospice where you worked?"

Janey hadn't thought about it before. She shrugged now. "I don't know, really. I just didn't."

"There's got to be more to it than that, Janey. After all, you'd worked there a long time."

"I...I don't know." She felt confused, suddenly trapped. "I just never liked him much. He was always so cold. So unfeeling. And then, when Bill died, he..." she trailed off.

"He . . . what?"

"Oh, it sounds ridiculous."

"Try me."

Janey wrapped both arms around her. Despite the warmth of the afternoon, she was back in Dr. Swanson's frigidly cold, air-conditioned office in Taos.

She could see him rising from behind his desk and coming around it, his hand stretched out in chilling sympathy. *I'm so sorry this had to happen to you, Janey. We'll all miss you, dear.* And when she'd said she wasn't leaving, that she

wanted to keep working, he'd looked startled, then calculating. Why? It hadn't struck her at the time; she'd been too
ensnared in grief. But it struck her now: why had he looked
calculating?

She described the scene to Dave.

"Then what did he say?"

"He asked me if I thought that was wise. I told him I
thought it would be the best thing for me. And then . . ."

He'd taken her fingers in both of his clammy, icy hands
and petted her fingers as though she'd been one of his
frightened cats he was soothing. *You haven't been happy
here for a while, Janey. You've been bucking management
at every turn. And now, while your mind is so fuddled with
this new pain, I can't believe that being with the patients
would be very helpful to your . . . health.*

"He waxed ecstatic about you over the telephone to me,"
Dave said.

Janey turned wondering eyes to him, surprised by the note
of sour sarcasm she heard in his voice.

"Did you have the feeling he was trying to get you to quit,
or was he more sympathetic than you made him sound just
now?"

"Now that I think about it, it sounds as though he wanted
me to quit." She looked at him squarely then. "You know
how it is when grief wraps you up, you don't see too many
nuances."

She was sorry she'd said that when she saw his face tighten
and the look of inexpressible sorrow she'd occasionally
witnessed crossed his face.

"I know," was all he had said, but Janey knew there was
so much more that he wasn't telling her, might never tell her.

"Do you think there's some significance behind my not
giving him my address and the guy who has been calling me
now?" Janey asked, as much to drag his mind away from
whatever horror he was thinking about as to understand why
he'd asked her about the address in the first place.

He sighed heavily.

"There is, isn't there? Something you've found out. Something that shows a connection between Taos and here?"

"Someone from Los Abuelos apparently bought Ed Buchanan's peacocks about three weeks ago. You haven't been back to work, so you wouldn't have known about them."

Janey sat perfectly still, her mind a total blank. She knew from his voice, from his tone, that what he was saying was important, but she couldn't think what he meant, couldn't imagine what he was telling her. Violet Deveroux was dead and he was worried about peacocks? Bill was dead and Violet was dead and Dave's lover was dead . . . and he was focusing on peacocks?

Slowly, as though through a gigantic filter, his words sifted through her mind.

She shifted on the porch steps, unconsciously edging away from him, as though his telling her, and not the menace dogging her, was the cause of her discomfort. Or maybe, she thought, it was because in order to speak the words aloud, she had to have some distance.

She said slowly, coldly, "Meaning you think that whoever called me telephoned from Los Abuelos."

"That's what I believe."

"Meaning that whoever he is, he probably has some connection with Los Abuelos."

"That's how I see it, yes."

"And probably with Taos."

"That's what I think, yes. And this letter only makes me more sure."

"This letter? From Violet, you mean?"

"Let's look at it again. This doesn't even sound remotely like the woman you were telling me about last night. See?" He pointed at the tragic lines of Violet's letter.

"But this is written after she knew the remission was false, and after they'd told her she didn't have much longer. And after her friend died."

"Think, Janey. Does this really sound like Violet Deveroux? The woman who faced her own death with some degree of calm? She'd already faced that. She even says that here."

Janey was getting angry. "That's true. But she also says, *right here* that she doesn't have that hope any longer. That she's frightened."

"Exactly! And that there are things she wanted to tell you, things she should have guessed before. And see where she's said that? Right after her friend dying. And she says her friend felt better and was going to contact her son . . ."

As if his words were a train wreck and she couldn't drag her fascinated, horrified eyes from the carnage, Janey could only sit and shake her head. Finally she murmured, "That's impossible."

"What's impossible?"

"What you're thinking. What you're implying."

"Tell me." He wasn't looking at her, he was staring across the street, watching Mrs. Aragon's grandchildren plundering her prize iris bed. His face held no more expression than that of tepid interest in their innocent destruction, but Janey could see the tension in his jaw.

"It's sick, Dave. That would be really, really sick." She felt her stomach heave as though her thoughts were taking concrete form.

"It's sick to saw a pregnant woman's steps clear through so that she could fall and get hurt . . . maybe killed. It's sick to shove a dead wasp in an envelope and send it to a new mother, a mother who might just possibly have that baby on her lap . . . like you *did*, Janey. And it's sick beyond sick to sneak into a hospital room and try to kill a new mother who's lying there as helpless as her newborn."

Janey couldn't say anything. He was right and she had never wanted to argue against that certainty so much as she'd wanted to argue anything in her whole life.

"Tell me how somebody doing all those things, and calling you and threatening you on top of it, is any worse than what I'm thinking?"

"These are old people," she cried. "They're fragile. They're frightened enough already. They're already going to die! No one, surely *no one* could do anything to hurry that along. Tell me that's impossible, Dave. Tell me!"

"I wish to God I could, Janey. Oh, honey, you don't know how hard I wish it. But if it's impossible, then it's also impossible that people can do bad things. And if that were the case, if people were that good, there wouldn't be any need for cops, there wouldn't be crime statistics, or torturing others—"

"Stop," she sobbed, grabbing at his arm. This couldn't be Dave saying these things. This wasn't the gentle, kind man who rocked her baby to sleep, this wasn't the tender lover of the night before. He sounded like Bill when he talked like that.

And the truth struck Janey with full force. He sounded like what he was: a cop.

"I can't stop, Janey. This is real. There is a nut out there and he's after you, honey. I'm a cop. I'm the sheriff in this town, in this county. It's up to me, and people like Charlie Dobson and your husband, to make sure the good guys do have a chance, that the bad guys are put behind bars."

Janey had known from the beginning that this moment would come. She had felt it since David's birth. She'd thought about it before going to sleep each night, and woke to it every morning. She had wondered about it earlier that afternoon.

Dave didn't have those transition periods like Bill had had, or like the young deputy she'd seen earlier. He was always Dave Reynolds, both tender and hard, strong willed and gentle voiced. And always, always a peace officer.

Slowly she reached out and traced the star pattern of his badge. "I told you last night, I couldn't go through it again. I didn't even know how truthful I was being. Now I do."

"Don't do this, Janey," he said. "You want all this nightmare over as badly as I do. Don't turn me into the bad guy just because I happen to have the same chosen career as your husband."

"You said it yourself, Dave. Wearing this badge is like wearing a target on your chest."

He was silent for a moment, then he took her hand from the badge at his breast and lifted it to his lips. He pressed a slow and strangely sorrowful kiss upon her fingers. Without releasing her hand, he said, "Listen to what you're saying, Janey."

"I know what I'm saying," she said, but at the look in his eyes, she wasn't so sure.

"No. You're not saying you don't want me anymore. You're saying you're afraid for me. *For* me, Janey. That's what you're worried about. That's the only reason you don't want to deal with a cop. You're afraid of losing one, you're afraid something might happen to one. You're holding back—and don't get me wrong—but you're only holding back because you're afraid your life will get blown to bits again."

Janey pulled back her hand as though the badge and then his lips had suddenly heated to molten levels.

"Is that so wrong?" she asked.

"No, it's not wrong, Janey. It's right to be scared. I'm scared. If you're not scared, you don't care anymore."

She relaxed slightly. "You do understand," she said.

"Yes. I understand. But you're missing something here, Janey. You're missing the feelings. My being a cop doesn't have anything to do with what you're scared of. You're scared of getting your life torn to shreds again. And that could happen no matter what I did for a living. That could happen if I step off a curb at the wrong time, or if I pull out at the wrong intersection.

"That's the way life is, honey. That's the way death is. I can't stop it any more than you can. I can quote you the statistics on cops versus firemen, on firemen versus doctors. I can twist and lie my way with statistics until I'm blue in the face. But not one single thing matters, not a scrap of it means a thing until you want to live again. Until you want to admit that what you're feeling is something real, something worth living for."

"And if I can't?" she choked.

"Then the bad guy whose bullet took Bill out wins. It's that simple. And if he wins, you might as well stick your head back in the sand, Janey, because unless you're willing to fight for what you believe in, what you love, then you're not really living, and the good guys are losing."

He stood then and shook his pants back down over his boots, and though he looked as though he wanted to walk away, he held out a hand to assist her up.

She stood and for a long time merely stared at him, her hand in his, her heart cold and her mind struggling to understand everything he'd just said so passionately, so earnestly. She felt the truth in his words, might even have said things like them once. But that had been a long time ago, and those truths no longer had validity in her life. In fact, she could point out a dozen flaws in his amazing speech.

She wanted to tell him that life wasn't comprised of the big things one fought for and cared about, it was made up of the small details of daily survival. It wasn't the huge, dramatic, sweeping changes that made life worth living; it was the small, seemingly insignificant routines of getting by without succumbing to grief, without caving in to the fears and lonelinesses of the long nights.

That's what life was . . . or, she had to admit, that's what life had been up until the night she'd fallen down the porch steps and Dave had helped her bring her son into the world. Since then, hadn't the sky been a little bluer, the grass a bit sweeter, the very smell in the air something fine and light, as effervescent as her heart had felt the night before?

Now, standing looking into this man's eyes, wondering if he could possibly, just possibly be right, she wished she could turn the clock forward, see him a year from now, two years from now, ten years.

She tried projecting his image into the future, painting his hair silver, extending the tiny wrinkles at the corners of the eyes, furrowing his cheeks with age. But the setting sun's rays glinted on his badge and blinded her, dispelling the images, causing her to see a different future altogether, a dark and frightening future, a time when she wore black once again and carried a folded flag on her lap.

"It isn't that easy," Janey said finally. "It just isn't that easy."

"No," he agreed. Sadly, she thought.

"I wish it were," she continued, equally sadly.

"It can be."

She shook her head. "No. No, it really can't."

He closed his eyes for a minute, looking as though she'd slapped him or, perhaps worse, dealt him a mortal wound.

"Bingo," he said. His voice was flat as the plains east of town. "The bad guys win."

Chapter 12

"Don't say that," Janey said sharply. "The bad guys haven't won."

Dave opened his eyes and looked down at this woman with whom he truly believed he wanted to spend the rest of his life. He knew she felt it, too. She was like a string on the same guitar; they thrummed to the same rhythm, blended to form a single, achingly harmonious chord.

Looking into her clear, mountain-sky blue eyes, he could read the doubt and the hope. And he could see both her resistance and her wishes.

He'd been telling himself since that fateful night of her baby's delivery that he'd been patient, willing to wait for her, willing to be whatever it was she needed him to be until she was ready—if she ever was—to take up the reins of living, really living again.

Now, as if she'd screamed the shocking truth at him, instead of standing there, so pale, so quiet, he could see that it was Janey who had been patient. It had been she who was patient all along, enduring the monstrous effects of change in her life, tolerant of the people around her, understanding of him.

She didn't need him pontificating at her, telling her how to live...she needed to have whoever was haunting her caught and locked up. It was that simple. And she'd never once said a word about the authorities' lack of having done so. She's merely accepted the slowness, the vague assurances, when she'd been receiving nightly threatening phone calls that conjured up every nightmare a human can have—loss of life, loss of child.

She had endured all of this and he'd had the audacity to stand there and tell her how she should be living her life.

"I haven't exactly been in any position to make any decisions about my life lately," she said, almost as though she could read his thoughts.

Her words flayed him. Someone had told her point-blank he was going to kill her. And he, Dave, hadn't done a single thing to stop the guy. Dave had told *her* not to run, had told her what to do and how to function, had told himself that he was ready for whatever life—and love—had to offer.

"I—" he began, but she interrupted.

"Don't say anything, Dave. You've already said your piece. Now it's my turn. Don't look away either. Look at me. Look at me as I really am, not as you *want* me to be. Just me. Here. Now. Janey Anderson, a full head or more shorter than you, face a mess from crying, some ragged old shirt of Bill's covering me. Look at me for what I really am."

He stared at her, frozen in place by the anger that turned her blue eyes to violet blaze, taking in the twin spots of color high in her cheeks and the lips thinned with the need for rigid control. Had he really been doing that? Seeing her only as an extension of his own wants, his own needs? Had he not seen Janey, the real Janey at all?

When he had thoroughly focused on her, she continued, "You tell me about living, about starting over. That's all

I've done for the last ten months of my life. That's all I've ever done. From the moment I was born I've never had a real home, a real life, until I finally ended up in New Mexico and met Bill Anderson. And we had a life. A real life.''

She broke off, never once letting her eyes slide from his. It was as if she had to make him look deep inside her and see the truth, feel it by falling into those fathomless pools of anger.

"It wasn't easy. *Real* life never is. But we hacked out a marriage together. It was made up of debt and sweat and a thousand other things that snared us every single day. And we fought, and we argued, and we made love, and we laughed. And then he was killed and that life ended. It just ended. A single bullet put a period to the only *real* life I've ever known.''

She did look away then, her eyes drenched with tears that she made no move to check. She stepped away from him a pace or two then whirled around so suddenly that it seemed her tears actually hung in midair between them. Tears he had caused, he thought, tears she had more than enough justification in shedding.

Again he tried to speak, to tell her that he'd been wrong to say anything, that he'd been speaking from selfishness only, but again she cut him off.

"I never once dodged starting over. Lord knows, I've had to do it often enough in my life. An orphan, shuffled from foster home to foster home knows all about starting over.''

She had glossed over the rough actuality of her life and he had never known, never realized—or had shied away from—this tragic addendum to her young life. He raised a hand to stop her, to tell her how sorry he was, to ask her forgiveness, but she brushed his hand aside and strode away from him. He knew her anger was propelling her, that her frustration required physical action. Every step, every tear was like acid on his heart.

She all but shouted at him, "I have never backed away from the hard, tangible truth of getting my life in gear. I've borne with the so-called hardships, or if you want to phrase it like the help books, I've *coped* with the shockingly tragic cards that life has dealt me. But I've never once had to stand and listen to someone telling me I wasn't doing a very good job of it! You know what you can do with your advice—"

"Janey!" he barked, as much to stop her tirade as to stop the effect her words were having on his bruised heart, the terrible effect they were having on hers. "Listen to me! I'm sorry. No, wait. Listen. I'm *sorry*. I...I was way out of line. I love you, and if that's any excuse for saying those things, then it's the only excuse I've got."

She stared at him as if he'd spoken Russian instead of English. Her breasts rose and fell beneath her shirt with the force of her still raging emotions. Her lips were parted and dry, her color high, and, as he watched, the anger slowly ebbed from her eyes and flush drained from her cheeks.

He looked at her now, as she'd asked him to do, for the first time not seeing her as the widow of a state hero, not looking at her as the pillar of silent strength he'd privately tagged her, not viewing her as the "frightened little girl" half the town had labeled her, but as a real person.

She had done all the things she said...plus. She had handled a near-fatal fall, the early delivery of her baby and a murder attempt on her life, with almost stunning equanimity. And now she stood before him, her face streaked with tears, and her nose shiny and red. Her shirt *was* some old castoff of a dress shirt that probably long since should have been pitched out, and she was the single most beautiful woman he'd ever seen.

She took his breath away. Her beauty was bone deep, like her honesty, like her courage. For a moment, while she was yelling at him, while her anger had gotten the better of her, she had scared him, because in that moment, when she was accusing him of not seeing her for what she really was, he had almost believed her. And in that dark, lonely moment, he hadn't felt as if he knew her anymore. He'd felt he was looking at a stranger.

But he'd done as she asked, looked and seen her and he believed...no, he *knew*...that what he'd seen in her all along was the real Janey Anderson. In some ways she might be that stranger he glimpsed for a moment, but she was a stranger he loved. And nothing she said or did could change that. Nothing.

Janey could read the full extent of his apology in his eyes, could see it in his loosened jaw and his drained color. She watched, almost amazed, as she studied her, and took her advice and *really* looked at her. And in his eyes she could see that he reached a vital truth of some kind, and the truth was far more beautiful than anything she could have imagined.

He'd said he loved her, and the simple words rocked the very ground she stood upon and made her want to cry out for joy or hit him for saying them now. She needed the anger to sustain her, to carry her through the conclusion of the nightmare. She needed the anger to keep the distance between her and Dave.

It wasn't until she heard him say "I love you" that she had to face the roiling truth in herself: she loved him in return. She did love him. *She* loved *him*. The thought stumbled around in her mind like a runaway looking for shelter, lost and confused.

When had it happened? How? Just as she had felt when she realized that sometime in the past month Dave had crossed the fine line between acquaintance and friend, now he had bridged another line, this one perilous and fraught with danger: friend to love.

Perhaps he had spanned the distance the previous night, taking her to greater and more glorious heights than she'd ever achieved before, but she thought he had really just reached this side of that chasm only in that moment.

And there wasn't anything she could do about it one way or another, because loving him still didn't alter the one absolute certainty that comprised her life right now: she couldn't open herself to the kind of trust it would take to live as a peace officer's wife again.

That's where Dave was wrong. All the statistics and data in the world, all the desire, couldn't give her the ability to stand back and accept the constant danger, the constant worry that comprised the life of a cop's wife.

But was he right, also? Was she dodging life, shoving her head in the sand, unwilling to peek over that fence she'd built around her and see what new and beautiful things were out there in the world?

"I feel like I should say something big. Something huge right now," she said. "And all I can think to say is that I'm so confused about how I feel."

"About us? About me?"

"Us. You. *Us.*"

The baby's wail from inside the house forestalled any response from Dave, and he watched her dash into the house as though from a great distance away. He hesitated before following her. He paced the living room, waiting for her return, wishing he could think of what he was going to say to her when she did.

He turned his back to the photograph of Bill Anderson. He didn't want to see his face, didn't want to feel the sense of betrayal and disloyalty he felt whenever he looked at it. And he didn't want to feel the strong surge of kinship or the overpowering wave of jealousy.

It was time to think of Janey, now. Not himself. She knew that he loved her, and she'd forced him to see her for what she was, not as he dreamed she was. And while she hadn't said she loved him in return, he knew that his words had moved her. And she hadn't run away from him.

She wasn't a runner. She'd proved that over and over again.

He had been the one who had convinced her to stay when the murderer had made his first attempt, had threatened her again. Dave had convinced her not to run away, to see it through, to let him get the bad guy for her. And she had done as he had asked. She had stayed, she had given him every facet of her self without reservation and with dignity.

And he had returned that favor, that tremendous trust with what? With himself? With his dreams and wishes? That couldn't be enough. The bad guy was still out there somewhere.

The ugliest facet of the truth was the last to hit home, but it was the truth with a double-edged sword, the one that could cut the deepest. He'd persuaded her to stay, dangling the carrot of a new life in front of her eyes, a new life with him. But it was *he* who was running away. He had been from the night in the hospital when the guy had tried injecting her IV with pentobarbital.

And he'd run again last night, after the phone call, after the threat to her life and the caller's awareness that Dave was leaving town.

He'd run, and he'd let her down dreadfully. Because Dave had known what to do then but hadn't done it. He should have set a trap that very night or the next morning, the next night, and he hadn't, because he couldn't face it.

He'd been lying to himself all along, he thought. She wasn't the one who couldn't forget the past . . . he was. He might believe he was ready to love again, but Janey was miles beyond where he was in actually *living* again. He'd told himself that the padlocks on the doors to his heart were rusty, where hers were new and shiny steel, but there was one door he'd ignored completely: the door that guarded the secret of having sent Patty Donahue to her death by using her as bait in an entrapment scheme. And the padlock on that door didn't have a single spot of rust anywhere.

"I'm sorry," he said aloud, as much to himself as to Janey, who wasn't even in the room, or to the ghost of the man behind him. And he was. He was sorry for misunderstanding, for having pushed her, even for having urged her to stay in Portales. At that moment he was truly sorry for everything he'd said and done with Janey Anderson.

"Dave . . . ?" she said from the doorway, and she smiled. The sight of that sorrow-filled smile on her wan face tore at him like an icy wind.

It there was a chance for them, a chance for him to hold out his arm and talk her into walking at his side for the rest of her life, he had to open that locked door and let her see what was hidden behind it. Some of it, if not all.

At that moment, Dave knew it was up to him to prove that the good guys did have a chance. It was up to him to prove that she could trust in someone else again, for things other than what he'd given her—and taken from her—the night before.

"All I have is supposition," he said now. "There's not a district attorney in the country who would listen to me at this point."

Janey didn't say anything, and, in all truthfulness, Dave hadn't expected her to speak. He'd stated a simple, irrefutable fact.

He waited until she sat down in the rocker, young David pulling at the bottle, his blue eyes on Dave, his tiny hand curled around his mother's forefinger. Dave sighed, his heart wrenching at the sight of the two of them, the two people most dearly held in his heart. Looking at them, he hesitated, feeling every bit as confused as Janey had said she was.

"But, I think there's a way we can pin this guy down."

She reacted then, as if she'd been electrically shocked. She jerked once, her hand tightening on the baby to the point that little David grunted and squirmed. She cocked her head in question, her lips compressed.

"How?" was all she asked.

"We...set...a *trap*." She would never know how hard it was to say what he had, never know how the past was crashing down on him, with the weight of the future lending its strength.

She studied him for a long moment, and he wondered what she could read on his face. Finally, as though reaching some sort of understanding, she nodded. "Tell me."

He wanted to wrap his arms around her, kiss her and tell her how wonderful he thought she was, but he held his distance, needing the space between them now. He couldn't tell her what he had in mind if he was touching her, if he was too near her, for he wouldn't be able to think clearly then, especially not while opening this dreadful door in his heart.

"What do you want me to do?" she asked when he didn't say anything.

He bit back an immediate outline of a plan, stunned that it should stand so clearly in his mind. He'd had the plan all along, he realized, but had hid it, even from himself.

He'd thought of Patty Donahue often while with Janey, too often, perhaps. He'd told himself, told Janey, that his former partner and lover had been on his mind because he was looking at loving again. But that wasn't all of it, he realized now. He'd thought about her because the past was repeating itself. He was again faced with the need to set a trap, flush a bad guy by using a lover as bait.

But this time, it wasn't his lover who would be there; he would be inside, waiting.

"I'll need you to make a couple of phone calls, then I want you to get David and clear out of here. Go over to Mrs. Lyon's or Mrs. Aragon's, or anywhere you want. And you stay there."

She considered him for a moment, then asked, "Who am I going to call?"

Relieved that she accepted his plan so easily, not even sure why he'd half expected arguments from her, he answered her question with a smile. "I want you to place a call to your

former boss, what's-his-name Swanson. I want you to tell
him that you know."

"I know?"

"That's all. I just want you to tell him who you are, and
where you are. And then say, Dr. Swanson...I know."

"And when he asks what it is that I know?"

"You don't answer for a long time, then say you know
what he's been doing, and you have proof."

"I say, 'I know,' I wait, and then I say, 'I know what
you've been doing and I have proof,'" she repeated slowly.
"That's all?"

"And then I want you to call the director of the hospice
here...what's his name?"

"The manager here is George Taylor. But the director is
Dr. William Swanson."

He closed his eyes for a moment. Had she told him this
before and his brain had just neglected to file it away prop-
erly? Had he been so blinded by her beauty, by the beauty
inside her, that he hadn't been thinking clearly at all? Or was
it that the need for setting a trap, and his running from that
notion, had blinded him to the information he'd needed?

"Dr. Swanson's our man, then."

"Maybe," she cautioned.

"Maybe. But it fits," he said. He had to pace a step or
two away, his thoughts demanding action, his eyes raking
the interior of her home, then looking out at the lawn, her
porch, and the pathway leading to the house. "And if I'm
right, we'll know soon enough."

"It's not Dr. Swanson who has been calling me."

"I know. I'm willing to bet everything I've got that the
guy who's been threatening you works for...or with Dr.
Swanson. You can't tell me that the guy who wrote that
pompous letter would sully his hands with doing something
himself."

He could see from her face that she was in agreement with
him. He swung around and strode on the far side of the

coffee table. "What is the hospice outfit, a chain of some kind?" he asked, turning back to her.

She half-smiled. "Not really. They have the same board, the salaries are paid from the same foundation, and they share the director... Dr. William Swanson."

"I know I've asked this before, but tell me again. How does the hospice get its money to run the two places?"

"From the foundation," she answered promptly. "It's a nonprofit foundation that relies, primarily, on grants and endowments."

"Explain those endowments," Dave said.

"Well, some of the endowered monies come from the patients themselves, donating some or all of their assets to the foundation in return for their care. Some comes from the families who place them in the hospice. Other money comes from charitable donations."

"What about a deal like this Angela Martinez, the friend of Mrs. Deveroux? Your friend said this woman was going to contact her son and leave all her money to her grandchildren. What happened to the money since she died before calling him?"

Janey stopped rocking long enough that the baby protested. She looked as though she'd been told her best friend had poisoned her. Perhaps it was closer to the truth than anyone would care to admit, Dave thought.

"The foundation," she said dully. "It would go to the foundation. I think there's a clause in the enrollment contract to that effect, but it's as much to protect the patient as the foundation, or at least, that's how it was explained to me when I asked one time. I never really thought about it until now."

"I'm sorry, Janey," he said. "I could be wrong."

"You aren't wrong," she said. "I can feel it. I don't like it, and it makes me feel ill... but I know you're right. They killed Mrs. Martinez because she was going to give her money away. And they killed V-Violet because she got in the way."

"That's what I think."

"And who knows how many other countless people they've...they've *murdered* over the years," she said, a frown marring her brow, her voice sharp with horror, her jaw tight with repressed anger or shock.

"We don't know that there were any others," he reminded her, hating her pallor, her stunned acceptance of the worst evidence of man's inhumanity to man that he'd ever heard about.

"There were," she said quietly.

"What? How do you know?"

"That's why Dr. Swanson didn't want me to come back to work. It was right before Bill was shot. An old man, Richard D'Agostino, was doing better. He was terminal, like the others, but he seemed to accept the end. But the day before...before he died he didn't want me to leave, said he was afraid of the night nurse. He told me he wanted me to call his granddaughter and have her come get him. Take him home."

"Did you?"

"His granddaughter had died a year and a half earlier. He didn't have anyone else."

"What did you do?"

"I went to Dr. Swanson and said that Mr. D'Agostino was frightened about something, the night nurse in particular." She didn't say anything for a few seconds, and Dave could see that her mind was on the past. "Needless to say, Dr. Swanson wasn't very happy with me. It wasn't the first time I'd complained about someone being dissatisfied with the care at his hospice."

"He didn't do anything, then? To take care of D'Agostino, I mean?"

"Mr. D'Agostino died that night."

"I see," Dave said. "Did you think there was anything suspicious in that?"

Janey shook her head and looked at the baby solemnly staring up at her. She tried to smile, but the intention fell sadly awry. "Bill was killed the next day. I wasn't thinking much of anything for quite a while after that. I didn't even know about Mr. D'Agostino for almost three weeks. And then, I have to honestly admit, I didn't consider anything unusual about it. He was terminal. His prognosis wasn't good."

Dave could actually feel every vestige of her pain deep within his own heart. "No. I suppose not."

"But I'm thinking now. It's too late, but I'm thinking now."

"Janey...nothing you could have said or done would have changed things. You couldn't have prevented their deaths. Honey, not to sound callous, but they were going to die anyway. What Swanson and his nurse-henchman did was hasten that death along—if they really *are* the ones behind it, and behind the attempts on your life. It's the worst kind of madness, the most despicable of crimes, but there wasn't anything you could have done about it."

"Until now," she said, looking up. That lost, defenseless Janey was gone now, and the strength she had was back on the surface. The icy wind that raged around his heart warmed a notch.

"Until now," he agreed, and couldn't resist the urge to touch her, to stroke the hair from her forehead.

"As soon as the baby's done eating, I'll call them," she said.

"I have to line up some backup first, and get you situated."

He thought for a moment she was going to say something important, argue with him, perhaps, or even add something she'd neglected to say earlier, but she shook her head instead, as though the argument were with herself.

She said, "Go ahead and arrange your backup, and then I'll go arrange things with Mrs. Aragon."

"Fine," he said, heading for the door.

"And Dave?"

"Yes?"

"Thank you."

"Don't thank me, Janey. I haven't done anything yet."

"You have. And you're going to."

"I wish I felt as certain," Dave said, and smiled bitterly.

"You should. I . . . you're one of the good guys."

She smiled, then, and though Dave could still see the reserve in her and could still sense the sorrow, the smile did much to restore his balance, his confidence and his faith in the rightness of things.

"Well then, I guess we'll just have to go after the bad guys."

Like a litany or a chant to ward off evil, he felt the phrase turning around and around in his mind, in his heart. When it altered, he wasn't sure, but after he'd called the department and after he'd talked with Charlie Dobson and outlined his plan, he could still feel the difference.

Capture the bad guys and get the girl. That was the phrase, that was the wish.

He'd at least try to do the first one. He couldn't even allow himself the luxury of daydreaming about the latter; it meant too much, it was too much like playing roulette with the rest of his life.

If he let her down now, if something went wrong . . . there would never be any facing her again. And if things went really wrong . . . he wouldn't be there to collect anyway. And Janey's heart would be shattered once more.

And in that flash of insight Dave understood the rest of the story about Janey Anderson. She might love him, but saw no future for them.

Neither did Dave. If things went wrong . . . all the king's horses and none of his own desire could ever put the pieces back together again.

Chapter 13

Janey changed the baby and dressed him in one of the soft terry-cloth jumpsuits that molded his round little body and transformed him to a picture child. He waved his hands and cooed, his innocent, wholly trusting eyes never leaving her face.

Outside, the sun still shone in that shimmery brightness peculiar to desert terrain, rays actually visible and golden, the thin, dry air apparently unable to blend the rays to a whole, but constantly producing a stunning light show.

Janey could hear children laughing somewhere, and the sound of cars breaking at the corner stop sign. All around her, at her hands, outside her house, life was going on, evidence of it everywhere. Inside her, she felt as if everything had stopped, as if her very heart were poised, waiting, scared to resume its rapid beating, reluctant to admit that she was frightened to her core.

Holding her baby up to the window, showing him the dazzling world beyond his grasp, she wondered if she was frightened of the trap they were laying, or was it the unanswered questions she had about her relationship with Dave Reynolds? Where did a relationship start and a friendship end? Did they cancel each other out, or did one make the other blossom into something so rare, so special that everyone in the world carried the atavistic memory of such a union?

He'd said he loved her, and she believed him. But that didn't clarify the feelings she felt for him. Were her feelings extensions of her desire to go on with her life? Were they evidence of wish fulfillment, a desire for the American dream of happy mommy, happy daddy, happy family?

These questions made her pause, made her heart beat erratically, but it was the deeper significance that made her frightened. What if she answered the questions with returned love for him? What then? What if they were real, weren't pipe dreams and compensations? What if, just maybe, she really did love him, just for him, only for him?

He'd still wear a badge and he'd still put his life on the line every day, every minute, and she'd still be somewhere, at home or at work, her eye on the clock, her ear on the phone, waiting for word of his safety.

As she was dressing the baby, she'd considered asking him to change his profession. Would he do it? Could she even ask it? And if he did, if he acceded to the fears in her, conceded to the need for absolute security, would he be the same man?

In Bill, in the young deputy on her doorstep, she'd seen men who were capable of shifting gears, of looking at life one way while in one uniform, and changing their entire outlook in the single blink of an eye, in the donning of different clothes. But Dave wasn't like that. His eyes still smoldered with the same banked fire, and his mouth still curved in that tender smile. And his cheeks, ever-ready barometer of his moods and thoughts, would always, forever, color with that earthy hue.

She couldn't ask him to change his life, his given profession, any more than he could ask her to be something different than what she was. And he wasn't asking her to be anything other than free to live...and love...again.

She couldn't ask him to change for her, to rearrange the universe into a tidy pattern for Janey Anderson. But she could take what he was offering her now: a chance to make a stand.

He was, through his plan, through his action, allowing her the opportunity of stepping forward and saying "I've had enough of this nightmare. I'm going to do something about it."

She had already called Mrs. Aragon and her daughter, Linda. Before she could even explain the reasons why she needed their assistance, they had assured her they would keep David for her, wouldn't let him out of their sight. Only then did Mrs. Aragon ask where Janey was going.

"There's been some trouble," she said cautiously. "The same man who rigged my porch steps, and, we think, tried to hurt me in the hospital...well, we think he might show up here tonight."

"Then you'd better come with your boy," Mrs. Aragon said. "And you'd better call Davey over there right now."

"He knows," Janey said, and was aware how little that actually said, and how much. She'd said "We think," and she didn't believe Mrs. Aragon wouldn't know who the "we" in question happened to be. She amended her statement, "Dave already knows. This is his idea."

Janey was aware, even as she told Mrs. Aragon that she'd be right over, that Dave really did know. And dimly, she was also cognizant that he knew things he wasn't saying, felt things he wasn't expressing.

She'd seen the desperation in his eyes, the torture his laying a trap had evoked in him. Putting the pieces together now, she thought perhaps she understood, and hoped she was wrong.

He had told her—reluctantly, she thought—that his former love had been a cop, also, like Bill. At the time, she'd thought he was only drawing the parallels in their lives. Now she wondered.

His love, Patty, had been a policewoman and she had been killed, that was all the significance that Janey had allowed herself to see. But during his speech that afternoon, he'd also mentioned a police officer being tortured . . . were they one and the same?

Now she wondered if there hadn't been some kind of entrapment situation that had resulted in the death of Patty Donahue?

Mrs. Aragon's voice interrupted her thoughts, "You come right on over here, then. And stay with us. We'll take care of you."

That's what Dave wanted her to do. That's what he'd asked her to do, take the baby and hide out with Mrs. Aragon, her daughter and her numerous grandchildren. And until that minute, that's exactly what Jane had intended doing.

But now, she realized she couldn't. She couldn't leave him alone to face this unknown assailant without her. But was that really the issue? She was a fairly good shot, yet, and she had a .38 police special tucked in her nightstand, but was protecting him really so much why she wanted to be there?

All she really knew was that by being in on it, by being with him, she wouldn't be sitting across the street, her eyes on the window, her ears attuned to the sound of car doors, her heart with the man waiting inside, serving as the bait in her stead.

If Dave was alone at her house, their mark—to use a phrase of Bill's—might never even come close enough to the house to be caught. He would escape them and be able to continue his killing, his disgusting, horrifying killing.

Whether Dave knew it or not, he *needed* her there. He needed her for the phone calls, if nothing else, and he'd even admitted that much. But on the off chance they called her back to see if she really was home and she wasn't trying to trap them, she needed to be there afterward.

And, though she scarcely acknowledged it even to herself, she felt she should be there to make certain, firsthand, that Dave was safe.

She kissed her baby goodbye and hugged Mrs. Aragon and her daughter before heading back across the street to her own home. It looked solid and stately, and until this moment, it had seemed a bastion of protection. Now it also looked easy to break into, easy to breach. She looked at it through Bill's eyes: the windows were all the old-fashioned slide-and-pulley variety, wide panes sliding upward on old, worn ropes sagging noticeably, intruders held out by a swivel lock that could probably be pried loose by simple pressure. The front door had a single dead bolt lock, but one that any burglar could open with a bobby pin or a credit card. The back door only sported a hook-and-eye lock, the kind that any swift yank would render broken.

In a town where a fender bender made front-page news and the theft of something out of someone's unlocked car was reported over and over until the culprit returned the item, a hook-and-eye lock and a single dead bolt were tantamount to sealing bank vault doors.

She tried looking at her house through Dave's eyes, but all she could see were the repaired steps, the evenings spent on the porch swing with him and the new bulbs sprouting in her flower beds. Why was it that when she tried to look at the place through his eyes, she saw a *home,* not a potential burglary in progress?

The lack of security measures hadn't mattered until the first of the threatening letters to reach her in Portales, and the first of the calls. Then she'd locked up every time she even went to the mailbox. After the hospital incident they hadn't seemed so problematical; the police drove by regularly and Dave spent practically every evening there.

She blushed, remembering that he'd spent more than an evening there the night before, but the sudden onslaught of color had nothing to do with embarrassment, only warm and tender reminiscence.

She paused, caught by the memories of last night, snared by the lure of the concept of a home—*I love you, Janey*— and stood still, wanting to believe that the world was as good a place as the sun on her shoulders and the scent of lilacs seemed to say it was. How could she be contemplating going inside her house and telephoning a potential murderer to try to trap him into revealing himself?

She drew a deep breath and continued across the street. Her baby was safe, Dave would be there with her in the house, and she wasn't running. She wasn't pulling back from anything now, she thought. She was meeting the enemy head on and confronting her own fears in the process. She was no longer the helpless victim, worrying when the next call, letter or attack would come.

Thanks to Dave, thanks to his plan, she was taking positive actions, and no matter what the outcome might be, she wasn't hiding her head in that sand anymore.

She pulled the door open with a steady hand and her head held high.

Dave was waiting for her, a shadow figure in the wide archway leading to her dining room. He smiled at her and held out his hand.

He was no ghost this time, and nothing about him triggered memories of the long-buried past.

"All set?" he asked.

She put her hand in his. "I'm ready now," she said.

"Absolutely not!" he said. "You promised. I told you the scenario, and you promised you'd do as I asked." Dave couldn't believe what she was saying, what he was hearing.

He paced the room, unable in his agitation to stand still let alone sit. He tried getting his mind to work, but his heart seemed to be holding the floor.

She'd come into the room, as fresh and vibrant as the spring afternoon. When she'd smiled at him and placed her hand in his, he'd known why Persephone had been captured and taken to Hades for most of the year. Persephone must have been much like Janey, the very personification of spring, the very essence of beauty.

When she'd said "I'm ready now," he'd felt she meant something different than setting the trap for a murderer. For a split second of infinity he'd thought she meant ready for him. Ready for a life with him.

She had picked up the phone, cool as you please, and told Dr. Swanson she knew what he was up to, and had the proof to boot. Ad-libbing, she'd added that she didn't think it might be totally necessary to involve the police or even a grand jury at this point...not if he was cooperative. She was willing to make a deal.

"That should do it," she'd said when she'd hung up the phone. "Of course, he sputtered and tried to act like he didn't know what I was talking about, but I think he should be on the phone to his cohort right now."

"I've already called the state police. They're going to wait for a signal from us...or in eight hours if anything goes wrong...and then they'll take Swanson into custody."

"For murder?"

"They'll try that, though there really isn't a thing against him that anyone knows right now. They've already arranged an order to impound his records. That might prove something's up. And there are the threats on your life to add to the coffers."

"Then all we have to do is wait." She said it so calmly that for a moment he hadn't understood her intention.

"Right. Why don't you get on over to Mrs. Aragon's now? If this guy really is in Portales, he could show up here any minute."

"I'm not leaving," she said. "I'm staying right here with you."

"Absolutely not! You promised to do as I asked."

"No, I didn't," she said.

"This is not time for games," he growled at her, not so angry at her as afraid for her. Didn't she understand the dangers?

He stopped his pacing, feeling off balance, more than a little stunned, as he watched her casually move to her rocker and sit down is if ready to nurse the baby or drink a glass of iced tea. Then he realized the significance of her posture. Her hands, loosely draped on either arm, were exactly placed so as to cling to the arms if need be.

He couldn't help it, his lips curved in a smile. "You're telling me that in order to get you out of the house, I'd have to carry you *and* the chair out the door, aren't you?"

She smiled back somewhat warily, he thought.

"That's about the size of it," she said, and her tone was saccharine.

"Janey, don't do this." He could still feel the smile on his lips, but it was fading fast. He wasn't kidding. She couldn't stay. Not now, not after placing that call, not after practically begging for them to come after her.

His mind raced, his heart screamed. *Don't even think it.*

"I have to, Dave. You accused me a while ago of sidestepping life. Well, you were right. I was actually allowing myself to be the victim. I wasn't fighting this guy on my turf. I was cowering in the corner, waiting for him to come after me. I'm not going to do that anymore."

"This isn't a game, Janey. That wasn't what I meant and you know it." He was relatively certain his face was hard and his eyes flint, but she didn't seem frightened or intimidated. She wasn't even shaking.

She sighed then and said, "Yes, but I mean this. I'm not leaving here without you, Dave. Either we both go across the street and watch from there, or we both stay here."

"This is ridiculous!" he snapped, feeling as though his mind were about to snap, too. "You can't stay here. It's too damned dangerous!"

"I have a .38 police special," she said, and added, "and I know how to use it."

"If I have to drag you out of here, I will—" he began but broke off at her sudden wave for his silence. "What?"

"A car door."

Dave crossed to the window in a single step and peered through the half-drawn drapes. "Someone's parked in front of the Judson place." He watched for a moment, then sighed with relief. "It's Tom Addersly," he said, and turned back to Janey. "One of the guys on the backup team."

She felt a wave of relief wash through her, as well. Not alone, she thought, they weren't in this all alone.

"Will you please leave now, Janey?" he asked her again.

"I can't, Dave. I have to see this through. I have to know I had a hand in stopping this. It's gone on too long for me, and has done so much damage to those I knew and loved. I owe it to Violet, and to poor Mrs. Martinez and Mr. D'Agostino. I want to see this through with you."

"Janey...I'm begging you, get out of here right now. You said you couldn't go through it again, well, damn it all, neither can I." His voice was so ravaged Janey knew what she had suspected was the truth.

"Because of Patty Donahue?" she asked softly.

"Sweet heaven," he murmured. "Yes. Because of Patty. Because we—*I*—staged an entrapment. Because we'd had an idea we could flush him if we sent someone out who looked like his other victims, and sent her in as a ringer instead of the girl who lived there. Patty went in. We all watched her go inside. She was wired, and if she heard so much as a peep she was supposed to yell like crazy."

When he stopped talking, his eyes wild and unfocused, Janey prompted him, "But you never heard anything?"

"No. The guy was already inside. He must have realized it was a setup from the first minute. Who knows, maybe he'd been dogging the target long enough that he recognized the difference, or maybe he was just smarter than we were. Anyway, he grabbed her right off, and that was the end of the wire."

"What happened to Patty?"

His smoky eyes met hers then, twin chips of pale ice. "He gagged her. And he tortured her until she died. Until she died, Janey."

Janey felt the bile rising up, and the tears welling in her eyes. She blinked them back, knowing this wasn't the worst, knowing there was more and she had to be ready for it. She had asked him to tell her, had forced him to give her this bit of himself. She couldn't refuse it now, or dissolve into empathy when he needed her strength.

"And we didn't know a damn thing about it until we went inside after we couldn't raise her on the wire." He ran a hand through his already ruffled hair and turned his back on her. His voice was muffled and dull when he continued. "We'd been sitting around, drinking coffee. It was a cold night. For L.A., I mean. We must have downed two whole thermoses of the stuff.

"There were four of us, and one of him. And the whole time we sat there, swapping stories and guzzling coffee, he was torturing Patty."

"I'm so very sorry, Dave."

"Don't be sorry, Janey. Just leave. Leave now!"

"I can't. I have to stay."

"I couldn't protect Patty. I may not be able to protect you! Don't you get it, Janey? You told me you didn't know if you could trust again, trust other people. Well, I don't know if I can either . . . but it's a different kind of trust. Maybe it's all tied up with the protective urges, whatever.

But I don't know if I can trust myself to be there at the right time, the only time it really counts!''

His impassioned statement flowed from him in a torrent, catching on the sob that ripped it from his throat.

He stared at her, shaken and horrified, and Janey suspected it was as much at the shocking release of emotions after all these years as it was at the horror of what had happened.

She wanted to run to him, throw her arms around him and soothe the aching hole in his heart, the wound left from this final piece of shrapnel that had been buried there so long and allowed to fester. She held herself still, however.

This wasn't something she could fix. Not with any simple homilies or platitudes. They could assuage some of the pain. Maybe. But the real healing could only come from within him. She knew that all too well from personal experience. But she could at least offer him the benefit of her awareness, the gift of her understanding. And perhaps, with her help, this wound, this fear, the self-doubt that had no business clouding his life, would be erased.

She pushed to her feet and walked to his side. As much as she wanted to touch him now, she didn't, she couldn't and still speak.

''You told me once that I had heart. More heart and more courage than anyone you've known,'' she said, hoping that her very stillness would capture his attention and hold it.

She waited until his agonized eyes met hers before continuing. ''I needed to hear you say that. I wasn't feeling very courageous right then, and I needed those sentiments. You made me believe in them.

''One good turn deserves another. You, Dave, saved my life and that of my baby's. No one else. Just you. I know, in my heart of hearts, that David—and probably myself as well—would have died that night but for your help. Your *protection*. You say you can't trust yourself. You don't have to. *I* trust you. I've trusted you since that first minute. I couldn't even admit it to myself until now, but I do.''

A tremendous shudder worked through Dave and he raised a hand to cover his eyes.

''Isn't this too sweet?'' a voice asked from the doorway to the kitchen.

Both Janey and Dave whirled toward the door.

Janey felt an immediate shock of recognition, and her hatred for the man who had been in her hospital room, who most certainly had called her, threatening her life and that of her baby, was so intense that she literally had to focus on the gun in his hand to keep from leaping at him.

He waggled that gun at her now. ''Well, well. We meet again.''

Chapter 14

When Dave whirled and saw the man with the gun trained on Janey, his first reaction was one of dull horror. What he had feared most had come to pass. First Patty, now Janey. Was history going to repeat itself? Was that the terrible fate that lay in wait for him each time he gave his heart, each time he loved?

It couldn't be that way, he told himself. Fate wouldn't have brought Janey and David into his life only to have them taken away. Second chances were forever, not to be ripped from his grasp right at the very moment his heart was fully whole again.

The notion that this murderer could sneak into Janey's house and try to steal her from him now, that he could harm her in any way, sparked such a powerful anger in Dave that it was all he could not to completely ignore the danger, damn the consequences and draw on the stocky man holding the gun on Janey.

But the man *was* carrying a gun, and Janey would be the one to suffer if the weapon were to go off.

I trust you, Dave. As if she were saying the phrase aloud now, he felt it take root in the lonely soil of his heart, growing there, strengthened by what he had read on her face, by the hope he swiftly nurtured it with.

In concrete danger now, the threat no longer some nebulous, vague menace, and fed by Janey's gift of trust and his own belief in the rightness of second chances, Dave found a new strength, a new courage, a feeling he'd never had before and wondered if he would ever encounter it again. He felt completely and totally ready to tackle this man, entirely confident of his ability to do so.

The only spanner in the works was the possible danger to Janey. His hands twitched with the need for action, the need to wrap his palm around the grip mere inches from his fingers.

"We've had a lot of fun together, haven't we, Mrs. Anderson?" the man sneered at Janey. "Imagine my surprise when I found out you were still alive. Luckily for me, I didn't have to hurry. I could take my time. All I had to do was wait till the watchdog left town. But he didn't leave, did he? And now, I get to kill two birds with two bullets."

The madman chuckled, and Dave felt the hairs on the back of his neck rise in primal hatred. This was a man who had tried to kill Janey, had tormented her, and possibly killed her friends, and he was standing there laughing about it all.

"I've enjoyed our little game," the man said.

"I haven't," Janey said softly. And only Dave, knowing her so well now, feeling as though he really were in tune with her, body and soul, knew that she wasn't speaking quietly from any fear, but from profound anger.

"You must have thought we were pretty stupid. Calling the chief and telling him you had some kind of proof."

"You're here," she said. "That's all we wanted."

"So you wanted me, did you? Well, you've got me. Or, wait a minute, are the tables turned? Could it be...yes, I do believe it's true...that I'm holding the gun!"

Dave studied the man across from him, noting the petulant set of the mouth, the film of sweat on the man's brow, over his upper lip. He saw a rent in the man's cotton pants and the bloodstains around his knee and idly wondered who's back fence the man had scaled to his discomfiture. Or had he tussled with Tom Addersly?

This creep was the type of perpetrator who had to make all the wise remarks, had to get the last word in, but in the end, always cracked, because underneath all that bravado, there was a morass of fear, a never-ending well of insecurities. He was the clown and juvenile delinquent turned amoral and adult criminal, but the insecure child was still inside there. How could he use those insecurities to their advantage?

"Yeah, I'm here," the man said. "But not for any bogus proof. I never leave any kind of clue. No. I'm here to get rid of you once and for all."

"There's a backup team right outside," Dave cut in. "You don't have a prayer, pal. Why don't you just give it up?"

"Correction watchdog...or should I say 'lover boy'? There *was* a backup. In a one-outhouse town like this, I didn't expect too much trouble. Or maybe the boys I saw were just nosy neighbors. At any rate, sheriff, they are out of commission. Maybe permanently. Sorry about that. But I didn't have time to make them look like accidents."

Dave had to hold in his instinctive lunge for the maniac. Ted Addersly had a wife and three kids; Johnny Delgado had a wife who was expecting their second baby any day now.

"You've just put yourself behind bars for life," Dave said through clenched teeth.

"We'll see. But I doubt it. I hate things so messy, but Swanson has this almost mawkish fear of you, Mrs. Anderson. He seemed to think that wherever you went the long arm of the law was one step behind you."

He paused to survey Dave with derision. "Looks like he was right and wrong at the same time."

"You can't get away with this," Janey said.

"She's right," Dave added.

"No. *You're* both wrong. I can get away with anything I like."

Janey knew she had to do something to tip the balance in Dave's favor. As alert as he was, he would be able to take any small advantage she could give him and turn it to good use.

She had given him her full trust, now she had to trust him to use it and to survive. Lord, he had to live, because she didn't want to make it without him. At first, her mind scrambled for some distractive attention device, she missed the significance of her own thoughts, then the real meaning settled in. She didn't want to make it without Dave, not she *couldn't* make it without him.

When Bill had died she had thought she wouldn't be able to survive, that life would be too overwhelmingly difficult, too much to bear. If Dave were killed, she wouldn't want to bear it; it wouldn't be worth bearing. He'd given her the taste of what life could be again, what it might have in store for her and her son, for all three of them. There was a tremendous difference.

But what to do? How to get through this nightmare and still have a new life, the life of picnics, baseball games and county fairs? How to switch the rules so that she could, for once, have it all? How to tip the scales so that she really could live with this love she'd discovered she wanted, she needed, now when it was almost too late?

"You were wrong about the proof," she said, and continued before the murderous evil standing in front of her could speak, "Dr. Swanson forwarded it to me himself, in the form of a letter from Violet Deveroux."

"Baloney, lady. I saw that letter. There wasn't anything in that thing that could incriminate a flea, let alone either of us. You really think he'd have been stupid enough to send something incriminating? You don't know us very well, lady."

"No?" Janey asked. "*You* obviously didn't know Mrs. Deveroux. She worked acrostics and anagrams all the time."

"What of it?"

"She had suspected the two of you for a long while. She says that she knew you killed Angela Martinez. She even hints about Mr. D'Agostino. But, it's all there. See for yourself."

She had taken him off guard, she could tell. Whether he believed her or not wasn't the issue, what mattered was if she could get him to look away from them long enough that Dave could draw his magnum. The time was now or never.

"It's right there on the end table. I'm sure you recognize it."

Her attempt was flimsy. It didn't have the remotest possibility of working, but every muscle in Dave tensed, nonetheless. His mind on lightning speed, his body already projected into the future a split second, Dave prayed what Janey was trying would work.

In the movies, directors often slow the film to show every nuance of time, hair flying, handing in the air, rain bouncing achingly slowly upward to fall again, or a bad guy turning his head away at a crucial moment. He'd never appreciated the technique before, but it happened to him now.

Time seemed to slow by a hundred thousand times the pace of normality. This cheap, conscienceless thug slowly lowered his eyes to the side table, taking in the lamp, a bill or two, and the crumpled bit of vellum that represented Dave's one chance at ending the nightmare.

The air seemed to rush into his lungs as he drew the steadying breath, and yet time still moved in that odd distortion. Dave had heard about people's lives flashing before their eyes seconds prior to their death, and this felt like that, but different, more vivid somehow. This was more as if his brain had gone into hyperdrive and all circuits were targeted on one object: vanquishing this evil standing before them.

He thought of Janey and of David, and he remembered the night he'd leaped over his porch railing, racing the clock then, too, trying to get to Janey before she actually hit the ground.

You saved our lives... he heard, though he knew she'd said these words what seemed like hours, days before.

I trust you...

He felt the truth of her gift now, felt it in his flexing hand, felt it in the invincibility that flooded his veins, corded his neck.

His hand eased around the grip of his .357 magnum and molded around it with the sure touch of expertise. His fingers tightened and his stomach tensed. It was now or never.

Out of the corner of his eye, he saw Janey shift slightly to her left, as if already hearing the gun's deafening roar. And his own weapon was free, even as the murderer's face registered recognition of Violet Deveroux's handwriting, as the creep involuntarily moved forward to retrieve it.

"Freeze," Dave said, and as if his voice had the power of the universe in that solitary note of command, time swung back into the proper sequence, slamming home with hard, sharp impact, bringing the scent of lilacs, the sounds of the street and the sweet whisper of Janey's breathing. The shift in feeling was swift, dizzying in its intensity and inexorable motion, and exhilarating.

But the thug didn't freeze; the killer of old people, and Janey's tormentor, panicked and fired.

Again Dave felt that odd sensation of time distortion. It almost seemed he could see the bullet as it left the murderer's gun. He heard his own weapon's nearly simultaneous explosion but couldn't remember pulling the trigger. He heard Janey's scream even as he saw the murderer stagger backward, crashing into her wall, into her paintings. Glass sprayed outward as the man slowly spun to the floor.

And he felt such a tremendous eruption of pain in his own chest, he wondered if he'd suffered a heart attack. He felt as if his body were empathizing with his would-be murderer. Janey screamed again, he thought, or was she calling his name?

If she could yell, she was all right. She wasn't dead, the past was not revisited in the present. She was okay. The bad guy hadn't killed her.

If only he didn't feel so tired and so oddly disconnected, he would answer her. But his legs wouldn't even hold him upright and his chest hurt so damned much. He had to lie down. That was right. That was what he would do, then he would answer her. There were a thousand things he wanted to tell her, things he wanted to show her. He wanted to take her arrow hunting, and to take her dancing some Saturday night over at Goober's, waltzing her around the floor, holding her in his arms, telling her he loved her.

"All those things," he said, unable to hold himself upright any longer.

"Dave! Dear God, no! No!"

He had to tell her something before he lay down, but he couldn't think what it was. Something about the future. But he really didn't have a clear sense of the future now. What was wrong with him? Had he been shot? Was this what it felt like? Strange, unreal, and the hottest damned pain he'd ever felt before?

He closed his eyes and tried to open them again when the dizzying sensation wouldn't ebb. But they wouldn't open. He heard Janey calling his name, but he couldn't seem to answer her.

Janey tried to catch him as he fell, but only managed to cushion his body as it slumped to the floor. She screamed his name, then cried a denial as his head lolled backward onto her arm, his mouth slack, his eyes closed.

Never so much as looking at the man who had done this to him, Janey focused every ounce of her energy and attention on Dave. His shirt was drenched with his own blood, and she knew with a spiraling sense of déjà vu that the murderer's bullet had cut through his chest and punctured something vital. *Just like Bill.*

But when Bill had been shot, Janey had been nowhere near the scene, hadn't cradled him in her arms, her hands were warm and sticky, her nostrils filled with the coppery scent of life ebbing away.

Not knowing she was echoing his thoughts earlier, she inwardly railed against a fate that would so cruelly force her to experience this again in one lifetime. "No," she whimpered. "It's not fair."

But it wasn't the unfairness to her in having to go through that pain a second time that made the tears well and fall. It was the unfairness to Dave. To both of them. They had both just admitted trust of the other, finally, shatteringly exorcising the sad ghosts of their past. Was fate as cruel a monster as the man who lay upon her floor against her wall, coming in to steal the chance to live that trust?

She had to do something... anything... to stop this callous twist of destiny's intention. Dave's heart was still beating and he was still breathing, though it was a thin, reedy whistle, not the steady deep breaths of someone merely unconscious.

She swiftly eased him to the floor and shot through the archway of the dining room and yanked the tablecloth from the table. Ignoring the shattering of china that struck the floor, she raced back to Dave and, after shoving a throw pillow against his chest, made a rough tourniquet of the fine linen.

She was back at his side in seconds, barely drawing him into her arms again when she heard the distant wail of a siren.

"You've got to live, Dave," she told him. "Hold on for me, darling. Don't slip away from me. I'm here. I'm not leaving. Please…please don't die. I couldn't bear it, do you hear me? I couldn't bear it!"

Dorla Dobson sat down beside her and said, "I called Carol Aragon and she says David is just fine, eating his lunch, watching one of her grandkids rub peanut butter and jelly into her hair. You don't need to worry. But you do need some rest. Charlie said he'd run you home."

"I want to stay here," Janey said dully, grateful to Dorla for her help but scarcely aware of the woman beyond that. Dave had been in surgery most of the night, and now, almost twenty-four hours after he'd been shot, the prognosis was still cloudy, the outcome uncertain.

Charlie Dobson had come to the hospital about five minutes after they'd brought Dave in. He hadn't talked much during the night, checking in first on Dave, but also on the two men from his department who had been wounded trying to stop the guy from entering Janey's house.

Tom Addersly had a hairline fracture on his skull, but was already out of critical, and Johnny Delgado was suffering a concussion and a broken arm but would be going home in the morning—that was, if his wife didn't have the baby today.

Charlie didn't talk to her much, but he'd been there. He'd brought her a cup of coffee now and then, and somehow always managed to be right at her side, touching her arm or placing his broad shoulder behind hers whenever the too-solemn doctors, McCall and Heythrop walked into the waiting room with the next round of bad news.

He'd been relieved by his wife at around ten that morning, and she had talked easily and calmly about the day's activities, about Janey's son, about the night her daughter was born or the day her son died, but never about Dave.

When Charlie came back a few minutes ago, he'd brought a bag of carry-out burgers from one of the local cafés. Janey had choked one down just to be polite, but was sorry afterward, for her stomach was too knotted to eat. When she'd sat quietly after the meal, Charlie had casually handed her an antacid, eaten one himself and walked a few feet away without saying a word.

Dorla rose now and, after kissing her husband farewell, walked down the hall, out of the so-called quiet lounge, and through the doors leading to the main waiting room. Charlie stood for a moment, then took his wife's seat.

"The state boys rounded up that Swanson fellow up in Taos. Between what you told us about him, the stuff they found in his files, and the confession from that scudsbag who shot Davey, he won't be seeing the sunshine for a long, long time," he said. "He's the kind of evil that makes a man believe in capital punishment."

Janey nodded, her thoughts not on Swanson and his brand of evil but on the man who had tormented her, had killed—by his own statement—at least ten terminally ill patients, and had shot Dave in the chest. His name, according to Charlie Dobson, was anything from Anthony Atkinson to Tobias Teller. He had a string of aliases a mile long, Charlie said, and was wanted in at least eight states, some for burglary, others for suspicion of murder.

With a sketchy medical background and a few instances of on-sight training, he'd had an easy time being hired by a large number of different medical facilities, usually those involving the terminally ill. He'd seen early on that hastening a death here and there could be extremely lucrative. But it wasn't until he met up with Dr. William Swanson that the full extent of his abilities rose to the surface.

Janey thought about the combining of two personalities: Swanson and this Anthony-Tobias person, Charlie and Dorla Dobson, she and Dave. In the Swanson-Tobias combination, a common evil, an element of amorality in both of them had melded to form a murderous unit, capable of such greed that no act or deed was too terrible to contemplate. In Charlie and Dorla Dobson's case, two fine people had worked together for years, weathering the ups and downs of life, fusing a marriage that still held romance, still fostered respect and a fierce protectiveness.

The last combination of personalities that had sprung to her mind was that of Dave Reynolds and Janey Anderson. They were already joined on some basic level, perhaps had been from that first moment she'd looked into his eyes and he'd told her that he'd be there for her, and a few minutes later he'd held her son—their son, it had seemed then, and seemed to her now—and had met her eyes again, forging a bond that could never be broken.

Or couldn't have, until now. Now he might not live to maintain that bond, that connection.

"Kind of gets me that this murdering scudsbag lives and is out of danger, while Davey . . . well, anyway, it gets me."

Janey murmured something, but whether it was agreement or mere acknowledgment of Charlie's presence, even she couldn't have said. *Dave!* Janey's heart cried, and her soul echoed the plea.

"You love that boy, don't you, honey?" Charlie asked.

"Yes," Janey said. She was beyond trying to evade the truth any longer. Far beyond it.

"Must be hell for you to have him get shot like that, right in front of you, and you just getting over your husband being killed thataway."

She looked at Charlie Dobson then and saw the sympathy in his faded eyes, the empathy stamped on his grizzled face. "I know it's hard for you, too."

Charlie didn't look away. "He's like my own boy," he said, his voice graveled, not from years, Janey knew, but from emotion scarcely held in check.

"I know. He told me. And he told me about your son, Johnny. I'm sorry."

"Violent death is always terrible," Charlie said. "Hell, I suppose any death is. But watching young'uns getting their lives snatched out from under them, that's when it really gets you."

"It's so unfair."

"It is that," Charlie agreed. He looked away now, down at the weathered hands in his lap. "If he gets through this, are you going to marry him, make an honest man of him?"

"Until today I would have said no," Janey answered.

"His getting shot changed your mind, did it?"

"Yes."

"Why's that?"

"Because until today, I thought I couldn't get through the fear of losing someone again. I thought I wouldn't have what it takes to face those hours of not knowing whether or not he would be okay."

"But things are different now?" he asked, but it came out more as a statement of fact.

"Yes, and no. You see, the worst has already happened. He was shot...exactly like Bill was. Nothing worse can happen now."

"He might not live, honey. You gotta face that fact."

"He has to. He's the one who convinced me to start believing in the good guys again. He's the one who talked me into living life fully again. I'm not going to let him take that away from me now."

"And just how do you plan on stopping him, honey?" he asked.

"As soon as they'll let me in there, I'm going to go tell him."

Janey knew she sounded like a child, refusing to accept the inevitable. And she knew that Charlie Dobson must have been shaking his balding head and wondering how long it would be before her mind just went away altogether, but he surprised her.

"You're going to let a bunch of guys in lab coats tell you when and where you can talk to Davey? Hell, honey, if I was him, and laying there not knowing if I was going to be pushing daisies or mowing 'em a month from now, I'd sure as hell like to know some young gal would come in and tell me to get off my ass and get on with the business of living. But that's up to you. You can wait, or you can get on in there now and say your piece."

Janey sat still a moment longer then pushed to her feet. Charlie didn't say anything until she reached the door. "I warned him once about cops' wives and women having babies."

Janey turned around and met Charlie's shrewd eyes. "What was the warning?"

"That a man can get lost in them," he said softly.

"Let's hope so," she said.

"Hell, honey, the boy doesn't stand a prayer of getting away now." He grinned, and something about that smile made Janey's heart lighten somewhat. "Go after him, girl."

No one stopped her as she pushed the door to his room open. Dave lay beneath an oxygen tent, almost as pale as the sheets beneath him. His body was covered with blankets and cloths, his face obstructed with tubes in his nostrils and his mouth. His body was perfectly still and Janey had the sense that his soul was thousands of miles away.

Her courage, buoyed by Charlie's easy acceptance of her simple goal, flagged and almost evaporated completely. It was one thing to believe she could talk him back to the land of the living, but she'd been sitting in a waiting room, imagining how he'd look, and now standing here, seeing the reality of how far he had to travel to come back was an entirely different matter.

But in her heart, in the deepest, most vulnerable and open places of her soul, she knew he could hear her, would listen to whatever she had to say.

Slowly, fearfully, she stepped to the side of the bed and slipped her hands beneath the plastic tent and the covers under it and took his cool hand in her own too-fevered fingers. Was it her imagination or did his fingers flex against hers?

"Dave...? It's me. Janey. I want you to listen to me. You've got to live, Dave. You've got to come back now. I need you. I don't want to go on without you."

She drew a deep breath, wanting him to respond so badly that she hurt all over, inside and out. "Dave. Remember when you delivered David? Remember how you told me to look at your eyes? Every time I thought I was losing it, that the pain or the fear would get too great, I'd look in your eyes and know I was going to be all right.

"I want you to open your eyes now and look at me, Dave. Open your eyes and let me save you. If you look there now, all you'll see is how much I love you. How much I want you. You'll see everything I know, and have ever known. You said one time that you wanted *everything*. It's here for you, Dave. You've got to open your eyes and see it. You've got to believe it."

When he didn't move, didn't twitch or turn his head or anything that gave any indication of having heard her, of having come closer to the surface, but continued to lie there, too still, too pale, Janey felt hope draining away. Her eyes welled with tears, and her entire body seemed to go numb.

She'd seen the bleak look on the doctor's face earlier, and saw in the averted heads of the nurses that Dave's chances weren't good at all. But she'd refused to believe it. She hadn't allowed herself to believe it.

Because if they were right, then life would hold no meaning at all.

But seeing him there, holding his unresponsive hand, trying to conjure some sign of life in his featureless face, hearing the high pings of his heartbeat echoing on the monitor, she was afraid the doctors and nurses knew the truth, a truth she didn't want to accept, didn't want to face.

"Please, Dave. Please open your eyes. Live for me, darling. Dear God, let him live for me. Don't take him away. I need him so much. My baby needs him. Don't take him away now, not after letting me see what loving him can mean. Oh, not now. Please, not now. Let him open his eyes and look at me.

"Please, oh, please...open your eyes, Dave. Live for me. Live for the love we have, that we both need. That we both want. Live. You have to live for me. You have to, Dave. I can't bear this, I can't bear for you to go away. Come back. Come back to me now."

The tears rolling down her face so freely momentarily blinded her and she started to pull her hands away to swipe at them, but his grip on her fingers prevented her. Startled, she blinked rapidly and half stood to better see his face.

His smoky eyes were open and met her tear-drenched, wondering gaze.

"Dave..." she sobbed, her heart suddenly too light for her body, her body weightless with joy. "You came back to me."

Slowly he nodded, and around the tube in his mouth, his crooked grin formed. "Always," he mumbled. "Forever."

"Charlie says I have to make an honest man out of you."

He didn't try to talk around the unwieldy device this time, letting his gaze say it all.

And it did. It said *everything*.

* * * * *

Silhouette Sensation

COMING NEXT MONTH

THE LIGHTS OF HOME
Marilyn Pappano

Eight years of waiting were over, and Jess Trujillo was coming home. Home to the town where he'd been born, and home to the only woman he'd ever loved, Caitlin Pierce, who had betrayed him just when it had counted most.

The chemistry between them was still strong, but Jess would never let himself love Caitlin again. However, that didn't mean he didn't want her in his bed—or his ring on her finger!

NIGHT SHADOW
Nora Roberts

A solitary figure robed in black was fighting a single-handed battle against crime. Nothing—not even love—could deter the man called Nemesis from his mission.

Deborah O'Roarke owed Nemisis her life, but she could not accept his methods of achieving justice. Still she felt a disturbing desire for this mysterious stranger who lived in the shadows. Who was he?

Silhouette Sensation

COMING NEXT MONTH

BLACK HORSE ISLAND
Dee Holmes

Keely Lockwood was determined to turn her father's dream of a refuge for troubled teenage boys into reality, but she had only one month in which to do it—and she needed Jed Corey.

Once a street-tough kid, Jed had been her father's greatest success. But now he was a dangerously attractive man who thought she was the wrong person for this job.

It was going to be a summer neither one of them would ever forget...

A LOVING TOUCH
Joyce McGill

Victoria Shelton's special gifts had never brought her anything but pain, so Michael Gallagher's urgent request—that she use her psychic abilities to help him find his missing friend and partner—was out of the question.

It wasn't easy to say no to a man as compelling as Michael Gallagher. But surely, even though he was desperate, he wouldn't seduce Tory just to change her mind...would he?

COMING NEXT MONTH FROM

Silhouette

Desire

*provocative, sensual love stories
for the woman of today*

THE SEDUCTION OF JAKE TALLMAN Cait London
COUNTERFEIT BRIDE Christine Rimmer
IMITATION LOVE Jackie Merritt
CASSIE'S LAST GOODBYE Shawna Delacorte
MOONLIGHT DREAM Noelle Berry McCue
BEAUTY AND THE BEASTMASTER Carol Devine

Special Edition

*longer, satisfying romances with
mature heroines and lots of emotion*

ON HER OWN Pat Warren
MARRIAGE WANTED Debbie Macomber
SHE GOT HER MAN Marie Ferrarella
RETURN ENGAGEMENT Elizabeth Bevarly
HERE COMES THE GROOM Trisha Alexander
LOVE ME BEFORE DAWN Lindsay McKenna